THE BOSS:

THE STORY OF A FEMALE HUSTLER

THE BOSS:

THE STORY OF A FEMALE HUSTLER

TYSHA

URBAN BOOKS

www.urbanbooks.net

Urban Books, LLC
78 East Industry Court
Deer Park, NY 11729

ISBN-13: 978-1-60162-437-6
ISBN-10: 1-60162-437-9

First Mass Market Printing February 2011
First Trade Paperback Printing February 2008
Printed in the United States of America

10 9 8 7 6 5 4 3 2 1

This is a work of fiction. Any references or similarities to actual events, real people, living, or dead, or to real locales are intended to give the novel a sense of reality. Any similarity in other names, characters, places, and incidents is entirely coincidental.

Distributed by Kensington Publishing Corp.
Submit Wholesale Orders to:
Kensington Publishing Corp.
C/O Penguin Group (USA) Inc.
Attention: Order Processing
405 Murray Hill Parkway
East Rutherford, NJ 07073-2316
Phone: 1-800-526-0275
Fax: 1-800-227-9604

I dedicate this book to the best grandparents in the world. Ruby J. Hill and Mr. John (Juin) M. Hill Jr., RIP (September 2, 1929–October 10, 1991). It is because of you that I am able to simply be. I am proud to be yours. Thank you for raising me, sacrificing for me, teaching me, loving me and molding me into the reflection of you.

Forever yours, Tishelle

Acknowledgments

It has been a long and treacherous road but my family and friends held on and traveled with me. For that, I am forever grateful.

I must first acknowledge and thank my cousin Malcolm Cash. It was he who saw my potential and fed my hunger to be challenged. I love you, Malcolm. Thank you for the inspiration for the courage to constantly search for knowledge.

My husband, Vincent McDougald, thank you for loving and supporting me. My boys, Je'Vohn and Reese, you both inspire me to be. I love ya'll around the world twice and back again. To my new children, Isaiah, India and Micah, strive to be the best no matter what, and remember, I got cha back! My brat of a sister, Tracey, and baby brother, Jay-Jae, we ride, we ride, and we ride. To my girls, Daria, Donnie, Gena, Nolicka, Tootsie, Marshell, Jodi, Tiff, Christine, Joy, Nickkie, Hylda, Marla, Dionne, Sheryl, Tonya, Tiffany, Ericka, Gena—I thank each of you for being a part of my life and supporting my dream. To my agent, Joylynn M. Jossel, words cannot express my gratitude for sharing your experience, talent and friendship with me. Thank you for pushing me toward the prize when I felt too weak to go on. My publicist, Earth Jallow of Down To Earth Public Relations, I love you, girl. To my first cousins who think of me as a big sister, Pam, Jessie, Nickkie, Tonne, Sirenna, Rosie, Marcus, Dyonna, I've tried to be a good role model to each of you. I love you all different but the same. To all of the strong women in my family who've inspired me to be the best at everything that I do, I pray that God continues to bless you all: My Aunts Juinie, Cherry, Toni, Ludie, May-Jimmy. My Great-Aunts Mary, Carol, Mildred, Inez, Carol, Sylvia, Gene. Uncle Jake, Jimmy, Sidney and Daddy Goose, I love you. To my daddy, Derick and my dad, Ronnie, all my love. My favorite cousins who've always looked out for me, I say thank you: Patt, Debbie, NeeNee, KeeDee, Johnny, Ronnie, Dwayne, Donna, Mark, Tonie Jack, Meshelle, Tommy, Lucille, Shimp.

Finally, to my mommy, when the evils of this world tried to knock you down, you fought back with a fury. When people talked about you and left you for dead, you called on God and walked each step in faith. I am proud of you and I thank you for all the sacrifices you've made for me and my sister and brother. The world is a better place because you walk the earth.

Please forgive me if I forgot anyone, I got you next time. Ty-Hill Baby!

Introduction

Meet Ms. Kayla Marie "Bossy" Tucker

What's it do readers? Let me holla at cha' for a minute. My name is Bossy—Kayla Marie Tucker to the government—and I'm a living legend on the city streets of Youngstown, Ohio. Truth be told, most of the rumors and tales about me are true but some have been exaggerated while others have some fiction peppered in. I must say that in my day, I was the best female hustla in the game. I was, and still am, that bitch.

You're probably wondering, "What does this chick know about the game?" Well, allow me to give you a little background. Daddy was a rollin' stone and he rolled his ass right out of our lives over thirty years ago. I really don't remember him; I just know that he was never around, so fuck 'im.

Since our sperm donor was missing in action, my mother had to work long hours and left me and my brother in the care of our grandmother. My mother was an only child, which made me Nana's only granddaughter. She used to spoil the hell out of me. The way Nana told it, I came into this world demanding attention from everyone. As I grew into a toddler Nana said no kids wanted to play with me because I bossed them all around. From that, Nana gave me the nickname "Bossy", with a capital B.

She taught me how to properly clean a house, sew a dress without the aid of a pattern, wash clothes, braid hair and most importantly, cook. My favorite meal is salmon patties, potato cake with some fried green tomatoes and fried corn bread on the side so that was the first meal I mastered. The time I spent with her was more educational than any time I ever spent in school.

Just weeks before my tenth birthday, Nana fell getting out of the shower and broke her hip. During her hospital stay, they ran all kinds of tests on her just to make sure her general health was as good as it could be. At least, that's what I remember them telling my mother but I think they ran those tests to hike up the hospital bill. One of the tests came back bad and she was diagnosed with lung cancer.

Nana wasn't taking that shit lying down though; she fought it up to the end and died eleven months later in my mother's arms. Nana was the strongest woman I knew back then and the strongest woman I know of today (God bless her soul).—She's been gone for twenty-three years but sometimes it feels like I just lost her yesterday.

With Nana gone, Devin was left to watch me while Mommy worked. Devin was ten years older than me and had always taken care of his baby sister. One day Devin and some friends concocted a plan to rob the neighborhood corner store. Their biggest problem was that no one counted on the Arab store owner having a shotgun behind the counter. Three armed men walked in and after the gunfight was over, only one walked out—Devin. He ended up taking a plea and was sentenced to twenty years to life for aggravated robbery and the homicide of the store owner. That left me alone at age thirteen to take care of myself. Trust me when I say that I write my brother weekly, visit him monthly and keep his books tight with money always.

That brings me to Mommy Dearest. She was a beautiful woman with long thick hair that changed colors with the seasons. Her caramel complexion was flawless and she had hips and ass for days. Yeah, Linda Tucker was the bomb in her heyday, but that was a long time ago. On my fourteenth birthday, Mommy Dearest caught her boyfriend of the month molesting me. She hollered, put on a show and hit him in the head with a cast-iron skillet. Never once did she hug me, say she was sorry, or vow to make the son of a bitch pay.

After he left, she cried all night and drank herself to sleep. I couldn't help but wonder why was she crying when I was the one being sexually abused? I should have been the one getting drunk and crying, but what was that going to do?

Her solution was to pick up a pipe, fill it with crack, and fire it up. Mommy Dearest was a pretty woman, but she was weak. After that first toke, nothing in her life mattered anymore, including me.

I've been hustling to stay alive ever since the pipe took over. Somehow Linda kept a roof over our heads. It was a roof in the projects but it was still shelter. Every month she would sell off her food stamps so I had to eat the best way I could: at neighbors, schools, shelters, trash cans. I did what I had to do.

One day a good friend of my brother's, Teddy Bear Sampson, asked me for a favor that changed my life. He gave me his car keys, a hundred-dollar bill, and an address.

"Bossy, get to this address, knock on the side door, and tell them Teddy Bear sent you. Stand inside the door but refuse to go any further into the house. Wait for a package, give them this roll, and come back to the jets," he instructed me.

I was like, no problem. By that time, I was sixteen, raising myself, and surviving off the kindness of others—what harm could it cause?

Teddy Bear was pleased with the job I'd done and took me under his wing. I've never been hungry since. Hustling in these streets will force you to grow up fast and you better learn quickly or these mean streets will swallow you up whole.

I have been able to make a pretty good living for myself. For me, the hustle is all about survival. The world is made up of all kinds of rules but in my world, there are three that I live my life by.

Rule number one: trust no one. There are no friends in the game. Rule number two: have a legitimate gig. Work a real job or open some type of business. Don't make it obvious how you make ya money. Rule number three: A hustler must make his or her own retirement plan. Money should be broken down into thirds. One-third of your money use to restock supply. Another one-third should be put up in case of emergency, legal trouble for example. Finally, the last one-third you live off of and try to put a little nest egg away for your future retirement. By spend, I mean on necessities. Keep a roof over your head, clothes on your back and food on the table. This plan requires discipline and self-control. One of the biggest misconceptions is that drug money is easy money. WRONG! A hustler works hard for it and should use it wisely. If you live in the heart of the ghetto, don't drive a Land Rover and have three plasma televisions in a house that's in dire need of a new roof and paint job. Possession of material trophies will always draw attention.

Miss Bossy has always been a private person but rumors still exist in these streets. People question my sexuality because I have to be hard in this game and I don't put my personal business out like that. My relationships with my girls Terry and Aisha are subjects of rumors and speculation around the city. What people don't realize is that the three of us are like sisters. We've been through hell together over the years and we've created a strong bond.

Truth be told, I love dick as much as a nymphomaniac. The difference is I don't let it consume me. I choose to keep my personal life personal and my business just that, business. I learn by watching others make mistakes such as mixing business and pleasure. Sooner or later, that mixture is guaranteed to explode.

Over the years, I've had "friends" but nothing serious. If it starts to become something more than sex, I cut 'em off. As a word of advice, I always let my "friend" know he's not the only one so don't claim me out in the streets, because he just might get his feelings hurt. So I guess people with too much time on their hands assume I'm a lesbian because my nose ain't wide open over some dick like most of these hoes. Whatever—they can think what they want; I'm still gon' be me—Bossy.

July 4, 1989

"*Bootsy, we want Bootsy,*" Bossy, Aisha, and Terry chanted along with the old school tunes as their game of bones (dominoes) heated up. The room was filled with a thick haze of smoke as the invited guest passed around a blunt filled with chronic.

"*Smack!*"

C-Lok slammed the domino on the oak table so hard that it echoed throughout the apartment.

"Put me down for another dub," instructed C-Lok. "Yeah, this is about to be another round for ya boy." No matter what the game, C-Lok loved to talk shit to his opponents. It didn't matter if he were winning or losing; he was going to run his mouth.

"Ah, nigga, whatever. That bullshit ain't flyin' up in here," retorted Bossy.

"Say what you want, I'm running this here tonight," replied C-Lok.

The rest of the partygoers in attendance laughed at the competitive spirit between the couple hosting the holiday party.

"Terry, we running low on this buffalo punch, can I get the other pitcher out the fridge?" asked Big Black.

"Do what it do, Big Black," answered Terry. She had soaked the melons, pineapples, and grapes in four different types of vodka for seventy-two hours. The norm was twenty-four hours but nothing about the annual festivities was ever normal. After Aisha added the condensed fruit punch juice and ice, the party favor was perfect.

Aisha and Terry spent the day before preparing potato salad, turnip greens, macaroni and cheese, and baked beans. C-Lok was up at six in the morning firing up the grill for the beef ribs, chicken breast, and shish kebabs.

Bossy had just moved into her own apartment after breaking up with C-Lok. They were both having a hard time letting go and kept trying to make it work. C-Lok was her air and Bossy his sunshine.

The couple was a dangerous combination and everyone knew it.

"How many houses y'all goin' to? Damn, let a nigga get on the table," complained Teddy Bear.

"Hold up a minute, man. As soon as I fill this last house, game over," bragged C-Lok.

"We should switch to spades after this, I'm tired of bones, let's mix it up," suggested Aisha.

"Cool with me 'cause whatever the game, you know I've already won it."

"There you go with that braggin' again. You just ain't gon' shut da fuck up until I beat dat ass into the ground," Teddy Bear joked.

Everyone in the room burst out laughing, including C-Lok. The two men had been friends for over twenty years and were as close as brothers from different mothers could be.

An hour later, the sun was setting and so was the mood at the party. Everyone had eaten, drunk, and puffed on blunts for hours, and had gotten tired. Teddy Bear, C-Lok, Big Black, Bossy, Aisha and Terry had gotten comfortable on the couch watching *Menace II Society* on the big screen TV.

Buzz!

The sound of the doorbell startled the group awake. Everyone looked around, trying to remember where they were and what the annoying sound was.

Buzz!

Bossy rose from her seat and walked to the front room to peek outside.

"Who the fuck is this?" asked Bossy.

"What, you don't know who at ya door?" C-Lok quizzed.

"Naw, it must be for one of y'all because I don't know this chick."

Aisha and Terry ran to the window to see what Bossy was talking about. Bossy was a very private person and did not surround herself with strangers.

The woman looked to be in her mid-thirties, with dark eyes and thick natural hair. Her jeans appeared to have been painted on and her spandex top looked like it was straining to cover her double D breasts. Besides her hair looking like it was in dire need of a Dark and Lovely perm, she was attractive enough.

Big Black got up off the floor and opened the door to find a woman he'd never seen before.

"Where is dat nigga? I know he been here all day. Where is he?" demanded the stranger as she pushed past Big Black.

"Bitch! How you just gon' walk up in my shit like I know you?" Bossy asked angrily.

"Naw, that nigga been here all damn day. All I want to know is which one of y'all bitches he fuckin'?" The woman shifted her weight to her left side and put her hands on her wide hips. She did not know Bossy, Aisha or Terry and they did not know her.

It became obvious that the woman was looking for C-Lok because that's who she pointed at when she talked. C-Lok had daggers in his eyes staring directly into the woman's eyes.

"What the fuck you doin' here? You ain't my bitch," C-Lok said, smirking.

"Oh, now I ain't ya bitch? I been that bitch every night for a week but now you don't know me?"

"I ain't even on this shit and if I were you, I'd

raise up out of here," suggested C-Lok. He never left his comfortable position on the couch and was more annoyed that the chickenhead had made him miss his favorite part of the movie.

"Oh, what da fuck you gon' do about it? These bitches don't know me and . . ."

Bam!

Thump!

Bossy hit the woman one time, almost knocking her unconscious before her body hit the floor. The woman lay still, trying to regain her senses when Bossy stood over her with her right foot pushing down on her neck. She was not strong enough to push Bossy off of her and it was becoming harder to breathe.

Looking down on her victim, Bossy said, "Ain't no bitch up in here but you. Don't you ever cross my path again because if you do, I promise you, it will be the last thing you do."

Bossy removed her foot, as the woman squirmed around trying to catch her breath. Beside the choking woman, the room was silent. Everyone knew that one wrong word or misguided move by the woman could cost her the privilege of living.

The woman staggered to her feet with the aid of the wall, still fighting to regain her composure. Bossy stood by the door while Aisha and Terry made sure the woman didn't suddenly pull out a knife or something.

Her legs wobbled and her throat felt as if she'd drank a cup of Red Hot hot sauce but the woman still had a small amount of will in her. She walked toward the door to leave but stopped to stand face-to-face with Bossy.

"Don't think dis is over bitch, because you ain't shit!"

Spit!

The woman spit in Bossy's face.

Bam!

Thump!

Again, Bossy knocked the woman to the floor.

Scream!

Bossy, Aisha, and Terry stomped the woman within an inch of her life. C-Lok, Big Black, and Teddy Bear stopped the women by grabbing hold of them.

"Naw, y'all right. Aisha and Terry don't need this on they back but I'm a ride wit' it," said Bossy. "Big Black, take this bitch out to McKelvey Lake and dump her ass beside it," instructed Bossy. "And all of y'all remember . . ."

"What happens at Bossy's crib, stays the fuck at Bossy's crib," everyone recited in unison.

My Office Hours Are . . .

Chapter 1

The sounds of Roger Troutman played in the background as Bossy stood over her stove watching the water boil. She was on a self-imposed deadline to have a kilogram of rock prepared for Twan to pick up later that day. The measuring cups sat on the counter, one contained powder cocaine and the other baking soda. Bossy followed her routine without missing a step and when she was finished, the potency of her product would be more addictive than the recipe most people followed. It cost hustlers a small fortune to have Bossy cook up they shit but it was well worth it.

The handles of the stainless-steel spoon and knife were beginning to burn her hand. This signified it was time to combine the two teaspoons of baking soda with the half ounce of cocaine. Bossy had discovered that using less baking soda worked better while cooking shit up one day after running low on supplies. Always wanting to be unique, Bossy invested in some real stainless-steel measuring cups, pots, and stirring utensils. The Imperial brand kitchen supplies put her back a grip but it proved to be well worth it in the end. Bossy also discovered that the dollar-store brand of baking soda was of more use to her than the name brand. The result achieved a potency second to none and thus, Bossy became the queen bitch of preparing crack cocaine.

Bossy was an attractive woman and often took advantage of her ability to catch men's eyes. She had a caramel complexion that turned bronze during the summer months and her straight, long, auburn hair hung midway down her back. Her body alone made men fall at her feet, but there was something else about her, something not easily defined, that brought them to their knees.

Bossy was seated at her cherry oak dining room table packaging the last of the freshly cooked crack cocaine with a joint balancing between her lips. She was racing against the clock to wrap up the latest shipment for Twan, a youngblood who reminded her of herself during her early years in the game. He would be knocking on the door at any minute. Just when Bossy thought she would finish on time, the phone rang. Annoyed, she walked over to the counter and removed the phone from its cradle.

"Hello," she said with an attitude, removing the joint from between her lips. She had answered the phone as if the person on the other end should have known that she had a deadline to meet and therefore should not be calling her.

"Bitch, stay the hell away from Twan. He got a family," a young female voice roared through the phone receiver in an attempt to sound threatening.

Many of Bossy's days began with stupid phone calls from immature females back in the day so she knew exactly how to handle the situation at hand. Bossy laughed to herself at the thought of dealing with crank callers in the current age of caller identification and star sixty-nine. Technology had made her life a lot easier and the person on the line lucked up and caught Bossy in a mellow mood.

Up until three years ago, Bossy's role in the drug cartel Teddy Bear put together was much more involved. She did everything from making the runs down south to buy the best cocaine money could buy to selling the shit to most of Youngstown, Ohio's high players. As if it were a regular nine-to-five, Bossy also set the schedules of the street corner hustlers Teddy Bear had out on the grind. Bossy helped him organize his workers like a W-2 form was on file. As a result, Bossy's apartment was the place to be when their shift ended. At times, there would be at least six fellas chillin' in the apartment. They all ate, showered, shitted and cheated on their main girls at Bossy's. That was when the late night hang-ups and threatening phone calls began. Once the insecure girls found out who they'd called, the "I didn't know it was you" apologies began.

Bossy knew the identification of this caller right of the bat because she had met her on an occasion or two and recognized her voice. It was Twan's girl, LaJetia. Twan sometimes complained to Bossy about LaJetia bitching about the hours he kept. She would also accuse him of fucking Bossy. The girl just didn't understand that hustlin' ain't got no time frame. It was not like hustlers, street pharmacists, pimps, and hoes could clock in and out. The streets never shut down. The need for drugs, sex, and money was never ending, and if a connection wasn't available when a client wanted them to be, there was always someone ready to take his place.

Bossy removed the phone from her ear, stared at it, and laughed. *Is this shit for real?* she thought to herself. She then placed the phone back up to her ear and spoke.

"You're just a young girl with stars in your eyes," Bossy said, snickering. "I'll give it to you though; you must be feeling pretty strong callin' my house trying to start shit over some dick. Or you're pretty insecure and thought making this juvenile call would run me off," said Bossy at a whisper while blowing out smoke from the joint she was tokin' on.

"I'll tell you why I called . . ." LaJetia spat.

"That's where you fucked up," interjected Bossy, "thinking I'd give a damn why you called!"

"Aw, bitch, I'll—"

"You'll what? You've already showed me your ho card. I care as much about that nigga as I care about you."

"I just want you to know that Twan has a woman and we got kids together," whined LaJetia.

"And what does that mean to me?" Bossy asked to piss LaJetia off even more.

"It means he stayin' wit' me!" quivered LaJetia.

"Good! That's where I want him, with you. I ain't feedin', clothin', or housin' no nigga. So keep him right there with you." *Click!* Bossy felt it was way past time to end that conversation so she could get back to her business.

Bossy could never understand why a woman would call another woman's house over some nigga. She felt that, even if she was sleepin' with another woman's man, it was him that needed to get checked. Bossy wasn't the one cheatin' and lyin' to her ass.

After slamming the receiver down in LaJetia's ear, Bossy walked, finished packaging the last of the coke. She then gathered it all from the kitchen table and placed it in a corner of her dining room. She looked at the crystal clock that hung on the wall and was relieved that she had completed her task before Twan had arrived. As she looked down at the product on the floor, she began to daydream about her part in "the life".

Hustlers do what they got to do in order to survive, she thought, justifying her role. *Those that come into the game believing they can change the rules one player at a time have set themselves up for a huge disappointment. It doesn't matter how wet a woman's pussy is or how deep her throat runs, the game can not be changed.*

Being a woman in a world dominated by men hadn't been easy for Bossy. Many had tried to take advantage of her, so she learned to be tough and ruthless. She didn't take shit from nobody. If she put in time on someone's product, she wanted her money. Thinking about the way some men treated her like, caused her to say out loud, "Hell, I got bills too. So what I was born with a money maker and I still got responsibilities. Even if I didn't, so what! I want my money!"

The sound of her doorbell summoned Bossy from her thoughts. She glanced up at her security camera before making her way through the living room and to the front door. She pressed the buzzer to unlock the security door to let Twan in.

"What up wit' you, boy?" Bossy asked.

Twan's muscular, but lean, physique walked through the door looking good enough to eat. The throwback jersey he wore complemented his chestnut eyes, and as usual, he was well groomed and put together. Bossy unconsciously ran her pink tongue across her thick lips as she thought about getting a taste of him. She never mixed business with pleasure though, and anyway, Twan was only twenty-six and Bossy never got involved with anyone younger than her. Twan came up ten years too short.

"I can't call it," Twan replied. "You all right, girl?"

"You know me, I'm straight. Your shit is over there," said Bossy, pointing to a corner in her dining room. "You want a drink or are you in a rush?"

Twan nodded his head yes as he walked over to the bar and mixed them both a drink. Bossy sat across from Twan at her dining room table and contemplated telling him about the call she received from LaJetia. Not in the mood for another session of Twan complaining about a problem he could easily get rid of, she decided against it.

"It took me a minute to cut that kilo down into those twenties. Whose shit is that anyway?" inquired Bossy.

"It's easier to keep track of my money by placing them in my various houses during the winter months. That way, I know who owes me money and who's slackin' on they hustle. You know how niggas get lacked in the winter," explained Twan before allowing the hot liquor to slip down his throat.

"I know you not still keeping track of ya money on paper. That right there will fuck you up one day."

"Naw, I got this. Don't worry about it," replied Twan.

Bossy shook her head. She didn't expect Twan to heed her advice. He had been hardheaded for as long as she could remember. Twan and Bossy met back in the day before she moved out of the Westlake Housing Projects on the north side of the city. They weren't related, and their mothers came from different stock but Bossy and Twan had some sort of connection from day one.

He lived with his mother and brother a couple of blocks away from the projects where he liked to hang out with the big boys. Twan would ride his blue Schwinn ten-speed in rain, sleet, and snow just to see Bossy. At age seven, Twan had the biggest crush on Bossy and would follow behind her like a lost puppy in search of a home. Bossy thought it was cute and called Twan her little boyfriend. He was cool with that until Bossy and her "big boyfriend" C-Lok got a crib together. Twan's heart was broken for a schoolyard minute but he would still ride that bike down the block, just to catch a glance of Bossy. Twenty years later, Bossy looked out for Twan as if he were her little brother and Twan would lay down his life for her.

Besides Twan, and her mentor Teddy Bear, Bossy only trusted her two best friends, Terry Benson and Aisha Woods. The three women were so close that they had identical tattoos on their upper left arm of a dove. In its beak was a ribbon that read *KAT69*; that stood for Kayla (Bossy), Aisha and Terry. The *69* stood for the year they were all born. KAT69 also figured in the name of their flourishing business, KAT69 Hair and Nail Salon.

The fellas from the projects often told Bossy and her girls that they were the coldest chicks on the north side. It wasn't just their looks that drew men to them, it was their attitudes. The three women would stand on a street corner, turn up a forty ounce of fo' five, roll a joint and toss dice. During the day, they were just one of the fellas but at night, the woman in them came out. Not many women could be gangster and sexy at the same time. Bossy, Aisha, and Terry cleaned up so well it was hard to believe they were the same women who had turned up forties and shot craps out on the block.

When Bossy first moved into her apartment, she threw a set every single weekend. Things were going on during the weekdays but only a select number of hustlers were allowed. KAT69 threw parties in the early nineties that P. Diddy would be proud of. They had it so tight that no cameras were allowed. After Teddy Bear bought the building, Aisha and Terry moved into the upstairs apartments. That way Bossy never had to worry about her neighbors calling the landlord to complain. Bossy never worried about anyone calling the police on her. That is something people in the Yo just did not do.

Over a decade later, niggas were still talking about the sets Bossy threw at 539 Falls Avenue.

Liquor flowed, weed went up in smoke, and the buffalo punch always marinated for at least seventy-two hours. If shit happened, Bossy made sure she controlled what went down, no ifs, ands, or buts about it. The sets were safe, they were fun, and what happened at Bossy's crib, stayed the fuck at Bossy's crib.

Meet My Girls

Chapter 2

Bossy, Aisha, and Terry were certain to always have each others' backs sharing the apartment building. The steel security door guarded against intruders and provided extra security, which was of the utmost importance in Bossy's line of work. Visitors had to be buzzed in and out by the residents. The brick building at 539 Falls Avenue held four two-bedroom apartments.

Terry and Aisha were both downstairs inside apartment B visiting Bossy when the buzzer signified a visitor seeking entrance. Terry, who was sitting on the couch reading *When Souls Mate* by Joy, opened the door for Twan.

"What's up, Twan? I haven't seen you in a week," greeted Terry.

"Girl, you know how my life is. One day I'm here, the next day I'm hundreds of miles away." Twan followed Terry to the couch, bent down to kiss her cheek, and walked into the dining room to speak to Bossy.

Aisha had been in the second bedroom that

Bossy converted into her Zen room when she heard Twan's voice. She called out to him as she walked up the long hallway. Aisha loved for Twan to come around because he was a comedian in his own right. He was always good for a laugh.

"Hey, Miss Aisha, with ya sexy ass," flirted Twan, "you thirsty, girl?"

"Oh, you want a drink with us after being MIA for a week? You sure you have the time or are you in a rush?" teased Aisha. She and Terry had become used to Twan showing up on their doorstep at least three times a week. He always claimed to be hungry but the women knew Twan was just making sure they were safe.

Twan nodded and accepted the drink offer. His intentions were to just pop in and check on his girls before making his daily runs, but who could pass up an offer to spend time with three beautiful down-to-earth women. Twan took a seat in the living room with Terry after Aisha made his drink. Bossy's living room was decorated in three different shades of blue. The oversized couch and love seat were sky blue. The mirrored end tables were always free of fingerprints and the black art was simply impressive.

Like most men, Twan often daydreamed about the three women in his company. They were all beautiful, intelligent, and hard to get with.

Bossy was caramel brown with hair falling off her shoulders, and petite, standing at five feet, four inches, not weighing more than 135 pounds. She had full heart-shaped lips and ass and hips perfect for her frame.

Aisha's features were breathtaking. A red bone

with hypnotizing light brown eyes, she kept her hair and makeup done to perfection. Aisha, at five feet, three inches, was what men call thick—hips, ass, thighs—just thick.

At five feet, five inches, weighing about 140 pounds, Terry was the shit. Skin color somewhere between mocha and cocoa, haircut in a short crop that complemented her face perfectly. Her glowing smile and those deep brown eyes of hers were dangerous. She was all about business and always had her head stuck in a book. If a black author wrote it, Terry had read it.

"What you dreamin' about? Or do we even want to know?" Bossy broke Twan out of his daydream.

"Ah, it's all good. If y'all straight let's get down with a game of bones. That is if Miss Terry can close that book," said Twan. "Terry, why is it that every time I see you, there is a book of some kind in your hands?" Twan asked jokingly but was really curious about the answer.

"Don't you know that there is more to the world than hustling, drinking, and playing games? I like to read, to expand my mind."

"So you what, thirty-five now and still trying to learn some shit? I'm straight on that."

"You never get too old to learn and grow. We should all want to better ourselves."

"Is that right, Miss Terry? I never realized you were one of those philosophical types," Twan said between sips of Belvedere.

"It's not even like that. Reading is my favorite pastime. There are a variety of authors just like there are a variety of rappers." Terry tried to break it down on a level that Twan would understand. "If you want to read about street life, pick up any book written by Donald Goines, Nikki Turner, or this new author, Tysha. Say you like poetry—there's Nikki Giovanni. This author I'm reading now, Joylynn Jossel, has written urban, romance, black erotica and even children's books. Her new book *Wet* is so good, I can't put it down," said Terry, smiling.

"Yeah, I hear you, but who has time to sit down and read a book when there's money out there to be made?" Twan questioned his longtime friend.

"I have time and will always make time to read. See Twan, one of the problems with our community is that we limit ourselves to what we can or cannot do. But I know my possibilities are endless," Terry explained with sincerity.

"I feel what you sayin', Terry. Yeah, that's what's up." Twan was letting Terry's words sink in.

Twan returned his attention to his now watered-down drink as Terry refocused on her novel.

The trio let Twan enjoy another drink with them, then explained that they had to get ready for their trip. As Twan rose from his seat to leave, the buzzer alerted them to the arrival of another visitor.

"Who the hell is that?" said Bossy. "Is one of y'all expecting somebody?"

Aisha and Terry shook their heads no and watched Bossy walk over to the intercom. Twan peeked out the window to see who it was. His eyes widened as he recognized the car. Just as Bossy pressed her intercom button to ask who it was, Twan stormed past her.

"Twan, what's going on?" yelled Bossy. Twan was

out the security door in the blink of an eye. Aisha and Terry ran to the window to find out who Twan was running after.

"I can't believe this shit. This chick got some nerve popping up over here," Twan mumbled to himself. Not only had LaJetia come looking for him but she had all three kids in the car with her.

"Something better be wrong with one of the kids, LaJetia," warned Twan.

"Why you over here again, Twan, if you ain't fuckin' with somebody who live here?" questioned LaJetia.

"Girl, what the hell are you talking about?" Twan was at a loss for words. He had no idea that LaJetia knew Bossy, let alone where she lived. As he waited for an explanation from LaJetia, Twan realized the kids were in the van listening to grown folks' conversation.

"I'm talkin' about you staying out till four in the mornings and going out of town every other week," fumed LaJetia. "Are you paying rent for some trick you got livin' here?"

"I am not going to stand here and have this argument with you. It's cold as hell and you got these kids out here in the middle of some junior-high-school type shit."

"Whatever, Twan. Just tell me who lives here."

"Take ya simple ass home, girl. We will talk about this when I get home." Twan turned his back on his immature girlfriend to walk away.

"Get back here, Twan," screamed LaJetia. "I ain't done and you better tell me who lives here. Today ain't the first time I saw ya car parked over here." LaJetia opened her van door to run after

Twan. She was determined to find out who Twan was visiting in the apartment building even if it meant ringing every doorbell in search of an answer.

LaJetia swung the van door open, yelled for Twan to come back and started to run after him. After taking three steps, LaJetia slipped on a sheet of ice and lost her balance. LaJetia tried to brace herself against her van but missed her mark.

Bam!

Bossy, Aisha, and Terry had been standing in the window watching everything. Their laughter made LaJetia feel such humiliation that she wanted to die on the spot.

"Twan, come help me!"

Twan never broke stride, refused to look back and embarrassed LaJetia more by slamming the security door behind him as he reentered the apartment building. Aisha and Terry stopped laughing once Twan walked through the door. Bossy kept her eye on LaJetia who was struggling to pick herself up from her fall. After the third attempt, LaJetia got up off the ground, brushed off the snow clinging to her coat and returned to her tirade.

"Twan, this shit ain't over. I know where ya bitch live now and I will find out who she is. You hear me, bitch? I will beat ya ass, fuckin' wit my man," fired LaJetia.

Inside the apartment, Aisha, Terry, and Twan all knew hell was about to break loose. Bossy did not tolerate someone bringing bullshit to her front door. She believed that if someone came to her house to start shit and disrespect her, they were basically begging for an ass kicking.

"Oh, hell, her ass done fucked up now," said Aisha. "Go talk to ya girl, Twan, and make her leave before this gets out of hand."

Twan had to think fast. He knew that Bossy would put a hurting on his girlfriend and LaJetia did deserve it but not with the kids in the van watching it all. The kids didn't deserve to see their mother get the living hell beat out of her.

"Bossy, I'm sorry about all of this. The kids are in the van and they don't need to be seeing all of this. Let me go out and talk to her, okay?" begged Twan.

LaJetia could see Twan talking to Bossy through the window and started screaming at the top of her lungs. Bossy never blinked an eye as she stared at LaJetia and spoke to Twan.

"She obviously came over here looking to find some shit and some shit she has found. You have exactly one minute to get a hold of ya girl and get her the fuck away from my home. If she is not gone at the end of those sixty seconds, I am going to whip her ass," promised Bossy.

Knowing Bossy meant every word, Twan's heart raced as he walked back outside. LaJetia was standing in the front yard, staring back at Bossy and making empty threats. She had no idea who the woman standing in the window was, she just knew her man had to be fuckin' her. LaJetia was determined to get her point across to both Twan and his ho. Seeing Twan coming back out to her gave LaJetia a feeling of victory. She thought that her actions had put fear in the woman and Twan was hers to keep.

"LaJetia, you don't know who you fucking with

and you don't want to find out. You can't just show up on somebody's door and talk shit . . . especially if you don't know whose door you knocking on. Now get back in the van and leave." Knowing the clock was ticking, Twan tried to keep his cool as he spoke.

"Fuck that bitch. She don't know who she's fuckin' with. Tell ya ho to come out here while she standing in that window. Tell her to come out here," bluffed LaJetia. Her heart did not match her words on any level.

"LaJetia, shut the fuck up and get out of here, please."

"Why, Twan? You don't want me messin' up y'all relationship so you going to choose her over me and the kids?"

"If you know what's good for you, you will get the hell out of here." Twan grabbed LaJetia by the arm and began dragging her toward the running van. Luckily, the kids had their attention on the video they were watching and were not paying any attention to their mother. They were used to their mother yelling and screaming.

LaJetia struggled to loosen Twan's grip on her arm to no avail. Twan opened the driver-side door and forced LaJetia behind the wheel. Inside, LaJetia was relieved because she couldn't fight one bit but on the outside she kept up her juvenile front.

"Fuck you and that bitch, Twan. I got something waiting for you when you get home."

"LaJetia, you have no idea what you've done. Don't you remember who that is standing in the window?"

"I don't know that girl so why don't you tell me who she is."

"Bossy," answered Twan.

LaJetia sat frozen with her jaw hanging open. She tried to will herself to talk but no words would come. Having grown up in the projects, LaJetia had heard all of the stories about Bossy wreaking havoc and fear in the hearts of women and men alike. LaJetia's heart was pounding and her hands were shaking as she tried to shift the gear from park to drive. After telling LaJetia to go straight home, Twan slammed the van door shut and watched it slowly disappear up the street. He had been so nervous he almost pissed his pants. Twan knew Bossy would put a hurting on LaJetia if things got physical between them.

Aisha and Terry rejoined Bossy in the window when Twan went back outside. As much as she did not want to, Bossy was prepared to beat the shit out of the young girl but was glad Twan had gotten her to leave.

"I'm too old for this fighting bullshit but if it's brought to me, what other choice do I have?" questioned Bossy.

"I'm proud of you, girl," answered Terry, "because there was a time when you wouldn't have given Twan or anybody the chance to defuse a situation like this."

"Yeah, you are maturing, girl . . . unless you just getting soft in ya old age," joked Aisha.

"Shit, that will never happen," laughed Bossy. "But on a serious note, Twan better watch that bitch. Her simple ass might kill him one day in a jealous rage or something." Bossy watched Twan as he stood in the middle of the street watching the van pull away. He looked up at Bossy, gave her a nod of the head, and walked over to his car. Bossy acknowledged him with a smile before closing her custom-made curtains.

"Now that the show is over, let me finish off my joint and we'll get on the road. I'm ready to have some fun," said Bossy.

The drive to Detroit would take an hour longer because of the weather. Living in the snowbelt area, natives were familiar with the snow, sleet, and icy roads. People who'd migrated north, however, couldn't seem to adapt to the winter road conditions.

The plan for the weekend included shopping at various malls, getting pampered at a full service day spa, and driving back to Cleveland on Saturday night to hit all of the hot nightclubs in the "flats" area, the place to be if you were looking to kick it.

"Whose shit is this anyway?" Terry asked Bossy, weighing her first bag.

"Teddy Bear is on some new shit. Y'all know I don't ask any questions on matters that don't affect me directly," Bossy explained.

"We know, but Teddy Bear always tells us more than we really want to know anyway. Has he mentioned anything about hiring a contractor to build the addition to the shop?" Terry inquired.

"Yeah, he wants to wait for the weather to break. Labor will be cheaper and more dependable in the spring. By the way, that was a great idea you came up with." Bossy commended Terry on her latest business plan to provide day care to clients receiving hair and nail services. It would be advertised as free, but actually the cost would be hidden in the new prices unveiled in the spring.

"What can I say, legal or illegal, a hustle is a hustle, but sometimes I even amaze myself." Terry jokingly gave herself a pat on the back.

Aisha and Terry lent a hand with their friend's hustle whenever her workload got heavy. They considered themselves to be part-time hustlers. Aisha could be described as "less ghetto" than Bossy and more street than Terry. Though the trio's backgrounds were somewhat different, they were similar enough to make their friendship genuine. They couldn't have been any closer if they were blood sisters.

Aisha came from a single-parent home just like Bossy. Beverly Woods had raised her only child, Aisha, on her own. Times were hard through the years but Beverly kept a full-time job and a steady hustle on the side to provide for her daughter.

When she was young, Aisha had book smarts but no streets smarts whatsoever. Her mother suspected that would be her downfall one day, but on the other hand, was happy to see the innocence she possessed. Beverly's work responsibilities meant that at an early age Aisha was left home alone for hours to care for herself. One spring day in 1983, when Aisha was thirteen, her innocence was stolen from her.

Shortly after Aisha arrived home from Hayes Junior High School, there was a faint knock at the door. She had walked home with a large group of kids and thought maybe one of them was locked out of his or her apartment or something. Aisha unlocked and opened the door without seeing who was trying to gain entrance. Before she knew it, the forceful opening of the door threw her violently against the wall, where she hit her head. She fell to the ground and heard the door slam. Aisha tried to get up from the tile floor and began screaming when a strange voice demanded her silence and a pair of hands grabbed her arms roughly. Fear overtook Aisha and she began to punch, kick, spit, and scream for dear life in an attempt to break free of the intruder's grasp.

The masked intruder was bigger and stronger than his victim was and was able to pin the young girl down, pull up her pink skirt, pry her fragile legs apart and brutally rape the child. Aisha continued screaming as pain shot up into her pelvic area. Then, as suddenly as the attack had begun, it ended. It seemed like forever before Aisha opened her eyes to find her assailant lying beside her with a kitchen knife in his back.

"It's okay, no one's goin' to hurt you any more." Bossy kneeled beside her neighbor and wiped her tears away. Bossy and her family lived next door to Aisha and her mother. Bossy was also at home alone when the screams of her neighbor demanded her attention. Instinctively, she ran into her kitchen, grabbed the biggest butcher knife she could find, and ran next door to help her neighbor. Like so many in the projects, neither Bossy nor Aisha's household had a telephone. As Bossy ran to help Aisha, she saw Terry Benson leaving her cousin's apartment across the way.

"Hey you, call nine-one-one, something's wrong

with my neighbor!" Bossy shouted as she ran through the door to see the neighborhood dope fiend raping Aisha. The knife went into David Lawford's back as if it were a steak.

As Bossy sat consoling Aisha, Terry ran for a blanket and held Aisha's hand until help arrived. The three had never let anyone or anything hurt them since.

The knife didn't kill David but months later his body was found hanging from the end of a rope in the Mahoning County Jail. His death was ruled a suicide although both his hands were bound behind his back. During the autopsy, it was discovered that shortly before his death, David had suffered four broken ribs, a split spleen and contusions to his back.

Aisha, Terry, and Bossy didn't care how the rapist had died—only that he'd paid for his crime.

Damned Either Way

Chapter 3

Getting a hair appointment with Sirenna Salas, KAT69 Hair and Nail Salon's best beautician, was hard, but LaJetia had been able to lock in a regular weekly time slot. Sirenna was said to be the best beautician in northeastern Ohio and her clientele list was a testament to it.

As always, KAT69 Hair and Nails was crowded with regular faces sharing new gossip and recalling last week's whispers. LaJetia flipped through an old *Essence* issue while she waited for her turn at the shampoo bowl. Seated next to her were two clients she'd seen on prior visits talking about their previous night out at Southern Tavern.

"Mmm girl, I see him in dere all the time. He and his boy always hanging out." A woman wearing a skin-tight Baby Phat knockoff dress spoke to her friend.

"They be buyin' drinks for everybody like that all of the time," stated her friend who was dark as coal and wearing a bright orange jumpsuit with matching lipstick.

"Girl, money ain't no thang to dem. They been ballin' for years. Shit, every time I see that cute one, he got on a throw back jersey with kicks to match," the first woman said matter-of-factly.

LaJetia had been half listening to the conversation as she looked through an outdated *Essence* magazine but after hearing mention of a baller splurging on drinks, wearing a throw back jersey with new tennis shoes, all of her attention became centered on the ghetto girl's conversation. She quickly sought a way to ease into the conversation in an attempt to obtain as much information about the mystery ballin', throw back wearing, big spender at the club, last night.

"I was at the wrong place last night, it sounds like I could have drank for free if I'd been with y'all. Them fool's at the hole-in-the-wall where I was at wasn't buyin' a bitch shit," LaJetia lied with ease.

Without hesitation, the two women allowed LaJetia to join their conversation.

"Yeah, girl, Southern Tavern had a nice little crowd last night and a couple of regulars bought a few rounds for everybody sitting at the bar," Neon Orange explained.

"What? Damn, I *was* at the wrong spot. My girl talked me into driving out to Warren, Ohio and that turned out to be nothing but a waste of gas, time, and money." LaJetia continued with her lie.

"Don't do that again. On Tuesday and Thursday if you want a drink, bring it on down to the tavern and drink free. My boys Twan and Ant will look out for us all. They both real cool, they not like some men. Think if they buy you a two-dollar drink you owe them some ass," Knockoff Baby Phat complained.

"Oh, they cool like that? What, they funny or something?" LaJetia fished for further information.

"Naw girl, they both straight. Ant is ugly as all outdoors and don't have a choice but to be nice because otherwise he couldn't pay a bitch to give his monkey ass the time of day. Now Twan and his fine ass, oooohhhhh! I'd give him some myself but he got a woman at home and that bitch must have a pussy lined in gold, 'cause he ain't catchin' nothing nobody throwin' at him. Believe me; many have tried, including me. Big baller got the nerve to say he 'straight, wifey at home holdin' it down'," Knockoff Baby Phat said with much attitude.

By the time Sirenna called LaJetia to her chair, Knockoff Baby Phat and Neon Orange had been serviced, booked for next week, and sent on their way.

"I heard what you and those two girls were talking about earlier," Sirenna said to LaJetia as she sculpted her hair.

"They obviously didn't know I'm the bitch at home with the pussy lined in gold."

"You know how some of these young-minded girls around here can be. They on welfare, got three or four kids by three or four different men, and looking for a man with money to take care of a family that the last man added to and walked away from." Having some idea that she'd just described her current client, Sirenna went on. "As you get older and get to know yourself, you learn that a relationship is give-and-take. It's about respect, communication, and trust. You have nothing without those three things. You must treat each other the way you'd like to be treated. Believe me, girl, I was young once and let a good man get away while a bad one stayed too long."

Sirenna knew LaJetia was young and didn't understand how good she had it with Twan. She just hoped her words got through.

LaJetia listened intently to the wisdom in Sirenna's words. She had a different view of her life now and she was going to take time out and study it. She was young but wise enough to know that if Twan wanted to, he could replace her in the blink of an eye.

"How many times do I have to tell you, LaJetia? My business is my business! The less you know, the better off we both are. Damn, girl, I'm taking care of home ain't I?" Antwan Marcus Glover was getting frustrated with having to explain himself day in and day out. LaJetia and her bitching were giving him stomach ulcers. All she did was complain about him being gone, make accusations of unfaithfulness and lay around on her ass all day. If it wasn't one thing with her, it was damn sure another.

"I'm so fuckin' tired of this shit! If I'm out making money, you want me home and if I'm at home you asking me for money. How the hell can I give you what you want if I'm not out there hustlin'?" Twan tried to regain his cool.

"I know you be messin' around on me. Don't deny it because my girls done already told me," LaJetia mislead Twan.

"Shit, what girls? Since I met you I haven't met any friends or family member of yours so don't try and play me for stupid." Twan felt a migraine headache coming on.

"You leave me in this house every day, all day while you out running the streets or going back and forth to Florida. All I do is cook, clean, wash clothes, and raise the kids. Shit, I'm nineteen and living like I'm thirty-nine."

"What you want me to do, LaJetia, sit here with you? How the rent gon' get paid? What about the utility bills, food, clothes, and whatever else? Not only don't you work, but you won't even take ya lazy, spoiled ass to welfare and get a check and food stamps. Why, you too good for the system now that you done reeled in a hustler? Shit, you want more of my time. Get up off ya simple ass and help me pay some of these damn bills!"

"Whatever Twan, I ain't gettin' back on the system and have them nosy-ass case workers all up in my business. You take care of us, right? You throw it in my face every chance you get."

Grabbing hold of his quickly growing anger, Twan lowered his tone and gave up trying to get his point across. Not once in his life had he hit a woman, but there had been countless times that he wanted to slap the shit out of LaJetia.

Twan couldn't figure the girl out. It's said that girls mature faster than boys do. Twan being twenty-seven and LaJetia nineteen it seemed as though they should be on the same level. But the reality of it was they were far apart. The relationship resembled that of a junior high school couple instead of two adults.

"I'm good to you, girl, and you don't even recognize it. Any other woman would appreciate what I've given you but as time goes on, I'm beginning to think that's the problem."

"What's the problem?" LaJetia asked, confused.

"You don't appreciate a good man because you're not a woman yet. You are nothing more than a little girl playing in an adult world."

LaJetia was livid that Twan considered her a little girl. Life hadn't allowed her to be a child in over five years and she couldn't fathom what Twan meant when he described her as *a little girl playing in an adult world.*

When LaJetia became pregnant at age thirteen, her mother, Kate Rose, asked her if she wanted to have the baby. Without hesitation, the naive girl vowed to have her baby. Her mother simply shrugged her shoulders, and as always, allowed her child to make an adult decision. At age fourteen LaJetia's body was nowhere ready to give birth. Because of that hard labor and delivery, her body would forever carry the marks of strain and stress. Two years later her belly began to grow again.

It wasn't until her teenage daughter became pregnant for the second time that Kate realized she'd done her daughter more harm than good by offering her freedom and condoning her loose behavior. By the time any adult noticed LaJetia's petite frame growing, it was too late to abort and once again she gave birth.

Twan had never questioned LaJetia about the whereabouts of her childrens' fathers and why they weren't around. But LaJetia knew exactly why the fathers of her two oldest children were missing in action. She'd never pinned the paternities of her five-year-old daughter Kiara or her three-year-old son Tyler on anyone. The girl had allowed six boys to run a train on her when she became pregnant the first time. LaJetia, like so many other young girls, mistook sex for love.

Twan and LaJetia Rose met at Southern Tavern. They had slept together that same night and for the third time, a baby was conceived. Growing up without a father Twan knew immediately that he wanted be a good father to his child. His nine-month-old son, Trayvon, was the spitting image of him and meant the world to his daddy. Being a good man, Twan promised to take care of LaJetia and his new ready-made family.

Twan moved LaJetia and her two kids in with him just two weeks after she found out she was pregnant with his baby. His mother and brother had warned him that the young girl wasn't looking for a boyfriend; she was seeking a savior. And that's exactly what Twan had become to the young girl—a savior. He'd saved her from the projects, welfare, and poverty. He'd protected her from loneliness, fear, and disgrace.

The family lived in a three-bedroom house on the west side of Youngstown. Tyler and Trayvon had every toy a boy could want and sported only name-brand clothes and shoes. Five-year-old Kiara was becoming a spoiled brat. Her room was decorated in pinks and whites. The queen-size canopy bed with lace and ruffles to accentuate it was fit for a princess.

The rest of the two-story house was comfortable and LaJetia drove her children around in a new, fully equipped Toyota Sienna, including two televisions and a DVD player. Twan never asked LaJetia to go outside of the house to work. All he asked for was healthy children, a clean home, and a hot home-cooked meal. He felt his requests were reasonable and fair. She wanted for nothing but always found something to bitch about. Shit, Twan sent LaJetia to get her hair and nails done every Thursday afternoon. Donna Simpson, a sales manager at Kaufmanns Department Store knew LaJetia so well that she'd put aside new arrivals in her size. A couple of the sales associates from various stores would call her when a good sale was coming up.

LaJetia felt that if Twan were truly in love with her, she wouldn't have to ask him to stay home or to come home at a decent hour. He would want to be with her instead of sponsoring her weekly hair appointments and shopping sprees. He would appreciate the fact that his woman stayed home and kept a clean house in spite of simultaneously caring for three children five and under. Shit, she even prepared three hot meals seven days a week. Her mother may not have taught her much, but she did teach her how to cook a good meal.

LaJetia complained excessively about Twan leaving the house early and returning late. She couldn't understand why any man, especially her man, would stay away from home all hours of the day and night unless he was out cheating. She didn't care what two lonely women at the hair shop said. For all she knew, Twan set up that whole scene just to get her off his back.

"Why you just now comin' home if you ain't out fuckin' some ho?"

"Look girl, you know how I make my money and it's late. I'm not in the mood for your bitchin' right now."

"Pull ya pants down, let me smell ya balls."

"Go ahead and smell 'em.. I ain't washed them in about eighteen hours so they nice and sweaty. Sniff away."

"You think you funny." LaJetia thought better of smelling Twan's privates and rolled over to get back to sleep.

Twan took a quick shower; just as he lay his weary head down on his pillow, LaJetia sprung into action again.

"I knew ya sorry ass was out fuckin' around. Who the hell is calling ya cell phone at four in the morning?"

"Answer it, LaJetia. Get ya ass up and answer it." Twan had no energy to fight. All he wanted was to get some sleep.

"Hello, who is this?" LaJetia practically screamed into the phone.

"Put Twan on the phone," commanded Twan's best friend Ant.

"He 'sleep and why you callin' so early?"

"Girl, don't you know the streets never shut down? Especially in the jets. Wake that fool up." Anthonie Quarles didn't like his best friend's girl, but he tolerated her because of the love he had for Twan. Ant had warned Twan many times that LaJetia's insecurities and immaturity would be Twan's downfall. And, in turn, Ant's downfall as well.

"What you want that's so important I got to wake him up? Sometimes I think y'all fuckin'!" LaJetia knew Ant would call her out her name for that remark.

"You know what? You are a phony bitch. All lovey-dovey when my boy got his peeps around and always bitchin' and complaining when y'all alone. Your days are numbered with ya two-faced ass! I just hope I'm around when Twan sends your stupid ass back to ya mama. Oh, that's right, she don't want you there either. Maybe the Samaritan House for the Homeless and Destitute can hook you up with some shelter and used clothes, bitch!"

Before LaJetia could reply, Ant hit the end button on his cell phone. She put the cell phone on the charger and tried to wake Twan to no avail. She was left to stew in her anger until Twan woke to start a new day of street hustling.

Countless times Twan had sat his young minded girlfriend down and tried explaining the number-one rule of being a street hustler. Be on call 24-7. In other words, if you're pushing a product, be available at all times to provide that product.

From Twan's point of view, he did everything to provide a comfortable life for his family; he was trying to make his girl happy. He was beginning to feel that doing his best just wasn't good enough for this young, easy lay from the projects.

No Rest for the Weary

Chapter 4

Terry woke up in a cold sweat again. She had been having the same nightmare for the past six months. The lack of sleep was wearing her down. She rose slowly to sit in bed, shoulders hunched, willing herself to begin the walk to the bathroom. Just as she prepared to step into the shower, she heard a light knock at the door and the turning of the dead-bolt lock.

"Girl, you ain't dressed yet? You didn't even set the coffee pot to auto . . . what's wrong with you lately?" Aisha yelled out one question after another more to herself than to Terry.

Without responding to any of the questions posed to her, Terry stepped into the warm shower and attempted to use the bar of Zest soap as a wake-up aid like the actors did in the old commercials. After lathering twice, she reached for a half-empty bottle of Victoria's Secret strawberries and champagne body wash when a scene from her recurring nightmare flashed in front of her eyes causing her to drop the bottle.

Startled, Terry shook her head, rinsed her body a final time, and stepped out of the shower. She caught a glimpse of her reflection in the mirror and didn't recognize the person staring back at her.

"Will you please tell me what is going on with you? I mean you always trip this time of year, but not this bad, Tee. What is it?" Aisha asked, concern in her voice.

"Aisha, you're always worried about nothing. Did you pour me a cup of coffee?" Terry tried unsuccessfully to sidestep her friend's question.

"No, I didn't pour you a cup of coffee. If I had, you'd complain that it was cold. Instead of trying to ignore my question, please talk to me. What is going on, Terry? You look like you haven't slept in weeks . . . and have you lost weight?"

"Like you say, I always trip this time of year. It is August and we all know how this month affects me."

"It's different this time and I want to know why. If Bossy and I can help you, please let us."

"I love you both but no one can help me with this, Aisha. It has been fifteen years since my parents forced me to give my baby girl away and I still can't get over the pain. I'm still grieving the loss and I don't know how to get past it." Terry broke down in tears as Aisha led her over to the oversized cream suede sectional.

Realizing her friend needed more help than she could offer, Aisha held Terry and let her cry out as much of her pain as she possibly could. A feeling of helplessness swept over Terry and she let out a scream that had been inside of her since the day that nurse took her beautiful baby girl away from her.

Unlike Bossy and Aisha, Terry was brought up on the south side of Youngstown. Both of her parents worked hard at Packard Electric to provide their only child with the best things life could offer.

Richard and Cheryl Benson began mapping out Terry's future the day she was born. They sent their baby girl to private schools, already envisioning her career as a successful corporate lawyer.

Mr. and Mrs. Benson were very protective of their little girl and kept her under strict lock and key. During her high school years when most teenagers were partying at the Union Hall or skating at the Skate Connection, Terry was stretched out on her queen-sized bed reading James Baldwin, Langston Hughes or Nikki Giovanni. Terry Lynette Benson was valedictorian of the class of 1988 at Ursuline Catholic High School. With her parents' blessings, she accepted an academic scholarship to the University of Toledo.

Terry was more than eager to escape from the strong grip her parents held on her. At first she chose to attend a college much further away from Youngstown, but that would have meant leaving her two best friends behind. Bossy and Aisha were more than friends to her, they were her sisters. Being able to stay close to them and preserving the bond they shared was more important than running away from her overbearing parents.

Freshman year in college was overwhelming.

Being away from home for the first time in her life, Terry discovered a whole new world. There weren't enough hours in a day. Classes, studies, parties, boys, pledging Delta, discovering herself; the list never ended.

While pledging Delta, Terry discovered she was pregnant. After being coldly dismissed and disrespected by her boyfriend, Terry didn't know what to do or where to turn. After crying her eyes out, Terry called Bossy and Aisha. They immediately rented a car and began the two-hour drive to lend support to their friend. Bossy sped the entire way and got them there in record time.

"What am I going to do?" stuttered Terry in between sobs.

"That has to be your decision, Terry. Whatever you choose, we will support you no matter what," Bossy assured Terry.

"I know and I love y'all for it. I'm worried about my parents. They expect so much from me and I've always done exactly as they've wanted me to," cried Terry.

"Tee, you may not like this, but it has to be said. There comes a time when you have to take responsibility for your own life and in turn, live it yourself. I know your parents mean well but they've lived their lives and made their mistakes. In order to grow and learn, we all gotta try, girl, and if we get knocked down, get up and try again." Aisha spoke wholeheartedly.

"You're right, but I'm scared of how they'll react to this. My parents have had me up on a pedestal my entire life. They are going to be crushed and disappointed," Terry worried.

"No one is perfect, Terry, no one, and that includes your parents. Sure, they'll be hurt at first but they love you and will forgive you of anything," said Aisha, consolingly.

Fifteen years later, Terry was still awaiting her parents' forgiveness. Terry was allowed to give birth to a six-pound, nine-ounce baby girl on August 31, 1989. She wasn't allowed to name her daughter, however, because the adoptive parents wanted that honor. After holding her beautiful baby in her arms for a mere five minutes, Terry handed her over to a nurse and never saw her again. Fifteen years later, she still dreamt of the baby she was forced to give away. In her heart, Terry called her daughter Anissa Renee Woods.

Terry never returned to Toledo to finish her education and her parents hadn't forgiven her for that either. In turn, Terry never got over the pain of being forced to give away her baby girl. She hadn't spoken to her parents in over fifteen years. Bossy, Aisha, and Mama Bev were all the family she felt she needed.

"Why don't you stay home today? I'll have Bossy come and help at the shop. You really need to take some time for yourself." Aisha thought this might be the right time to suggest Terry reach out to her parents. Aisha felt that in order for Terry to find peace, she not only had to forgive herself, she also had to forgive her parents. But after seeing the pain in her friend's eyes, Aisha decided to remain silent. At least for the moment.

"Remember, the Model Me Role Model Project?

I'm interviewing two teenagers from the Mahoning County Youth Focus Program today. Anyway, it's Thursday and you know Bossy won't be seeing the light of day. I'll be all right, girl. Just go open up without me and let me have a cup of coffee," Terry said. "I'll be up the hill in about an hour."

Aisha understood that Terry was asking to have a little time for herself and made her way to the door. Before leaving the apartment building, Aisha stopped to share her concerns about Terry with Bossy. Bossy appeared to be in deep thought, her brow furrowed, lips pursed.

"Girl, I'm thinkin' real hard about letting this hustle go. Shit, we all thirty-five years old and I'm still doin' the same shit I was doin' when we were twenty-five. These young girls callin' my damn house all hours of the night lookin' for some dick that ain't stickin' nothing here! Twan's ass gettin' too bigheaded lately. If he ain't already, he's gon' draw some negative attention to himself. Out at the clubs buying rounds and shit," Bossy vented.

"Bossy, I hear you on all of that but we need to talk." Aisha went on to explain her visit with Terry and voiced her concerns with Bossy.

"Her baby girl will be fifteen years old this summer but the pain of losing her is so fresh it could have happened just yesterday. Maybe we should suggest she start seeing a psychologist."

"I don't understand why this year is so different from all of the others. We all know that August is the most difficult month for her. Has she made contact with the family that adopted her baby?" Bossy questioned.

"No, not that I know of. All she'll tell me is that

she's been having a recurring nightmare and hasn't been sleeping much."

"What are the nightmares about?" Bossy asked as she walked towards her kitchen to pour a second cup of coffee.

"She won't tell me, but I think the two are related."

Aisha and Bossy decided to sit Terry down to discuss the possibility of her seeking professional help or maybe tracking down the baby daughter she was forced to give up for adoption. They both agreed to wait for Terry to get back to herself before they opened a door that might send her over the edge. After Aisha left to open the shop, Bossy returned to her dining room table and the fresh package of cocaine waiting to be stepped on.

KAT69 Hair and Nail Salon had been a profitable establishment since the first day the doors opened for business. The building had been renovated numerous times over the years but the foundation remained strong. The previous owner, Matt Pierce, had remodeled the place to accommodate both barbers and beauticians. After he was busted for running numbers, the establishment became an after-hours nightclub run by some bikers. Once their membership started dwindling due to death, imprisonment, and plain old age, they locked the doors. About five or six years ago, Teddy Bear bought the property and opened the first beauty and nail shop to operate seven days a week. Bossy, Aisha, and Terry were the legal owners, operators and, managers of the prosperous business. The shop employed three nail techs: Donnie Barnett, Virginia Faircloth, and Bianca Hill. On the other side of the establishment were the best beauticians to come out of Youngstown: Sirenna Salas, Jessica Hopkins, Nolicka Williams-Robinson and Diane Jackson.

Working with such a variety of personalities could be challenging but everyone respected each other and loved working for Terry, Aisha, and Bossy. Terry never hired a new employee without the approval of the veteran beauticians, Sirenna and Nolicka. It was important to Terry for her employees to feel like family. Unlike many salons, the turnover rate there was low because the employees were involved in the daily running of the business.

While no drugs were warehoused there, it was a good front to justify the illegal money the three women had coming in. Terry never returned to Toledo to complete her education, but she was able to obtain a business management degree from Youngstown State University. Running the shop was right up her alley. Recently, she'd decided on adding to the building's structure for it to serve as a day care for the children of clients receiving hair and nail services. The new benefit would be offered free of charge and, Terry believed, in turn would draw in more business. By year's end, she planned on bringing in three barbers. Her five-year business plan had the company transformed into a full-service day spa, offering everything from a shampoo to a full body massage, maybe even yoga and Pilates classes.

By the time Terry pulled herself together and

got to work, the girls from the youth program were waiting in her office.

"I apologize for keeping you girls waiting," Terry said sincerely, "but now that I'm here, why don't we get started?"

The youth program had chosen Talissa Croomes and Caron Johnson to work at KAT69 based on their current interests and plans.

"I'd like to start by getting to know you both a little. I'll start by telling you about myself, the other two owners, and how the salon operates." After Terry provided even more information about the business than she'd initially intended, she let the girls talk about themselves. Caron spoke first and her bubbly personality dominated the meeting.

"Miss Terry, I just want to thank you for bringing us on and taking us under your wing. I don't know about my girl Talissa, but I've always wanted to be a part of KAT Sixty-nine. My mom and I ride by here every day and it's always packed. My mom gets her hair done by Miss Nolicka and . . ."

Terry's thoughts wandered off as Caron continued to talk for another ten minutes. From time to time, Terry would tune in and wonder how a person could talk so long and never stop to take a breath. When Terry couldn't stand the sound of the girl's voice any longer, she interrupted her. "Thank you, Caron, I think Talissa and I have both learned a lot about you today. Now Talissa, I understand you're a member of the honor society and want to attend Spelman College after graduation."

"Yes ma'am, that's right."

"What else do you like to do?"

"I love to read," Talissa spoke softly. Terry waited a moment for her to continue but Talissa sat quietly.

"What do you plan on studying at college?"

"I'd like to obtain a degree in English and creative writing. I'd like to become an author," Talissa said with a smile.

"What a coincidence, that's exactly what I wanted to study in college but ended up with business management. You probably keep journals too, don't you?"

Talissa felt herself relax as she spoke with her new boss. She had been worried about feeling out of place, especially when she compared Caron's outgoing personality to hers. Now, however, she was beginning to believe that KAT69 would be a good fit for her. She and Terry seemed to have so much in common.

Not All Teddy Bears Are Cuddly

Chapter 5

Theodric "Teddy Bear" Sampson ruled the Youngstown drug scene. There wasn't a nickel bag or a brick of cocaine sold or bought without Teddy Bear's fingerprints on the deal.

Teddy Bear looked as if he could have been the brother of the lead singer of the old-school band the Time. He and Morris Day both had "high yellow" skin; baby soft complexions, relaxed hair, and a petite built that gave strangers the wrong impression about the men when initially meeting them. Inside, demons dwelled, emerging when provoked by greed, others' deception, or the desire for revenge. His reputation on the street was that of a ruthless businessman who kept his enemies six feet under and his loved ones living high on the hog. Behind closed doors, there were secrets long buried that only he and his wife knew; Teddy Bear chose to act as if he'd forgotten them all.

"Look here, we have to be on the same page about this shit. I've made the same run many times myself so I'm familiar with the time frame," Teddy Bear lectured his student.

"I feel you on that—but we just made a pit stop in Atlanta on our way back from Jacksonville," argued the young man.

"Let me tell you something, son, and I'm only going to say it one time so listen up closely. First, that run to Florida is business; keep it that way. I have a schedule I like kept tight. Second, if you want to make a pit stop in Atlanta, Florence, Alabama, or anywhere else for that matter, you do that shit on your own, personal time." Teddy Bear spoke slowly and clearly to ensure his message was heard.

"That's what's up man; it won't happen again," Twan said and was sure to make eye contact with his mentor.

"I got big plans for you, youngblood, and I'm trying to teach you by giving you hands-on experience. If you can't handle the shit, let me know now. My time is valuable and I got plenty o' soldiers who'd love to be in your shoes."

"We on the same page and I'm ready for this. Teddy Bear, man, I swear I won't fuck up again."

"We cool, youngblood, we cool."

Teacher and student finished their pool game and business transaction just as Marie Sampson woke from her early evening drug-induced nap.

Teddy Bear saw Twan to the door and remembered how naive he was in his mid-twenties. Twan reminded him so much of himself that he felt an obligation to look out for him. Since Teddy Bear decided early on in life that he never wanted any children of his own, he'd sort of adopted a son and daughter—Twan and Bossy.

For a man who had never held a legitimate job in his life, Teddy Bear had done well for himself. He and his wife of ten years lived in a six-bedroom, seven-bathroom mini-mansion in Trumbell Township, about a half an hour's drive east of the city limits. The house had been custom built to fit Marie's specifications and the lavish decor was expensive yet inviting. The Sampsons liked to entertain, especially during the holiday seasons, and it was very important that their guests felt at ease. Molly Maid was contracted to come clean the house from top to bottom twice a week and Teddy Bear was considering hiring a live-in cook. Marie was a great cook but the hold of that monkey on her back was changing her and in turn, undermining the foundation of their marriage.

On November 19, 1994, Teddy Bear and Marie became man and wife after living together for eight years. As a result of his own upbringing, Teddy Bear was adamant about making not bringing any children into what he saw as a cruel world a precondition for marriage. As a result, Marie had her tubes not only tied, but clipped and burned to further deter her body from naturally healing itself.

For years Teddy Bear was a dedicated and loyal husband to his one and only love, Marie. Teddy Bear's dedication to Marie was much to the dismay of his parents. Teddy Bear was born and raised to be a drug dealing pimp. Kane's parents on *Menace II Society* didn't have shit on Paul and Eunice Sampson.

It was a proud day on April 14, 1964 when Eunice bore Paul a son whom they named Theodric Leon Sampson. There was never a question as to what the future held for the heroin-addicted baby boy. He would follow in his father's footsteps and be one of the best hustlers of northeastern Ohio.

Paul Sampson began bragging about the player his son was born to be the moment he entered the world. Big Daddy Paul groomed his son to become the biggest and most feared pimp in the Youngstown–Warren, Ohio area, and was proud of it. Eunice Sampson supported her husband's plan for their son and promised to show Teddy Bear the right way to keep his fleet of hoes in line. Like all kids seeking parental approval, Teddy Bear did, said, and acted as his parents instructed him to until that fateful day in 1983 when he met Marie Ruth Faye at one of the Afro Dogs Bikers Club after-hours parties.

The moment he saw her walk through the doors sporting a juicy Jheri curl and tight-ass black-and-white Adidas jogging suit with matching tennis shoes and puffing on a Newport, he knew his heart would forever belong to her. For over twenty years, Teddy Bear and Marie had stuck together through thick and thin, from hell and back again. The fairy tale ended the day Marie showed her love and need for the pills overpowered what she felt for her husband; that was the same day he went running across town into another woman's arms.

After the sterilization procedure, Marie was sent

home with a prescription of Percocet for pain. Weeks later, Marie's body began craving the narcotic; she had been addicted to prescription painkillers ever since. In the beginning she went from one doctor to another to acquire the drugs.

It didn't take long for her body to become immune to the medication and she began taking the pills with shots of expensive brandy. She tried Vicadin but they weren't as strong as Percocet. Not long after Marie was introduced to a new prescription drug, OxyContin, used to treat chronic pain. Some cancer patients relied on it for pain relief. On the streets, the pills sold for one dollar per milligram. Taken correctly, only one tablet should be swallowed every eight to twelve hours. The drug came with a warning not to chew, snort or crush. As a way to obtain that ultimate high, drug addicts crushed, snorted, and chewed the pills.

One night, Teddy Bear and Marie lay in bed, both waiting for the other to make the first move. Just as Marie rolled onto her side to face her husband, there was a knock at the door. Teddy Bear's eyes followed his wife's body as she stood; he'd always enjoyed the vision of her as God had made her—perfect and flawless in form.

As she rose from their bed, Marie slowly covered herself with a robe, knowing her husband enjoyed looking at her nude body, and exited the room to answer the door. Stunned didn't begin to describe Teddy Bear's reaction to seeing his wife's fragile frame. She had always been a petite woman, standing at only five feet, weighing 120 pounds even, but she was tight and firm. Marie had always taken pride in being in shape. The sight before him made it obvious that her addiction had taken over and was slowly sucking her spirit away. It looked as if she hadn't eaten in months, there were dark rings around her eyes and her hair was thinning. For the first time ever, Teddy Bear no longer found his wife attractive.

The next day, Teddy Bear found himself visiting Betty Terrell. When the affair first began, Teddy Bear felt so guilty, he couldn't get an erection. Embarrassed, he left the woman alone with wet panties, an eleven o'clock check-out time, and a hundred-dollar bill on the night table. A couple of months later, he had set Betty up in a three-bedroom house on Parkwood Avenue. The house was furnished to accommodate her and her two small children and Teddy Bear paid all of the monthly expenses.

In the past year, Betty had gotten very relaxed in her role and demanded more and more of her married lover's time. Teddy Bear saw nothing wrong with fulfilling the needs and wants of his girlfriend—hell, his wife was married to the drug.

Marie struggled to open her eyes and raise her head off the pillow when she heard her husband walk into their oversized bedroom. Instead of napping in their custommade Texas king-size bed, she'd fallen asleep on the love seat on the northeast side of the room. This area was specifically for reading, lounging, and enjoying the fireplace during the winter months.

Teddy Bear didn't acknowledge his wife as he

walked past her. His only purpose in being home now was to shit, shower, shave, and head out into the night air. To Teddy Bear, the way Marie had let herself go the past few years was unforgivable.

There was a time when Teddy Bear was proud to have his wife on his arm. She always kept herself together. Hair appointments two times a week, manicures and pedicures once a week, Fashion Fair makeup and designer clothes. Marie was prissy.

Since she got hooked on the pills, she had let herself go to the point that Teddy Bear refused to take her anywhere with him. He had even started beating her for leaving the house in search of pills.

Because of their history together, Teddy Bear had tried to help his one love fight her demons. Finally, to his dismay, he was forced to accept the fact that until Marie wanted to let go of her addiction, the demons would prevail.

"You got something for me, Teddy Bear?" Marie asked in a raspy voice.

"No," Teddy Bear replied without looking in Marie's direction.

"You want me sittin' in this big-ass house all the time by myself and you won't even help me get what I need to feel good," Marie said, pouting.

"I'm not helping you kill yourself by supplying pills to you."

"You are such a hypocrite, Teddy Bear. What business are you in again? Oh, yeah, that's right. You're the biggest drug dealer in Youngstown," Marie said sarcastically as she stood and walked over to the door of Teddy Bear's walk-in closet. "It seems logical to me that a man who sells drugs to his community would expect to have someone close to him craving those drugs. Shit, Teddy Bear, you ain't above reproach!"

Marie's last word was met with a backhanded slap that sent her fragile body sailing across the room. Before she could pick herself up off the floor, she was kicked in her ribs; this was followed by a punch to her right eye.

"Bitch, one day you're going to learn to keep ya damn mouth shut; you talk too damn much!" Teddy Bear's anger with Marie was not merely because of the truth in her words. He also felt she was trying to justify her craving for prescription painkillers. He was hurt that Marie had betrayed him repeatedly by loving the drugs more than she did him after all they'd meant to each other over the years. Revenge was the code he lived by and beating her was the only way he could think of to cause her as much pain as she'd caused him.

Marie lay on the bedroom floor watching drops of her own blood form a small puddle just under her chin. She didn't know if the blood was coming from her nose or from her bottom lip, she just couldn't muster up enough strength to tend to her wounds. From experience, Marie knew that at least one of her ribs was badly bruised, maybe even broken. Teddy Bear may have been angry with her for asking his help in obtaining some pills, but he'd actually done her a favor by beating her up. She needed medical attention and the emergency room doctor would most certainly send her home with a narcotic strong enough to mask any physical pain she felt.

Class Is In Session

Chapter 6

Twan sat nervously staring down at his well-done T-bone steak. His stomach was in knots and Teddy Bear's lecture wasn't making him feel any better.

"What you youngbloods don't understand is that respect is earned not demanded. You can't force a man to respect you by inflicting bodily harm. Respect is given to a man who knows himself and walks around with head held high, no matter what his status in life," Teddy Bear said directly to Twan.

When Bossy informed Twan it was time he joined her and Teddy Bear for their monthly dinner, Twan was both nervous and elated. The invitation was validation of Teddy Bear's trust in him. Climbing the hustler's ladder is easier when the person ahead of you reaches back to help pull you up. Twan had two hands pulling him, Teddy Bear's and Bossy's.

Twan realized that with responsibility comes a certain expectation. Both Teddy Bear and Bossy expected Twan to be a model pupil with a perfect 4.0 grade point average. At times, the pressure seemed unbearable.

"Are you listening to me, son? See, the problem with your generation is lack of respect for life." Teddy Bear paused to allow his words to hit Twan hard. He enjoyed the status that the adulation of the younger man and the role of mentor had brought him. However, Teddy Bear wanted Twan to feel more comfortable around him. He knew his position caused people to both fear and revere him—that came with the territory—but his protégé had no cause to fear him. As long as he didn't cross him.

Twan cleared his throat and reached for a glass of water before answering Teddy Bear.

"Yes, I hear you. I'm following every word. I feel what you sayin' and I'm puttin' in work."

"And besides the obvious, what's your motivation for living this life?"

"What else am I gonna do? I mean after taking a wrong turn early on in life, it's hard as hell to get back on the right track. The problem is that even if you do, people ain't gon' let you forget the mistakes you've made in your past." Twan felt that not only was it hard out here for a pimp, it was just plain hard out here period.

"Youngblood, what you must remember is this situation isn't new to your generation. Curtis Mayfield said, 'Been told I can't be nothin' else just a hustler in spite of myself, I know I can make it.' That's from *Superfly*, back in the seventies shit on the streets were the same as they are today," reminisced Teddy Bear.

"I've heard of Curtis Mayfield, Marvin Gaye, and Al Green. My mom and her friends love them and Barry White, Earth, Wind and Fire, Parliament Funkadelic, and all the funk classics."

"Okay, you know who the heavy hitters from the seventies were but do you know what they stood for? Do you know Curtis Mayfield's lyrics? Marvin Gaye's messages? People today like to say that the legend saw the future and sang about it, but the truth of the matter is that it's the same shit, just a different damn day. See, you learn your history from the old players, their music, lyrics, and legacy."

"I hear you, Teddy Bear, and I feel what you sayin'. Wasn't it Marvin Gaye who said, 'Crime is increasing, Trigger happy policing . . . ; Oh, make me wanna holler.'"

Bossy and Teddy Bear gave Twan a look that said they were proud and impressed with him. In unison, the three said, "Inner City Blues." Twan had impressed Teddy Bear and he felt good about himself for the first time in many years. The tension at the table faded away and it was back to business less than an hour later. While Bossy updated Teddy Bear on the plans to renovate KAT69 Hair and Nail Salon, Twan sat back in his chair and let his mind drift off to a different time in life.

Discouraged with his life and frustrated over how he and others like him were viewed in America, Twan carried a weight on his mind more often than he'd like to admit. He felt as if he had been backed into a dark corner surrounded by nothing but roadblocks and detours.

Twan's mother, Tracey, raised him and his brother, Aaron, in a working-class community on the north side of the city. The neighborhoods surrounding Alameda Avenue were considered some of the better for Youngstown, Ohio with their tree-lined streets, garbage cans on the curb, and sedans in driveways but most importantly, few sightings of police cruisers rolling through. In reality the neighborhood was no different from its counterpart—Westlake projects. Both areas housed a mix of hardworking people trying desperately to make a better way of life and hardworking drug dealers and hustlers determined to do the same.

Despite Tracey's efforts to keep her boys away from the temptations of the streets, she failed. It's difficult for a single woman to raise boys into men. The relationship between mother and son is a special bond. It is the boy's first love affair with a woman and for his entire life, he will love and protect his momma. A woman loves her son with an indescribable devotion and protectiveness, sometimes feeling her son is the first man in her life she can trust wholeheartedly not to betray her.

Tracey worked hard at a physically grueling and demanding job in order to provide for her boys. Commercial Sharon Metal and Steele was one of the last profitable manufacturers of its kind in the midwest. The work required employees to spend anywhere from six to seven days a week and ten to twelve hours a day on their feet, often lifting forty pounds above their heads.

The salary was equivalent to that of a two-income household. For Tracey, the job was a blessing because it allowed her financial security and the ability to have one less worry as a single parent. Twan and Aaron were born eighteen months apart but their selfish, sex-addicted daddy, Sammy D. (as he was known on the streets), was gone before Tracey even knew she was pregnant with Aaron. The Temptations sang that "Papa Was a Rolling Stone," but Sammy D. was a runaway boulder. He had more kids strewn around the city than Evander Holyfield and George Foreman put together.

The big house, nice car, and name-brand clothes all came at a price. Working first shift meant Twan and Aaron had to wake themselves up for school and lock the doors behind themselves at very early ages. Twan was responsible for getting his little brother home safely after school and making sure both had their homework and chores completed by six o'clock every school night. Tracey did her best to be home and have dinner with her boys every evening at seven.

Like most single mothers, Tracey sacrificed her needs for the wants of her boys. Twan played basketball and attended various camps during the summers. As he grew older, he became very interested in clothes, shoes, and always being well-groomed. As puberty took over and questions of becoming a man began to arise, Twan naturally turned to his mother for answers.

Junior high school also provided answers to Twan's questions. Since most of the answers came from boys his age also in search of answers, the majority of the information was wrong or of dubious worth. Like, oral sex wasn't really sex.

Twan was a good student, a great son, and a protective big brother until the unexpected changed his view of life, death, and the time in-between. Tracey had called her boys into her bedroom for a serious talk. Twan and Aaron silently worried about what the talk could possibly be about.

"I got a phone call today from your grandmother," Tracey began, trying to find the right words to say. "I'm sorry to have to tell you this, but Sammy D. passed on today."

The boys never had a close relationship with their father but Tracey still had no idea how they would react.

Twan was numb, Aaron was silent, and Tracey was afraid to say another word. She knew from firsthand experience that not having a father in your life is one thing but having him die is something altogether different because when he was alive, there was always the hope that things would change.

"What happened to him?" Twan stared at a small stain on the tan carpet.

"I don't know any of the details yet but it was health related."

Twan took his mother at her word because he knew she'd never lied to them and there was no way she'd start now. Not with this.

Five days later, Tracey accompanied her boys to their father's funeral. She held their hands, massaged their backs, and made certain that no one, friend or foe, said anything stupid to her sons. Tracey's personality made her seem soft but to see the ghetto in her, all a person had to do was fuck with one of her boys.

Twan retreated into himself when he found out about his father's death. Somehow his personality seemed altered, even damaged. He hadn't wanted to talk about how badly his heart ached for the father he'd always dreamed of having.

From time to time, Twan would bump into Sammy D. around town and they'd speak, exchange handshakes, promise to keep in touch and move on. Twan mourned for the father of his dreams that taught him how to throw a football, bounce a basketball and how to shave. His heart ached for the type of father who'd sit him down and talk to him about the changes happening with his body and why his dick would be hard whenever he saw Shawnie Brown wearing that dark blue mini skirt of hers. Even before his death, Twan often cried himself to sleep because he knew the chance of the father in his dreams coming into his life was slim to none.

Tracey tried with all her might to reach out and save her baby from the pain he was in. She knew instinctively what her son was feeling inside. Though she sometimes found herself wondering how you could miss a person you hardly knew, still, she sensed the pain his father's absence caused.

The attempts to communicate with her teenager failed time and time again. Tracey was at a loss and felt backed into a corner. She knew that the type of pain and confusion Twan was swimming in could easily make him feel as though he was drowning. A good mother would sacrifice her own life to save her drowning child and Tracey was no exception. She tried to suggest outlets for both Twan and Aaron; she even offered to take them to professional counseling.

After a few weeks of her anxious mothering, Twan

began feeling as though life was suffocating him. His views on life, however, became blurred and doing the right things just didn't seem worth the effort any more. Months after the death of his father, something inside of Twan snapped. His personality, mentality, and soul took a left turn and he had yet to find his way back. Twan saw no use in working hard to get into a good college when tomorrow wasn't promised to anyone. To Twan, the future was just a pipe dream his mother had sold him.

Twan stayed home long enough to barely graduate high school and to take care of his brother. Shortly after graduation, Tracey gave Twan an ultimatum: he could live in the streets or with his family but he couldn't do both. Twan's influence over his brother was too strong for Tracey to take for granted. The streets may have won the first round but she'd be damned if she'd let them claim both of her boys.

Twan made his choice and never turned back. Life in the streets of the Yo' wasn't no joke. A person only needed to get caught slippin' one time and that meant death or prison for sure.

After dinner, Twan and Bossy decided to make a stop at the local nightclub for another drink and a little more relaxation. Twan was tenser than he had realized, having his first dinner with Teddy Bear. The ride from the north side of the city to the south side took less than fifteen minutes and the sounds of Rick James accompanied the two through the city. Bossy sat in the leather passenger seat enjoying the lyrics of "In the Ghetto" and wondered if Rick James had ever been to Youngstown.

"Bossy, you all right over there? You're too quiet," said Twan, adjusting the music volume to a moderate level.

"I'm straight, just listening to the song and wondering if every ghetto in America is the same," answered Bossy.

"Every one that I've seen is the same. People hungry, tired and in search of a break. Cars broke down, kids playing ball, men on street corners and women on the stroll. Shit, the ghettos of Youngstown, Brooklyn, Detroit or wherever are all the same—just in a different location."

Bossy looked out of the car window and Twan turned the volume back up as they approached the parking lot of Larry's Lounge. It was happy hour and people were scarce but it was exactly as Bossy wanted it to be—near empty.

After taking a seat at the back bar, Twan put a few quarters into the jukebox and allowed some jazz to fill the room. The waitress on duty, Yvonne Wayne, knew each of her customers like she knew her kids and giving her a drink order was rarely necessary. Twan returned to his seat to find Bossy sippin' on Hennessy, and a Belvedere and cranberry juice waiting for him.

"So how do you feel dinner with me and Teddy Bear went?" Bossy could see how nervous Twan was before he'd even sat down at the dinner table but near the end he was more himself. She knew Twan would do just fine once he found his place in the trio.

"It was cool; I mean I didn't have any expectations

or anything like that. Teddy Bear is a cool cat and I can see how much he cares about you," said Twan between sips.

"He's like a father to me and has been since Devin got sent up. As long as you are real with him, even if you don't agree with him, he'll respect you. Never take his respect as weakness," warned Bossy.

As Twan listened to Bossy a group of women walked through the door. Twan was instantly ready to leave the bar. Bossy was a true hustler and she had no problem letting you know where she was coming from. Her bite could be as big as her personality and everyone in the city knew it. For years, all hell broke loose whenever she and her enemies went head-to-head. Unfortunately for them, two of her main enemies had just walked into the bar and deliberately sat directly across from Twan and Bossy.

Yvonne was preparing to freshen Bossy's drink when she looked up to see Brianna and Sheila Phillips stroll into the bar. *Oh shit,* Yvonne thought to herself, *don't let these bitches start shit today. I am not in the mood.* As Yvonne put a fresh drink in front of Bossy, she hit the call button alerting security to impending trouble.

Twan shifted in his seat and gave Bossy a sideways glance. He knew she wouldn't be the one to start it, but Bossy would damn sure be the one to finish any bullshit the twins might be in the mood to start.

Since they were kids, Brianna and Sheila Phillips thought they were the queens of the projects just because their parents lived together. They were always teasing and goading the smaller and younger kids—a group that at one time included Bossy.

From day one, she wasn't having that shit. The three were mortal enemies and nothing was going to change that as long as the twins thought they shit didn't stink.

"This must be 'fuck with a bitch night' if her stuck-up ass is up in here," said Brianna loud enough for everyone sitting around the bar to hear her.

"Damn, them bitches just don't get enough. Bossy, you know I got ya back," said Yvonne just as loud. Bossy gave her favorite barmaid a wink of the right eye and lifted her half-empty glass to her thick lips for the last time.

Twan was not in the mood for drama. Most men loved to see women fight with hair and titties flying everywhere but Bossy threw punches with brute force and she wasn't the typical female fighter. She would step to a man and stand her ground and from what he remembered of their last meeting, Twan knew that the twins must have wanted an ass whippin'. Trying to deter the inevitable, Twan attempted to persuade Bossy to leave.

"It's getting late and I know you got work to do, why don't we head out the door," pleaded Twan.

"Not yet; I want one more drink. Anyway, them two ugly- ass bitches don't want to see me. The last time we tangled they left with a piece of me that will last a lifetime." Bossy stared straight ahead as she spoke knowing damn well that the twins were looking dead in her mouth.

"And what was that?" inquired Twan.

"My initial tattooed on they ass." Bossy reached inside her left pocket for the ivory pocket knife her brother Devin use to carry and bragged, "like Denzel said in *Training Day*, I'm surgical with this bitch, Twan."

Twan and Yvonne couldn't help but bend over in laughter at Bossy's comment. Brianna and Sheila didn't find anything funny and in fact had become angered by it. They sat nursing their drinks and talking to each other about double teaming Bossy there in the middle of the bar. Sheila wasn't sure she wanted another physical altercation with Bossy. The scene from their last encounter played out in her mind.

Brianna and Sheila had been shopping in Southern Park Mall for the latest in Baby Phat gear when they spotted Bossy trying on a pair of shoes.

"There go that bitch Bossy right there and it looks like her dumb ass is alone. Let's get her," suggested Brianna, the more aggressive of the two.

"Shit, I ain't fuckin' with her out here in Boardman. The last thing I feel like doing is being locked up in a suburban jail. Let's ride to the south side and wait outside her spot. Aisha and Terry ain't with her so we can give it to her ass tonight," suggested Sheila.

With that, the twins made their way to Falls Avenue and waited for their prey to arrive. Unbeknownst to them, Bossy saw their pear-shaped asses at the mall and she had her guard up. She pulled into her driveway and noticed the two-toned broke down hooptie the twins drove parked halfway up the block. Bossy spotted that shit the minute she bent the block to the house.

After parking her car, Bossy pulled her blade from her left pocket and unlocked her door. She decided to leave her packages in the trunk and walk slowly to her front door. As Bossy made her way up the stairs to the door, she heard faint footsteps behind her. Anyone born and raised in the projects knows to listen out for things that go bump in the night.

The twins never knew what hit them as Bossy slashed away with vengeance. Aisha and Terry opened the security door to their apartments to find Bossy standing over two bloody, beat-down figures moaning on the grass.

The mention of their last encounter caused Brianna to think twice about fucking with Bossy again but Sheila was feeling strong thanks to the three shots of Grey Goose she had just downed.

"What Bossy? You goin' soft on a bitch?" stuttered Sheila.

"Oh, I got cha' bitch," responded Bossy.

Brianna swallowed hard at the thought of tangling with Bossy again. The scar on her ass still itched when it rained or the air was full of humidity. Besides, even she knew they were too old to be out in a bar catfighting over nothing. They had walked away from the last altercation with a few slashes; Brianna was afraid that might not be the case the second time around and wanted to diffuse the situation.

"Come on Sheila, let's just go. This shit ain't dat serious," Brianna pleaded with her sister and tried to grab her arm to leave.

"Naw, fuck dat, I ain't going nowhere. Shit, I'm tired of walking on eggshells every time that ghettofied, self-proclaimed queen of the hustlers is around." Sheila continued to slur her words. Brianna tried again to get ahold of Sheila and again she failed. Sheila jerked her arm out of reach, accidentally hitting her sister in her chin.

Bossy remained perched on her bar stool hoping Sheila would not force her to show her ass.

"Get off of me! I'm 'bout to fuck dat bitch up. Get off of me!" screamed Sheila as she headed across the bar towards Bossy.

"Come on, Bossy, not tonight, please not tonight," begged Twan.

"Shit, nigga, she bought the ticket so I'm obligated to give her a show."

Bossy's timing was perfect as she threw a punch that connected squarely with the left side of Sheila's face. Sheila stumbled backward and tried to catch herself from falling by grabbing onto Twan. There was no need for Bossy to fight dirty so she allowed Sheila to regain her balance before meeting her with an open-handed slap to the face. The sound seemed to echo over the tunes coming from the jukebox.

Yvonne and Twan watched the fight unfold purely for amusement. Sheila had resorted to closing her eyes, putting her head down and throwing windmill blows. That technique left her open to each jab being thrown her way. As much as she knew her sister deserved the ass beating, Brianna could no longer stand by and watch.

Bossy was reminded of the other half of the tag team when she felt a punch in the back of her head. Before Yvonne could make it from behind the bar, Brianna had pounced on Bossy from behind. This only enraged Bossy. No longer willing to take it easy on her, Bossy reached back and grabbed Brianna by the hair. Her body twisted sideways until she was in a position to knock Brianna on her ass. She landed at Twan's feet just when Yvonne got to the action.

"I'ma kill you Bossy! Look at my sister!" screamed Sheila.

Bossy looked down at Brianna and landed a kick dead in the square of her back. Bossy body slammed Sheila and fell on the floor with her. Sheila's arms were pinned under the weight of Bossy's legs. The blows Bossy gave Sheila forced blood from her nose and mouth. It seemed like a force of nature had taken control of Bossy and Twan was hesitant to call the fight. However, he was more afraid that if he didn't, Bossy would kill Sheila.

"A'ight, girl, that's enough," said Twan. "Come on Bossy, she's had enough." Twan caught her left arm in midair and brought Bossy out of her trance. She looked up at him as if it were the first time she had ever seen him. Bossy was frozen in place; she didn't even blink her eyes. "Bossy, come on baby, let her up," Yvonne whispered. Bossy looked down at the bloody sight in front of her and snapped out of her trance. With the help of Twan and Yvonne, Bossy stood up, leaving Sheila rolling on the floor in pain and Brianna still knocked out cold.

"Come on, girl, you've had enough exercise for today," joked Twan.

Bossy grabbed her glass off the bar and swallowed the last of her drink before following Twan towards the door. Before she left, Bossy kicked Sheila in the face and asked, "Who's the bitch now?"

Housewives Deserve Respect Too

Chapter 7

Not long after Teddy Bear began playing the field, his game started slipping, not in business but in his personal life. He found out the hard way what happens to a man after he's left a woman scorned.

Betty Terrell was a professional at being a well-provided-for bitch and if you asked her what she did for a living, she'd simply reply, "Whatever it takes to get my rent paid, baby."

Even Betty had to admit she hit the lottery when she hooked and reeled Teddy Bear in. It took her less than a month to get a furnished house, mid-sized car, utility bills paid and a monthly spending allowance. That was record time, even for a pro like Betty, especially when all she had to do was deep throat him twice and toss his salad once.

It was now one year later, Teddy Bear was spending more time and money with Betty, and she couldn't have been more pleased. With each visit came an expensive gift. Soon Betty would need to purchase a third jewelry box to hold all of the treasures her sugar daddy had given her. Betty's game was so tight; it never crossed her mind that her personal ATM might be making nightly deposits at other addresses around the way.

Once Teddy Bear decided to play the field, he operated off the lessons his daddy tried to teach him about the game. In addition to Betty, there was Ruth, Bonnie, and Alicia. Teddy Bear didn't treat his stable mean or unfair and never did he get them strung out on drugs. Actually, he didn't pimp them at all. Quite the opposite, Teddy Bear was being pimped and played by his four young things. His nose was so wide open that he failed to see it.

Bonnie, Ruth, and Alicia all got a car, an allowance, and playtime with Teddy Bear. They were also all living in the Plaza View Apartments, just doors apart from each other. Each one knew about the other and even compared the quantity of material possessions they'd acquired from the community sugar daddy.

Teddy Bear's pimping game was not kept under lock and key the way his drug hustle was. Everyone in the Yo' knew about him housing and providing for his sideline women and soon enough, so would his wife.

Marie had swallowed her last OxyContin pain pill less than an hour ago and she was still fiendin' for anything to calm the cravings. As she rummaged through her husband's home office in search of her next high, the room began to look as if a tornado had swept down destroying everything in its path.

During her search, Marie happened upon paid rental receipts for different Southside addresses. In her heart, Marie knew Teddy Bear had begun stepping out on her because their relationship had deteriorated at the same rate as her health and beauty. She had caught wind of the rumors on the street but dismissed them as lonely women seeking company at their pity party. Now that proof was in her hands, she could no longer ignore it. Marie fished through more desk drawers and file cabinets and found mortgage papers to a house at 1015 Parkwood Avenue. In the same files were nude photos of different women, posed exotically and touching themselves. All of the women pictured appeared to be at least twenty years younger than Marie.

"What the fuck are you doin' in my shit, bitch?"

Marie hadn't heard Teddy Bear come into the house. Although his presence initially caught her off guard, she quickly regained control of her senses and immediately started her verbal attack on her now proven-to-be unfaithful spouse.

"What the fuck am I doin'? Shit, you the one that got some explaining to do. What are you doing? Housing all the new hoes in the city?" Marie stared into Teddy Bear's eyes in search of the truth.

"Why are you in my office ransacking it like you've lost what's left of your mind?" Teddy Bear angrily ignored Marie's questions.

"Don't fuck with me today, Teddy Bear, I ain't in

the mood. So, you not only out slangin' dope but you slangin' ya dick too?"

"Why do you care what I do? Marie, you don't even care about your damn self. Now clean up this mess, bitch!" Teddy Bear grabbed Marie by the arm and with little effort, swung her fragile body to the floor.

Feeling betrayed by the man she'd sacrificed not only the ability to bear children but at one time, her dignity, Marie jumped to her feet as quickly as possible.

"I've been with you for over twenty years. Stayed by ya side when you couldn't even keep a roof over our heads. Slept next to ya ass on the WRTA bus station floor because I loved you, because I believed in you. I sold my body to put food in ya mouth and heroin in ya arm."

Tears began rolling down Marie's face as she recalled all the struggles they'd endured the first few years of their relationship. Teddy Bear's face became somber as he stood witnessing the pain Marie had been holding inside over the years.

"When you went through withdraws from heroin, I held you all night, covered you with blankets, wiped your forehead and wiped your ass for you!" Marie continued to shout. "Now, twenty years later, you turn on me because I got a problem and I need you the same way you needed me then? You the bitch, Teddy Bear, you the bitch."

Teddy Bear could feel the weight on his heart as he realized that every word Marie had said was true. Once he'd turned his life around, he blocked out all of the hard times of the old days. Hearing Marie's hurt and anger, Teddy Bear knew he owed his wife so much more than what he'd given to her. The only problem, as Teddy Bear saw it, was his status on the streets.

For years, Marie was able to lure him away from the path originally penned out for him by his parents. Marie was his strength, his backbone, his crutch and he had no idea how to stand on his own without the security of knowing that Marie would catch him if he fell.

Feeling both embarrassed and helpless, Teddy Bear looked around his home office and the clutter left behind by Marie, and he caught a glimpse of his reflection in the cracked mirror hanging over the fireplace mantel. He saw a man without a soul looking back at him. Teddy Bear's heart told him to stand by Marie, hold her, vow to love her unconditionally, to beg for her forgiveness and a second chance at rebuilding a good life together. However, the streetwise hustle had a tight grip on Teddy Bear, forbidding him from righting this wrong. Something inside was telling him to stand tall, be a man and lay down the law just like daddy taught him.

"I don't know what's going on in your head but pull that shit together and get started cleaning up my office." Unmoved, Marie sat staring into space with her back toward Teddy Bear.

"Marie, did you hear me? Get off ya ass and go clean up my office!" Teddy Bear barked even louder, to no avail.

"Don't make me repeat myself again." Teddy Bear moved closer to the gray velour love seat that held Marie. He stood in front of her in a military stance and shook his wife by her shoulders. Marie remained unmoved.

"Marie, you pushin' me too far, woman, do you hear me?" Teddy Bear slapped Marie across her face with an open hand.

No response. Just as quickly as the first one had come, Teddy Bear delivered another slap to Marie's face, and another and another. Soon the slaps were hard, vicious punches.

Teddy Bear beat Marie until he became physically tired. He was so lost in delivering the punishment he felt Marie had earned by reminding him of days he'd chosen to forget that he didn't realize Marie didn't fight back, cry, scream or attempt to protect herself from his powerful blows. Marie's only movement was that of her head rebounding from each blow it received.

When Teddy Bear finally noticed that Marie sat soaked in her own blood, he stopped the beating.

"Bitch, for as long as I live, don't you ever throw shit up in my face again. I know who the fuck I am and I don't need you to remind me of it."

Marie remained dazed as blood seeped from her nose, split lip, and a space in her mouth that once held a tooth. Teddy Bear took three steps back before continuing his verbal abuse.

"You ain't shit to me no more. The only reason I ain't put your ass out on the streets is because I felt sorry for your ass. You stepped over the line today."

Not reacting to anything Teddy Bear said, Marie remained dazed.

"I'm not carrying this deadweight on my shoulders any more. You can pack up as much of your belongings as you can and I'll put you in one of my houses on the south side. Your time is up; I'll move one of my new hoes in here. One who will appreciate the luxuries." Before heading into the master bath to shower, Teddy Bear advised his wife she had exactly one week to vacate the premises. Marie remained unmoved. She'd heard nothing Teddy Bear had said to her, for her mind had left her body before the physical beating began.

The sounds of the running shower drew Marie back to a night in the spring of 1985. She and Teddy Bear had been living and surviving strictly on the money Marie earned selling her body on the streets. The heroin held Teddy Bear prisoner in his own body, but Marie served out his sentence with him. He had developed a three-hundred-dollar-a-day habit shortly after being introduced to the drug.

A steady rain had left the city drenched and gray for two straight days with no end in sight. Marie and Teddy Bear lay resting behind the His and Her Beauty Salon when the drug began calling out to Teddy Bear.

His small frame shook uncontrollably and they both knew convulsions weren't far behind. The choices were medical help or another hit. Knowing Teddy Bear would never agree to receiving help, Marie prepared her mind for the sacrifice she'd have to make in order to help the man she loved—her body.

Three men standing on the corners of Chicago Avenue and Market Street propositioned Marie. She quickly agreed to suck all their dicks for a mere thirty dollars. The men walked Marie behind the Sparkle Grocery store to complete the transaction.

A piece of Marie's soul was stolen from her that night. The three johns gang-raped her for what felt like an eternity. When they were finished, Marie lay battered, bruised, and degraded but she'd more than earned her agreed-upon fee. The men left her behind without a second thought but not before tossing five twenty-dollar bills at her where she lay.

Teddy Bear got his next hit and the couple stayed at the run-down Wee Motel for a week.

The sound of falling water always brought back memories of that horrific night. Marie never wanted to feel as low as she had then. For years, she'd been stronger than that memory but tonight, Teddy Bear brought it all back.

Teddy Bear pulled his pearl-white Lincoln Navigator up to the house his girlfriend Betty called home. His thoughts were occupied with what had just happened with Marie. He walked toward his destination with his eyes to the ground. In his heart, Teddy Bear knew he had done wrong by his wife. Turning his back on her and blaming Marie for allowing the addiction to control her life was hypocritical and Teddy Bear knew it. Marie was right about laying facedown in the gutter with him; she'd even allowed him to sell her out in order to get a hit. His conscience had been eating away at him for years, but with each step up the drug chain Teddy Bear took, the less concerned he was about the welfare of his wife. The power he held on the streets had become his new addiction and the only important thing in his life. That left Marie on her own to fall deeper and deeper into her addiction.

Unable to get herself up, Marie lay on the expensive carpet for hours after Teddy Bear beat her into the ground. Her left eye was swollen shut and blood was oozing from her mouth. Marie turned her body slowly, trying to avoid increasing the amount of pain she felt in her rib cage.

"Fuck you, Teddy, I don't need this shit no more," cried Marie. Twice Marie struggled to stand on her feet and twice she was unsuccessful. On the third try, something white on the floor caught her eye. Marie fell back down and crawled over what she thought was a pill only to discover it was her own tooth. Teddy Bear had caused her major damage. Just how much, they were both about to find out.

With a .38 caliber pistol in hand, Marie grabbed her car keys and began her mission of tracking Teddy Bear down. Something was guiding her as if she were watching herself in a movie.

Something inside of Marie had snapped. She'd sold her body and soul for Teddy Bear, sacrificed the ability to have children for her man. Now Teddy Bear would not get away with treating her like a dog.

Just as Marie bent the corner, she saw Teddy Bear's car parked in the driveway of a moderately cared for two-story house. The pale yellow paint was peeling and the roof looked to be a couple of years old. Some of the gutters looked too weak to hold the melting snow draining down the sides.

Marie slowly pulled up to the curb in front of the Parkwood Avenue house. Oblivious to her own actions, Marie grabbed the gun, exited the car and as if in a trance, walked slowly toward the porch. Driven by betrayal, Marie cocked the gun before knocking on the door. A voice asked "Who's there?" Marie mechanically took a defensive stance, preparing for Teddy Bear to meet his fate.

Hearing no response, the owner of the voice on the opposite side of the door began turning the doorknob.

Before the door opened completely, Marie found her voice and ordered the poorly dressed middle-aged stranger to, "Tell Teddy Bear his wife is here."

Seconds later, the rickety door opened to an enraged Teddy Bear. The sight of his badly beaten wife made Teddy Bear sick to his stomach. For a split second, he felt sorry for what he had done to the onetime love of his life. That sentiment was fleeting—he soon noticed the metal in the hands of the woman he had come to loathe over the last few years.

"What the fuck are you doin'—"

Bang! Bang!

Teddy Bear lay facedown at his wife's feet with two bullets through the heart.

Screams and wailing from inside the house left the assailant unfazed. Inside, Marie felt hollow, betrayed and worthless. Her soul had died hours before she pulled the trigger; she was now the walking dead.

Marie turned on her heels and strolled back to her car as calmly as she had walked up to the door.

The loud blast was a common occurrence in the

lower south side neighborhood but when screams rang from inside the house, neighbors came running from all directions. Oblivious to the presence of men, women and children running toward Teddy Bear's dead body, Marie opened her car door, sat behind the steering wheel, turned off the ignition she'd kept running and fired one more bullet. The fatal shot pierced Marie's heart, finally ending the agony of her life's trials and tribulations.

Blink and the Game Changes

Chapter 8

Winters in the Yo' could seem harsh and cruel to a newcomer but Twan was a veteran and everyone knew that the corner of Falls Avenue and Hillman Street was his claimed territory. Twan walked out of his house into the cold February winter's night with one goal in mind: to replenish his stash of street candy and start making money. Twan first started hustling weed, but wasn't no real paper in that. To make some real money, Twan had to step his game up and so began dealing rock. Teddy Bear had also put Twan in charge of running six drug houses on the south side.

Managing the houses required him to make road trips but he continued to make time to return to his roots in the concrete of the street corners. He wanted to stay connected to the people, the action, and the city.

As Twan maneuvered his three-toned hooptie toward his block, the sight of police cars and medics parked one block away sent a chill down his spine. Police car number seventy-three was occupied by two of the Yo's worst. Officers Powell and Meeks were as crooked as any public servants could be. They were notorious for kicking in the doors of drug houses, robbing the occupants of all money and drugs and leaving out the same door they'd entered, making no arrests.

There was no reason for Twan to suspect the officers were burglarizing one of the houses he managed because, after the first time they'd hijacked him, Teddy Bear Sampson kept the men paid to leave his associates alone. Twan knew the blinking lights meant someone's life had been unexpectedly suspended.

"Yo, Meeks, what y'all after this time?" Twan asked the officer standing closest to the curb.

"Another life taken by gunfire." Officer Meeks spoke with caution.

"Who got popped this time?"

"It looks like a friend of yours, Twan." The officer knew the south side of the city would be affected one way or another by this latest homicide. This one was big.

"Meeks, you know me, I ain't got no friends. Who got popped?"

"Teddy Bear Sampson," Powell said, smiling with a sly grin. "Some woman just shot and killed ya boy Teddy Bear."

Twan couldn't believe what he was hearing. There had to be some kind of mistake. Teddy Bear Sampson's stature and personality were in vast contrast to his physical appearance. A small man with a baby face, he was still the biggest supplier in the city. He profited from his many drug sales and lived high and mighty.

His father had passed the family business down to him and Teddy Bear transformed the drug connection into a profitable corporation. He owned a six-bedroom house, a fleet of cars and wore only tailored suits and custom-made shoes.

He had invested his ill-earned money into day spas, clothing stores, and area bars and taverns. Teddy Bear was well liked because he kept it real. He took care of his people; at the same time he supplied the poison they were killing themselves with.

Twan stood there trying to make sense of the killing. He later learned that Teddy Bear's wife had shot him down after taking one too many beatings from him. Only those close to Teddy Bear knew the real man. He treated his wife like property and often disrespected her.

For years Teddy Bear had been grooming Twan to take over the south side of the city. Twan was certain of two things: one, the streets would soon become a war zone for those seeking to fill Teddy Bear's shoes, and two, if he kept his head right, he'd be the man to fill those shoes. After all, who was more qualified to take over Teddy Bear's empire than his understudy?

Teddy Bear and Twan's relationship of teacher and student began the day after one of Teddy Bear's drug houses on the lower south side was raided by two of Youngstown's finest crooked cops, Officers Powell and Meeks. At first when the front door of the small house on Plum Street was kicked in, Twan and his best friend Ant thought it was a raid. However, it soon became clear that the two officers were not there on official business. Instead of serving the occupants with a warrant, they threw a pillowcase at Ant and demanded all the money and drugs be placed inside.

Thanks to the snowstorm burying the city under eight inches of ice, business had been light. Officers Powell and Meeks left with only a quarter of an ounce of weed and two ounces of cocaine.

Twan immediately called Teddy Bear to notify him of what had just transpired. Because Twan was responsible for the house and the drugs, he took the loss and gave Teddy Bear the money he would have made off of the stolen products. Teddy Bear gained respect for the young man and began giving him more and more responsibilities. The following day, Teddy Bear met with the two officers and never had another problem with them again.

Now, with Teddy Bear gone, Twan was more than eager to assume his new responsibilities in the drug game. He was hungry for what he saw as the respect and glory, and material wealth that would be his as Youngstown's drug lord. Twan had to think, to map out his plan to take over the streets. With Ant as his right hand and Bossy on his payroll, he knew nothing was standing between him and power.

February of 2006 would be forever etched in the mind of every man, woman, and child residing in the northeastern Ohio city once known for its manufacturing of steel. In the three months since the death of his mentor, Twan had been catapulted to the head of the drug chain. It was a role he had no trouble keeping pace with. Besides Bossy, he was the only other person that personally knew Teddy Bear's contacts and how his cartel operated.

Spring and summer are the seasons when hustlers are in full swing. The players in the Yo' were no different. The streets of Youngstown literally light the hell up with people making moves and flossin' their new material possessions acquired during the winter months. Although Bossy had sat him down and reviewed her rules of street life with him, Twan was among the flossers. He'd moved his family from their three-bedroom two-story house on the west side of Youngstown to a four-bedroom ranch in Boardman, a suburb just off the south side of the city. Twan now pushed a 2005 fully loaded pearl-colored Escalade. LaJetia still had the Sienna for when the kids were with her but she also drove a 2006 silver gray Lexus.

Twan's age and mind-set were reflected in the ways he recklessly spent his money—clothes and jewelry were bought on a whim. Patrons at Larry's Nightclub and Southern Tavern loved for Twan and Ant to walk through the doors. The two were always springing for bottles of Moët and Alizé for any and everyone fortunate enough to be sitting about the bar.

Seeing the lifestyle changes the two friends were experiencing caused men to envy them and women to want them.

Ant often took advantage of his new status in the city. He'd never been popular with women because of his large frame and hard features. All his life people called him ugly. Ant thought it was funny how money could make a monster look good to some women. He had been a virgin until the age of twenty and even then, he paid for the experience. Life had changed with money and he was making every minute count.

Being local celebrities brought the men attention all around the city.

"This run tomorrow will be the biggest since Teddy Bear died. Bossy, are you sure you can handle the weight?"

"How much weight are you talking about and what type of turnaround time are you looking for, Twan?"

"I'm looking at twenty pounds of weed to be broken down into twenty- and fifty-dollar bags. They'll be distributed out to six workers. Then I'm looking at fifty kilos of white girl. I know it's time consuming but I need half of those keys cut into twenty- and fifty-dollar rocks. The other half packaged the same, but keep it in powder form," Twan explained in his most professional sounding voice.

"Twan, when do you want all of that done? You know how I feel about rushing my work," said Bossy while she freaked a blunt.

"You're the best in town when it comes to this shit. I still have you breakin' down my weight because you don't waste a crumb and after you put your magic touch to it, the potency is outrageous. Each bag and every rock hikes my profits way up," Twan complimented her.

"Whatever nigga, when do you want it done?"

Bossy knew that Twan was trying to soften her up before stating his deadline.

"Don't trip on me but I need dis here on the streets in two months at least." Twan took two steps away from Bossy and waited for the storm to strike. He had just picked up a delivery from her a few weeks ago and that was the third one in less than four or five weeks. Twan knew Bossy wasn't stupid and sooner or later, she would start asking questions about the extra product but until she asked, he damn sure was not telling. Twan read the look on her face and quickly changed his request.

"It's cool; I can stand to wait a few more weeks for this load. You know I don't want you to rush and fuck up my shit."

"See, you trippin', I ain't ever fucked up nobody's shit!" Bossy said defensively. "I got to eat, sleep and shit at some point so at least give me ten to twelve weeks. And I'm NOT cleaning that entire shipment of weed. Now that's what's up."

"Girl, you know I'm just playing with you. Just think of this shipment as your own personal property. That will motivate you to complete the assignment in record time. How does three months sound to you?"

"Yeah, three months Twan, three months."

"Cool but check this out, I'll pay you and your girls a thousand dollars extra per day if you get it done early."

"Oh, I was chargin' extra for this load no matter what but you'll have it before August rolls around. It's May now, so yeah, you'll have it before the block party," promised Bossy. As with each business transaction and agreement, they shook hands before Bossy received a third of the cost of her services as deposit. She loved Twan like a little brother but business is business.

"A'ight, girl, let me rise on up out of here and

let you get back to whatever it is you do during your downtime," Twan said, jokingly.

"Before you go, I just want to remind you not to forget about that contribution to this year's Kenmore block party. Danny got the entire weekend lined up and Terry wants KAT Sixty-nine to be the biggest sponsor for 2006."

"Isn't the annual Kenmore block party the last weekend of July?"

"No, it's always the first weekend in August. I know it's three months away but Danny needs the finances to roll in now. Terry got him to let No-Joke and Dollar perform at the free concert but there is still cost in doing this thing."

"Ah, for real? I didn't know my boys were doin' a show this year. Yeah, that's what's up," Twan said.

"You know both of them boys are nasty and blowin' up the underground scene. After they perform, Rufus Black takes the stage. The block party gets bigger and better every year." Bossy decided there was no time like the present to speak with Twan about his recklessness, so she changed the subject.

"Before you leave, have a drink with me so I can holler at you about a few things."

"Anything for you Bossy, what's goin' on?" Twan asked as he cracked open a new bottle of Belvedere.

"Word on the streets is that you and ya boy Ant are flossin' and puttin' ya business out there. Slow down, boy, everybody ain't ya friend and we both know there are a lot of haters out there."

"You worry too much, but I hear you loud and clear."

"I hope you do because if you get popped, that affects me and my girls and let's not forget about that family you got out there in Boardman."

"Bossy, don't worry about nothing. I'm straight and won't nothing happen to any of us. That's what's up."

"Now that we have that out of the way, I want you to join us the weekend after the block party for a small, informal set. It's going to be here at the crib, you and Ant are both invited. Y'all both more than welcome to bring a date, just keep in mind one thing."

"I already know what you about to say," Twan interrupted Bossy: " 'Be careful who you and ya boy bring into five-thirty-nine. You know I don't trust anybody.' "

"That's what's up and while we're on the subject of trust, you need to slow your roll, Twan. I'm hollerin' at you from the heart, baby boy—be careful," Bossy said with sincerity and concern.

Bossy saw Twan to the door and returned to packaging and weighing the product of another longtime associate. It puzzled her as to why Twan and others of his status would take the time to have drugs packaged for street distribution on someone else's behalf. In the end Bossy decided it didn't matter why they did it, only that they continued to do it. She preferred dealing with one top-notch person as opposed to six mid-scale players.

Time for a Change

Chapter 9

"You have to be fuckin' around on me otherwise you would be home at four in the morning," LaJetia cried into the phone.

"Man, I'm so sick of this shit. Take ya ass to bed and I will see you when I see you," said Twan.

As LaJetia lay recalling the argument she and Twan just had, tears began streaming down her face. The tears were flowing from years of pain and neglect. In her heart she felt the love Twan held for her was genuine and unconditional. Yet, years of feeling neglected by her mother, not to mention her father's suicide, convinced LaJetia that Twan would one day betray her, just as everyone else in her life had done in the past.

After Barry Rose placed a .32 caliber pistol to his temple and pulled the trigger, LaJetia's life was forever changed. Kate Rose did her best to raise LaJetia on her own after finding her husband's body in the family room. She was so determined to have a good relationship with her daughter that she became a close friend instead of a good mother. La-

Jetia was free to do as she pleased and as a result, she'd make the first of many mistakes she'd be paying for the rest of her life.

LaJetia felt alone and insecure as a result of her father's suicide. She was always seeking attention from strangers in an effort to feel love. Because love was foreign to her, she couldn't recognize what Twan was offering her. Unlike most people, LaJetia didn't allow herself to dream about tomorrow. She kept her focus on today and today only.

She couldn't figure out why she was so unhappy and angry. To anyone looking at her life, things appeared good. Twan had given her and the kids a nice home, clothes, cars and all of the material necessities. If happiness were measured by material possessions, LaJetia would be ecstatic. Twan was a good provider but fell short when it came to giving of himself emotionally.

Twan had had enough. In the time he'd been in this relationship with LaJetia, he felt he'd given his all. He couldn't understand why his best was never enough. Lately the weight on his shoulders had gotten so heavy, he was becoming physically ill. Uncontrollable headaches were becoming common, not to mention the stomach ulcer he'd recently developed. Twan knew his only option was to walk away from the relationship. He just couldn't figure out how to get LaJetia to understand that his leaving the relationship didn't mean he would be walking away from his responsibilities.

Things had gotten so bad that Twan dreaded going home at nights. He knew that an argument would greet him the second he walked through the door no matter what time it was. That's just how bad things had gotten. Home is supposed to be the place a man can lay his head and rest. Twan's home was a battleground and it seemed that his mere breathing could ignite a fight.

Twan walked into his new home with caution and was surprisingly met with quiet and calm. The kids weren't running around ignoring their mother's threats of beatings if they didn't calm down and LaJetia didn't attack him with a verbal assault, accusing him of sleeping around on her.

After walking further into his home, Twan heard the sounds of Teedra Moses sing about her man standing her up. LaJetia was sitting in the study with an aromatherapy candle lit, wearing a pair of lilac satin lounging pajamas.

"Hey baby, what's up with you?" Twan asked cautiously.

"I didn't hear you come in. Nothing's up, I'm just taking a minute to myself since the kids are all asleep." LaJetia turned to face Twan as she spoke. He saw evidence of recent tears on her face.

"Are you okay, LaJetia? Please, tell me what I can do to make you happy," Twan said gently. He had to figure out a way to handle the situation with care because LaJetia's emotional state seemed fragile. Looking at the mother of his only child, Trayvon, Twan began to rethink his decision to leave the relationship. In addition, he was the only father her other two children had known. Seeing LaJetia like that caused Twan to fear that one day she might harm herself or him.

"If I tell you, will you do it for me?"

"Yes, what do you need?" pleaded Twan.

"I need your time and attention. If you not in

the streets, you paying the kids more attention than you do me. I need you too, Twan, why can't you understand that?"

"Damn girl, I'm trying to be as patient as I possibly can. Like I told you countless times before, the streets don't close down. I'm a hustler and I'm my own boss, shit, I ain't punchin' no time clock. If I'm home you got ya hand out for money! How can I give it to you if I ain't puttin' time in?"

"See, that's what I'm talking about, Twan," LaJetia snapped, throwing her previous cool, calm demeanor out the window. "You don't listen to me at all. I may as well be a single parent because you ain't helpin' me raise these kids. You come and go as you please while I do everything around here by myself. You climb into bed and don't even touch me so you must be touchin' another bitch."

"Come off that shit, girl. How many times I got to tell you I ain't fuckin' around?"

"As many as it takes!" LaJetia replied as she stood up, exited the study and stomped down the long hallway. Once inside their bedroom, she threw herself across the bed and forced herself to cry. She knew how it affected Twan to see her cry and she was going to milk the situation until she got what she wanted from him.

Twan refused to run after her but her crying seemed to echo throughout the house. *Shit, this bitch must think I'm one of those weak-ass niggas from the jets she use to fuck with. It's Sunday night and the streets are moving slow because everybody is either having family time or chillin' at the skating rink. I'll chill at the crib tonight but if she thinks she gon' keep a nigga on lockdown she got life fucked up.*

After pretending to cry ten minutes, LaJetia realized that Twan was not going to cater to her. She had to regain control over the situation. *Get it together, girl. You're about to lose this fight. Pull it together and go talk to him.* LaJetia gave herself a pep talk before walking into the kitchen in search of Twan.

"A break, Twan, I really need a break. Do you think we can go away on vacation for a week? Even a weekend? I'm tired and just need a break."

"Yes we can do that. Do you want to take the kids to Disney?" Twan asked, not fully understanding what his girlfriend was asking of him.

"No, Twan, I don't. I want us, just me and you to go away together. I love the kids but I need a break, please." Tears began falling from her brown eyes again. "I'm tired and sometimes it feels like I'm inches away from having a nervous breakdown. It's hard being a good mother and committing all of my time and energy to the kids. All I'm asking for is to have a few days to myself."

Twan completely understood what LaJetia was trying to tell him. Growing up, he'd watched his mother run herself into the ground in an attempt to be both a mother and father to him and his brother.

"Baby, I want to do whatever you need me to but I need to ask you one question. Do you need to get away alone or do you need to be with me?"

"Twan, I want us to go away together. No kids, no friends, no business. I need you to make time for me sometimes. Can't you understand that?"

It now became crystal clear to Twan what LaJetia felt was missing from her life—his time. He concentrated so much on hustling and building his status in the streets that he'd neglected his family. The next morning, Twan got on the phone with Aisha and asked her to contact a travel agent to book a five-day cruise for two. Aisha would also hire someone to stay at home with the kids while they vacationed.

Twan and LaJetia were so excited about the trip that neither of them could sleep the night before. The plane was scheduled to leave Cleveland Airport at 7:00 AM. Twan arranged for a limo to pick them up at 4:00 AM. The limo was a surprise for LaJetia. Twan wanted her to feel special and pampered.

Royal Caribbean cruise line was heavenly. On the first day of the cruise, they gambled, sat out by the swimming pools, visited the day spa and enjoyed his-and-her body massages. When the boat docked in Key West, they shopped at various stores and enjoyed a lobster lunch together. They rented wave runners and drove them for an hour as if they were little kids on a roller coaster.

On day three, the ship docked in Cozumel, Mexico, and the couple signed up for a party boat excursion. They snorkeled, kayaked and drank tequila and Coronas with the other partygoers. When they returned to the ship, they showered and went back out to shop in downtown Cozumel. Twan bought himself some reasonably priced platinum jewelry and LaJetia bought outfits, shoes and souvenirs for the kids.

That night the couple enjoyed an elegant dinner with the captain and sipped on apple martinis under the moonlight.

"This is wonderful, Twan. I would have never

imagined myself doing something like this. My life feels like a fairy tale right now."

"I'm happy that you're enjoying yourself, this is the way I want you to feel. I know you deserve things like this and I'm going to do better by you from now on. I get it now." Twan reached out to hold his woman in his arms as he spoke.

"People have talked about me my entire life. For the first time, I feel like I'm somebody. I feel like I can do anything and it's all because of you. Would you believe that I'm thinking about taking some college classes?"

"LaJetia, you can do anything you put your mind to. Remember it's you doing it, not me. Whatever you do, I'll support you."

Twan and LaJetia returned home with a new outlook on their life together. For the first time since they been together, they were on the same page. Twan prayed that LaJetia would trust him and feel more secure in their relationship. For the sake of their family, he hoped the changes surfacing in LaJetia would be permanent. If not, he was going to bounce and not look back.

STREET LIFE 101

CHAPTER 10

The private life of Twan's best friend Anthonie "Ant" Quarles was in vast contrast to that of his street life. Before he went to work each day, he checked in on his mother to ensure she was safe and wanted for nothing. This morning was no different from any other.

"Hey, Mama, do you need anything done before I head out to work?" Ant asked between bites of his homemade sausage burrito.

"No, baby, ya mama is fine. I keep telling you not to worry about me; the good Lord will keep me safe."

Olivia Quarles was a strong, God-fearing woman known for her kind spirit and enduring faith. She dedicated her life to serving the Lord after the senseless murder of her oldest child, Davis. He was a customer at the local bank when it was robbed and he ended up being one of five people murdered during the crime. That was almost twenty years ago, and her youngest child, Ant, was still trying to come to terms with the loss of his brother.

Ant had been only four years old at the time of the murder and Davis was the only father figure he had known. As he grew older, seeking revenge and someplace to direct his anger, Ant began running the streets, dealing drugs and robbing people for sport at ten years old.

Each day, after ensuring his mother was okay, Ant went to the only job he'd ever known: slinging dope. After being in the game for seven years and getting away with so many crimes, Ant felt invincible. Any true hustler knows the future holds only one of two things if you stick around for too long: prison or death. Ant Quarles tried to put up a facade that said he wasn't afraid of either doing time or dying but the truth of the matter was that the thought of both scared him shitless.

The only reason Ant was hustling drugs was because Twan talked him into it. All his life, Ant had been a follower and he followed behind his best friend like a puppy in training. Ant had recently begun feeling secure in the streets after realizing he had gained himself some clout. His relationship with Twan was paying off by earning Ant some attention from the streets and women. The streets of Youngstown, Ohio didn't allot any young black man the option of fearing the unknown and Ant would soon learn that lesson the hard way.

As Ant drove down Warren Avenue he cracked open his second forty ounce of White Mountain citrus wine cooler as the clock struck 9:00 AM. The powerful sounds of Parliament coming from the charcoal gray duce and a quarter could be heard coming three blocks before he got there. Everyone in Youngstown had one thing in common—listening to the hypnotic sounds of funk. George Clinton, Bootsy Collins, Roger Troutman and Zapp have contributed more to the rearing of young men than their absentee fathers.

"What it do, pimpin'?" Twan greeted his boy of fourteen years.

"Ah, man, I can't call it. How ya livin', playa? Ready to do this?" Ant questioned between sips. The partners in crime were up early to meet with their runners and tally up the week's earnings.

Sitting inside the two-bedroom drug house situated on the corner of Warren Avenue and Overland Street was Ant's south side chick, Shadaisy Davis. She was a "high yellow" high school dropout, dope-dealing, mother of four, and a money-hungry freak. She kept her dirty brown hair covered with a cheap blond weave and her ass hiked up in leather pants whether it was winter, spring, summer or fall. Because of the instability of her lifestyle, the state removed all four of her children from her care. Her mother got custody to keep the children from being lost in the system. That was two years ago and Shadaisy had no plans to get them back. The freedom just tasted too good.

"Come on, girl, let's move this shit. You already rollin' and ain't even washed ya' ass yet. We call that 'ready rollin', and it ain't cool for chicks to do that shit. It's nasty for a bitch not to change her panties," Ant snapped at his ghetto queen. "Shit, you knew I was coming."

Shadaisy was tagging along to double count the money collected and play chauffeur for the day.

"Ah, nigga, fuck you. We got three hours to do this, why you sweatin' me? I just got in a minute ago."

"Ain't nobody tell ya' hot ass to close down the afterhour spot. Go wash that ass before I tap that ass," Ant threatened as he finished off his liquid breakfast.

Ant kept his work car, a 1986 Ford Escort, parked at the Warren Avenue drug house. The car needed some bodywork and a paint job but the engine purred like a kitten. Before making their rounds, the trio headed north to hit up Perkins Restaurant for breakfast.

After scarfing down enough food to feed a small country for a month, the trio made their way to the various drug houses Twan kept around the city. After all of the money was collected and bills were paid, Shadaisy was dropped off at home and the partners headed to Sharon, Pennsylvania.

Shortly after Teddy Bear was killed, Ant put the wheels in motion so that one day he would be able to break away from Twan and stand on his own feet. He loved his boy like a brother but was tired of standing in the shadows while Twan received all the glory on the streets. Today was their first meeting with Ant's new contact. The product wasn't as good as what they were getting from their Florida connection but Ant needed this relationship if he was going to make his move. It took a lot of doing, but he was able to get Twan to go along with the deal. Ant reasoned that Pennsylvania was a lot closer than Florida and expanding resources was a good thing.

There was only one problem resulting from the

new connection: where to house the additional weight. After their last conversation, Twan knew Bossy wouldn't be happy but he had to take a chance with her helping them out. He knew it was a long shot but like Teddy Bear would often say, "Nothing beats a punk but a good beat down."

"Twan, what the hell is all of this? I know damn well, you're smarter than this. Just like a little kid, you got ya hands in too many cookie jars!" Bossy had tried relentlessly over the past six months to calm Twan down. He was acting like a teenager rebelling against his parents because he thought he knew all of the answers to the world's problems and everyone else was just getting by in life.

"Come on Bossy, don't trip on ya boy. You like gettin' that paper just as much as me. All I'm doin' is stacking our paper higher and faster."

"Twan, this is already fast money. What type of race are you running?"

"The same one as you and the rest of these hustlers in these streets. You know how it is out here, every baller for himself."

Twan was right. Bossy understood firsthand what it was like on the streets. That was exactly why she'd bent over backward to continue teaching Twan after Teddy Bear was killed. Frustration grew daily for Bossy because Twan refused to listen to her teachings, to recognize her experience. It was one thing for Twan to increase the amount of weight he was moving but Twan was stepping into an arena he was totally unfamiliar with.

Like a carry-out restaurant, Twan's products could

now be listed on a menu: powder cocaine, crack cocaine, heroin, weed, Percocets, OxyContin, Valiums, meth—and the list grew weekly.

"Listen to me, Twan, because I'm only going to say this once." Bossy paused for effect. "You are making too many trips up and down the highway. You are making too many drop-offs and pickups here. Every day your name is mentioned at the shop because the night before you and Ant were out flossin' at the clubs."

"Not this again," Twan sighed.

"I wouldn't be surprised if some wannabe gangster is measuring you up looking to take your place. In fact, I wouldn't be surprised if five-O ain't already on ya trail. And if that's the case, you might have unknowingly led them here to me."

"What you trying to say to me, Bossy?"

"Since Teddy Bear died, you have been acting like a sheltered child getting his first taste of freedom. Slow the fuck down or I'm going to stop fuckin' with you!"

Twan never expected to hear those words come from Bossy's mouth. Now that she put them out there, what could he do? Only two choices were on the table, either do as Bossy said or find someone to take her place. Twan may have been a naive hustler but he knew Bossy was not replaceable. What the fuck was a hustler to do?

Business is Business—Personal Ain't

Chapter 11

Terry walked out of her office to hear two familiar voices engaging in a heated discussion. She had no idea what Aisha could possibly be arguing with Twan about.

"Excuse me, but would the two of you please join me in my office?" Terry's request was more of a demand than an invitation.

Aisha sprinted into the office and immediately began pacing the floor. "Terry, do you know Twan has the nerve to want us to keep some of his shit here until Bossy's ready for it?" Terry couldn't believe what she'd just heard. Twan knew better than to make such a request. In the beginning, KAT69 turned bad money into good but since then, no illegal activity ever took place in the shop.

"Why y'all trippin'? Tryin' to act all brand new like y'all hands ain't dirty. Shit, it's only this one time," Twan tried to reason.

"You must have lost ya damn mind, Twan. I told you 'no' outside and I'm telling you 'no' again," fumed Aisha.

"Come on girl, y'all know I ain't bringing any heat up in here. Just let me stash a couple of keys here till Bossy ready for 'em."

"Terry, you talk to him, the longer I stand here, the more my head hurts." Aisha slammed the door behind her and walked toward the phone to call Bossy. She knew Terry could and would handle Twan and his careless request but Bossy needed to know what was going on.

Twan stood contemplating his next move. He knew he was wrong for making this request but he felt he had no choice. He and Ant had made a deal with the new supplier, Clifton "C-Lok" Boyd, without thinking ahead. Ant had made the deal sound so inviting, there was no way Twan could have said no. Now they were stuck.

Before approaching his friends, Twan contemplated hiding the stash in his basement or even at Ant's mother's house. His conscience wouldn't allow him to deceive Ms. Quarles and he didn't want to take the chance that one of his kids would find the drugs at home. He would ride around with the drugs in his trunk before he stored them at home and put his kids in harm's way.

Terry calmly walked around her cherry oak desk and sat down in her black leather high back chair.

"Have a seat, Twan, we need to talk about this request of yours," Terry calmly stated.

"Listen, Terry, I'm not trying to disrespect. You know me, we go way back. I wouldn't ask if it weren't an emergency."

"How many times did Teddy Bear say to you no

business but hair business to take place at KAT Sixty-nine?"

"Yeah, but Teddy Bear ain't here any more and what I need ain't that deep. It's just this one time."

"Twan, I'm all about business and this place is my livelihood. Teddy Bear set down rules for a reason and just because he's gone doesn't mean everything changes."

"What you want me to do, beg?" asked Twan.

"No, I don't. But I do want you to think about the possible consequences to your actions."

"Look, I don't need you lecturing me too. LaJetia and Bossy bitch at me enough. So what's it going to be, Terry? Are you with me or not?"

"Simple: it's going to be no, and I resent you trying to take advantage of our friendship this way."

As Twan stood to leave, he looked into Terry's eyes and said, "Teddy Bear and Bossy were right, ain't no friends in this business." As he walked fuming out the front door, Twan ran right into LaJetia. She was there for her weekly appointment with Sirenna. Twan explained he was in a hurry and would see her at home later. After reminding her man about the promise he made to the kids, LaJetia stepped aside and watched as Twan got into his car and sped off down Hillman Street.

LaJetia left KAT69 feeling like a queen. In the two weeks since the trip, Twan had been making her life a little easier. Per her request, Twan had been helping with the kids in the mornings and coming home from the streets by two in the morning. Her man had even been attentive and taken time out to join his family for dinner every other day.

Today was Thursday and Twan had promised the kids he'd be home when they got in from school. It was coming up on eight o'clock and becoming obvious that Twan's promise had been broken.

"Mommy, where's Daddy at? He said he'd be here to watch a movie with us after I did my homework," whined Kiara.

LaJetia's nerves were already on edge and having to answer questions from her five-year-old daughter was the last thing she wanted to do. LaJetia's disappointment gradually turned into anger. She'd suspected the honeymoon wouldn't last long but lying to the children was inexcusable. Letting her down was one thing, letting the kids down was something else altogether. LaJetia knew all too well the pain felt when the person who's supposed to love and protect you breaks your heart.

Twan turned his key in the lock and braced himself for the impending fight he was about to be a party to. The search for a place to store his newly acquired stash had taken much longer than he or Ant could have ever imagined. The last thing he wanted to do was disappoint his kids but today it just couldn't be helped. It was now three in the morning and all he wanted to do was lay down but Twan knew LaJetia wouldn't let that happen.

The house was eerily quiet and that sent a chill up Twan's spine. No voices coming from the family room and no soulful sounds playing in LaJetia's private room. This really took Twan by surprise. LaJetia used that room as her place of refuge. The walls were a soft lilac and housed a state-of-the-art stereo, a plush cream-colored sofa, and two matching wing back lounge chairs. The maple wood bookshelf matched the end tables and aromatherapy candles filled the room. This was the room LaJetia retreated to when she needed to relax, escape the responsibilities of motherhood and/or mentally prepare for an argument with Twan.

A plate covered with a paper towel caught Twan's eye as he walked through the kitchen. He took a minute to place his dinner in the fridge and pour himself a glass of water. Twan thought that just maybe he'd dodged a bullet and LaJetia had fallen off to sleep. The idea allowed him to relax his shoulders and breathe a sigh of relief.

Inside the bedroom, Twan undressed and slowly got into the custom-made four-poster bed trying not to wake LaJetia. The second he closed his eyes, LaJetia spoke to him.

"All of my life people have talked about me. They can say anything they want about me but there is one thing they can't say. No one can ever say I'm a bad mother. Even at age fourteen, I was a good mother and I work hard at being there for my children.

"If you ask some people what it is they aspire to be, you might hear a variety of things. If someone were to ask me what I aspire to be, I'd answer, a good mother." LaJetia paused to collect her thoughts and Twan waited for her to finish what she needed to say so he could get some sleep.

"You're a very good provider, I can't deny that. From what I hear on the streets, you're even a good hustler but you fail where it counts, Twan.

Kiara, Tyler, and Trayvon worship the ground you walk on. No matter how many times you let them down, all is right in their worlds when Daddy walks in the door." LaJetia's voice cracked as tears streamed down the sides of her face. "A little girl should always be able to count on her daddy, always. He's the only man in her life that will be there no matter what. I say that because Kiara cried herself to sleep tonight because her daddy let her down. It appears to me that you're aspiring to be a sorry-ass father."

Twan lay tense and speechless. He'd never taken the time to measure himself as to what type of father he'd become. He felt that providing material things, shelter, food, and raising another man's child made him a prime candidate for the father of the decade award. LaJetia's words must have held some truth because no sleep would come for Twan that night. . . . *you're aspiring to be a sorry-ass father.* As the words replayed in Twan's mind, he mumbled to himself, "Damn, that was personal."

We Don't Call 911 'Round Here

Chapter 12

Twan was up the next morning before the rest of the family. To make up for breaking his promise to the kids, he decided to cook a special breakfast of waffles, scrambled eggs, bacon, and fresh orange juice, Kiara's favorites. Twan was willing to hold off running in the streets for a couple of hours because he had to make things right with Kiara before his day got started. After the kids ate, Twan planned on driving his baby girl to school.

The love Twan showed for LaJetia's two oldest children, Kiara and Tyler, was the same love he showed for his and LaJetia's only child together, Trayvon. He loved them so deeply that he vowed to never allow anyone to hurt them, including himself.

Still hurt by what her daddy had done, Kiara walked slowly into the kitchen, eyes still red from crying, to pour herself a bowl of cereal. Upon entering the eat-in area, Kiara's eyes lit up when she saw her daddy sitting at the table with her favorite breakfast in front of him.

"Daddy! You're home," Kiara sang excitedly, for an instant forgetting the pain he'd caused her the night before.

Twan stood and gave his daughter the hug of her life. "Good morning, sweetness. How are you today?"

"I'm fine but you made me cry last night. You promised to be home and watch movies with me," cried the five-year-old.

"I know, baby, and Daddy is so, so sorry. I completely forgot. You know that I'd never hurt you on purpose don't you?" Twan's heart ached as he saw the hurt in Kiara's eyes.

"Yeah, Daddy, but I made popcorn and poured you a big cup of Pepsi," whined Kiara.

"Please forgive Daddy. I can't stand to have you mad at me." Twan and Kiara ate together and began making plans for a mini–family vacation. Kiara reasoned that since her two brothers were small, it wasn't a good idea to take them on an airplane.

At only five years old, Kiara was very bright and mature. Thanks to the attention and dedication from her mother, she was reading at a third grade level and prided herself on being a good helper to her mother. She could never understand why, but to Kiara, her mother seemed sad inside. Even when she was smiling and laughing, she was sad. It was Kiara's mission to try and make her mother's heart smile.

On the ride to school, father and daughter decided Cedar Point Amusement Park would be a fun getaway for the family during the summer. Twan promised they'd go as soon as possible and even spend two nights at a hotel with an indoor pool. Kiara promised not to spoil the surprise by telling her mother and brothers. Knowing a breakfast and weekend getaway wouldn't be enough to make things up to LaJetia, he told Kiara their plans would be a secret until the weekend.

"Baby girl, you be good and have a great day. Mommy will pick you up."

"I love you, Daddy, see you later," sang Kiara as she skipped away from the car.

"Love you too," Twan hollered behind her.

Kiara ran into school with a smile on her face and happiness in her heart. After making sure his daughter got into the school safely, Twan pulled off toward his other life—in the streets.

The air was humid and all the players were strollin' the strip trying to be seen. Making his rounds from the south side, to the north side, up the east side and back south, Twan saw which runners were working and which were missing in action. He made mental notes on who to call into the office on re-up (replenish) Thursday. Lazy doesn't amount to money and hustlin' wasn't a game for those not willing to put in the sweat, tears, and the risk required to make it. The incompetent would have to find another player to work for, especially since Ant had decided to step the game up.

Twan bent the corner and made a left hand from Hillman Street onto Evergreen Street to see if the fellows were out chillin' on the green (nickname for the block of Evergreen Street where the

Williams family lived). As expected, Big Dell, Tonie Jack, Kev Ruff, Mike and Kev Davis, Sean Simms, Rick and Ruler, and a few other veterans were standing there reminiscing about Red Barn Restaurant and South High School football games. The group watched as Twan pulled into Granny Williams's driveway, knowing it was forbidden. Chillin' in front of the house was one thing but Granny had made it clear years ago that her driveway was meant for her and her alone.

"What up, nigga? You tryin' to get us all cussed out," Tonie Jack asked Twan, "Nigga, you better move ya ride to the lot." Tonie Jack pointed to the open parking lot across the street as the others began to mumble about the parking infraction.

"Chill dude, I'm only gon' be a minute," replied Twan as he gave each fella dap.

"And in a second Granny gon' be yelling out that door," laughed Big Dell.

Twan did as he was told and rejoined the group for a walk down memory lane. After an hour, they handled some business and each hustler was off to begin his workday while a couple of the fellas were just putting their previous workday to an end.

Two hours later, Twan sat inside his pearl Escalade debating whether or not to go inside and face the music. He knew word had made its way back to 539 Falls about what went down between him, Aisha, and Terry three days ago. Before stepping into KAT69 he knew the women were going to have a baby over his request. The confrontation with Terry had actually gone smoother than expected. Knowing things with Bossy wouldn't be as easy, Twan gulped down a few shots of vodka before ringing the doorbell. Bossy was one woman not to be fucked with and Twan had done just that.

Inside the apartment, Bossy sat tokin' on a blunt, sipping' on E&J and listening to Curtis Mayfield. It had taken her longer than expected to weigh and bag that last shipment Twan dropped off but she'd met her August first deadline. In addition to her workload, she, Aisha, and Terry were still planning their annual summer party and finalizing the business plans for the shop. She had enough on her shoulders without Twan's immature ass pulling that stupid stunt knowing it would piss her off.

As Curtis Mayfield told the story of Freddie being dead, Bossy drifted back to the days when she'd been immature and reckless. Her early twenties were something for the books and most things that happened back then were never to be spoken of again. There was no noticeable difference in Bossy's appearance. *Shit, I may be in my mid-thirties but my ass is still being carded at the liquor store. Too bad I can't see the reflection of my soul in the mirror.* The ringing doorbell drew Bossy from her thoughts.

After sitting outside for twenty minutes and getting a nice buzz going, Twan finally worked up enough nerve to face the music. He held his breath when the door slowly opened permitting him to come in. Bossy had seen him sitting outside but decided to wait for him to make his move. Lately Twan had made so many bad choices that Bossy began questioning his loyalty to her and her girls. She had practically raised him and had tried to teach him the rules of the game just like Teddy had taught her and this is how he wanted to show his gratitude? Bossy looked Twan in his eyes and wondered if she even knew who he was anymore.

"What's up with you, girl? You all right?" The minute Twan heard the music Bossy was listening to, he knew this visit wasn't going to be easy. That new artist from Toledo, Lyfe Jennings was serious and his story was that of so many. Bossy felt every word of his songs and was living his story.

"Yeah, ya shit is over there. Leave my money on the table," Bossy said harshly.

"Look Bossy, I know your girls told you about me coming into the shop and asking for their help. I know it was wrong and it won't happen again." Twan apologized without making eye contact, making Bossy question his thinking even more.

"Sit down."

"I know we need to talk but I got go—"

"Sit down," demanded Bossy, "don't make me say it again." Twan did as he was told and sat on the couch across from her. They sat quiet while the disk changer switched to Bootsy Collins and "Hollywood" began playing.

"Some of the things you do remind me of myself when I was a couple of years younger than you are now. Other things you do are so reckless it pisses me off."

"I know and—"

"Twan, just listen to what I have to say. Pay close attention and hopefully when I'm done, you'll understand why I'm asking myself if you can be trusted anymore."

Twan swallowed as his body stiffened and the room closed in on him. He had always had anxieties about the unknown and at that moment, he was afraid.

"I know you've heard stories about me, how I was back in the day. Some stories good and some bad but they're probably all true. I've had my fun clubbing it, robbing cats out on the streets just for the fun of it, fuckin' with three and four different playas at one time. Shit, one time I caught this nigga fuckin' around on me and I went to his bitch's crib and kicked his ass." Bossy reflected on her wilder days and smiled to herself at the memory. "People used to call me a pimp. I hate that word because it has become too generalized these days. What your generation doesn't understand is that sometimes pimps got to ho too." Bossy paused to let her last sentence sink in. "Aisha and Terry hung with me at the clubs but they never committed any crimes. I love and respect them too much to put them in danger that way. Even today, I only let them get in so deep with what I do and truth be told, I don't want them involved at all. See, when you love someone, Twan, you protect and look after them." The ice in Bossy's drink had melted and all she tasted was water as she took her last sip. She stood to pour herself a fresh drink and brought Twan back a beer to sip on.

"About ten years ago, I was hanging out with my boys Big Black and Poppy. We were real tight. Most people thought they were fuckin' me but it wasn't even like that. We looked out for one another and to them, I was just one of the boys. Anyway, one day we started drinking around noon and didn't stop until three in the morning. Man, we kicked it that day. I think I won over five thousand dollars from them playing craps, spades, and dominoes down in Mill Creek Park. Poppy won half of it back when we hit Corky's and played a few hours of pool.

"That night, we rode out to the Sharon line and paid the after-hours spot, the Davis's a visit. Just when the spot started jumpin', shots rang out. Me and Big Black were on the dance floor and Poppy was off in the back smoking with some chick. Shots being fired in that joint were common, so everyone hit the ground and waited for the bouncers to grab hold of the situation. When all was cool, the DJ would start spinning the tunes again and the crowd would return to partying like nothing happened.

"Not that night though, when the smoke cleared, three people lay dead, one being Poppy. Big Black and Teddy lost they minds over that shit. By the time we laid our boy to rest, word had hit the streets that some bitch from the 'Brooks' (Kimmel-Brooks housing projects) had set him up. That's who was all up in his ear that night. He'd beat her ass a month before and she wanted payback. I understood the payback but not to the extent of taking my boy's life. Teddy found out who pulled the trigger and plans were in the works to lay them down." Twan remained quiet and listened closely to Bossy.

"Big Black took that shit to heart and it was all he could talk about. We were out one day reminiscing on old times when we spotted them fools that killed Poppy. What happened next was reflex, it seemed so natural. All I could see was my boy lying in a pool of blood with half his face blown the fuck off." Tears began flowing down Bossy's face as she remembered the love she had for Poppy and the sin she'd committed that night. "I grabbed my thirty-eight, Big Black whipped out his nine and we both started blastin'. When the bullets stopped flying, some eastside niggas named Eddie 'E-Low' Brown and David 'Slim' Collins were on their way to hell."

Twan was shocked. Although Bossy could be very violent, he was surprised to hear she had gone to the extent of taking someone's life. For a moment he wondered if she was making all of this up to make a point but the tears and sincerity of her words told Twan that everything he was hearing was true.

"We hauled ass out of there and drove straight to Teddy. A lot happened that night, including the guns and car we were driving never being seen again. You have no idea how difficult it is to live with the fact that someone is no longer on this earth because of me. I didn't even know their names until I read that shit in the papers. No matter what they did, just like Poppy, they were sons, brothers, maybe even fathers. We all chose this life and we live it the way these streets demand but we all deserve respect because we breathe. I tell you this story and say all of this to you just to say this: do not disrespect the game, the hustle, or my girls' livelihood ever again. And Twan, most importantly, do not disrespect me. Just because we don't call nine-one-one 'round here don't mean they won't come for you when you slip."

AND MAMA BEV SAID . . .

CHAPTER 13

Mama Bev, as Bossy and Terry called her, stood in her modest-sized kitchen preparing lasagna, garlic bread and a tossed salad for her three girls. A bottle of red wine and strawberry cheesecake chilled in the refrigerator. The four-bedroom house on the east side of the city had become too big for the single woman since Aisha and Bossy moved away from home; however Bev had no plans to move. She felt there might come a time when Aisha and/or her adopted daughters, Bossy and Terry, needed to move back home and she vowed to always have room for them.

Terry and Aisha arrived for dinner on time and the aroma of Bev's homemade sauce was inviting and they were both ready to enjoy the feast, made with such love.

"Hey Mom, we're here. How are you today?" asked Terry. Aisha and Terry both hugged and kissed Mama Bev on each cheek simultaneously.

"I'm fine, how are my girls doing?" The three

women caught up on the week they'd had and explained that Bossy should be arriving shortly.

Bev took the main dish out of the new oven the girls had given her as a Christmas present and prepared her dining room table for the four of them. Bossy arrived just in time to hear the food being blessed. After finishing up with dinner, the ladies sat out on the deck sipping red wine and relaxing.

Before the girls had even arrived, Bev had made up her mind to take advantage of the gathering to get a few things off her chest. Bev was never one to bite her tongue or mince words, especially when it came to the welfare of her girls.

Since the day Aisha was raped and Bev saw the way the little neighbor girl (Bossy) and frequent visitor to the projects (Terry) took care of her daughter, Bev had loved them as her own.

"All I'm saying is that you three have to stay alert at all times. We all know ain't no love on the streets and people will kill they own mommas to be where y'all are right now," lectured Bev. "Keep a close eye on Twan and Ant. I don't like the things I've been hearing about them boys lately. I don't trust 'em."

"Ma, you know we got this. Don't worry so much, please."

"I'm always going to worry about my girls, especially you, Aisha. No matter how old you get or how many kids of your own you have, you'll always be my baby." Being an only child to a single mother, Aisha cherished the relationship she shared with her mother.

Aisha had somehow become the nurturer of the threesome. Her role was chosen for her, she didn't choose it. She was the only member of KAT69 maintaining a good relationship with her mother and had been married—although briefly. Her girls often teased that she was a clone of Mama Bev's. Aisha took it as a compliment because she thought the world of her mother.

"I had a long talk with Twan a couple of weeks ago. I let him know where things stood with us. He's used up all of his chances with me and he knows that his next fu—I mean mess up, is his last," explained Bossy.

"Good, I'm glad to hear it . . . but you still keep your guard up. If you get relaxed, the ax will fall," warned Mama Bev.

Terry wanted to change the conversation because as far as she was concerned, Twan was no longer a friend. No true friend would ask a friend to put his or her livelihood on the line.

"Mama Bev, did Aisha tell you about our updated business plan?" Terry asked.

"Yes she did, baby, and I think it's wonderful. Adding a day care and bringing in barbers will attract new clients."

"Terry's being modest, her five year plan includes a full-service day spa and yoga classes. KAT Sixty-nine Hair and Nail Salon will be attractive to men and women of all ages," explained Aisha excitedly.

"Are you still working on the permit to build the addition?" Bossy chimed in.

"Yeah, it's very involved. I don't foresee a problem. For a minute I thought we'd have to hire a lawyer to do the paperwork," answered Terry.

"Are we going to have the two girls from the

Model Me Role Model Project help set up the day care facility?" Aisha wondered.

Terry explained how the girls would be able to gain hands-on experience, learning how the business operated from A to Z. The conversation then floated to the bad vibe Aisha and some of the techs at the shop got from Caron. Her personality came off as very manipulative and fake. When asked for her opinion on different things, she always agreed with whoever was dominating the conversation. Terry let Aisha know that she'd gotten the same vibe but was willing to give the girl more time to come into herself. She went on to explain that if their instinct proved true, Caron would be let go from the shop and the program would have to place her elsewhere.

"Talissa is a totally different story. She's very smart and intuitive. You can tell her parents have raised her to want something out of life. In fact, she reminds me a lot of you, Terry. She could have been your clone back when we were teenagers." Aisha revealed what she and Bossy had both noticed.

Terry laughed at her girls, agreeing with their observations. Soon, they began to realize how late it had gotten. Mama Bev asked Aisha and Terry to clean up the dinner dishes while she had a heart-to-heart with Bossy. Aisha had confided in her mother about Bossy wanting to walk away from the game. Mama Bev thought the idea was long overdue but also knew that Bossy would find 101 reasons to allow Twan, Ant and their mommas to hold her back.

"I heard that you want to make a life change," Mama Bev opened up the conversation.

"I was considering leaving the business before Teddy was killed and even more so since. Things out here on the streets have changed drastically in the past ten years. I just don't know how much longer I can do this," confided Bossy.

"You know how I feel about it. So far you've been lucky, damn lucky. Years ago you were able to walk away from tragedy," Bev reminded Bossy of the incident surrounding Poppy's death, "next time you *won't* be so lucky. Baby, I know this is all you've done but you have the shop to keep you busy and make you money." Mama Bev paused to allow her words to Bossy to sink in.

"So tell me, sweetie, what's it going to take for you to walk away and live life the way it was meant to be lived?"

"How is life meant to be lived?"

"Without the daily threat of death or imprisonment. So what's it going to take?" Bev was right and Bossy knew it. Her time could be up any day, but living and hustling on the streets of the Yo' made it feel more like her time could be up any second.

"I don't know, Mama Bev, I wanted to look out for Twan but he doesn't seem worthy any more. I still feel responsible for him because Teddy Bear wouldn't and didn't leave me for dead."

"Girl, after Teddy's funeral you told me that replacing him was not for you because you couldn't imagine yourself taking another person from this earth. Don't you know that you don't have to be that high up on the totem pole to have to make that call? When it comes down to it, Twan is going to look out for self. Keep in mind, ain't no friends in the game."

These conversations with Mama Bev meant the world to Bossy. She spoke from wisdom and experience. After promising to do what she had to do after packaging this last shipment for Twan, family time was over. The three women said good night to Mama Bev and headed home. Once there, Aisha and Terry couldn't wait to gather in Bossy's apartment and find out what Mama Bev had said to her. When asked, Bossy reported, "Mama Bev said the usual: 'Baby, I know this is all you've done but you have the shop to keep you busy and make you money.. When it comes down to it, Twan is going to look out for self. Keep in mind, ain't no friends in the game.'"

That night Bossy lay on her king-size bed and reflected on her life to date. Thinking back to her childhood, teenage years, twenties, and now thirties, Bossy couldn't help but wonder why God had even created her. She wondered what she had done so bad that caused her to be born and raised by a crack fiend woman and a heartless daddy who'd disappeared so early on in her life, he may as well have not existed at all. Bossy thought about her big brother Devin, sitting in prison for the rest of his life and hoped with all of her heart that he was safe. She hated thinking about him being on the modern-day plantation because she was unable to have his back or protect him as he'd done her as a little girl. Devin had been her daddy, her male role model, her first true love. Him being snatched away from her life felt like death to her.

After Devin was arrested, Bossy had no one to comfort her when things went bump in the night. As Bossy lay with "Moon Child" by Rick James playing softly in the room, she needed Devin. The bumps in the night as a child were nothing compared to the damn boom headed her way. Bossy had no way of knowing that, in order to protect herself and her girls, she'd have to reach out very far.

Can I Have A Minute To Myself, Please?

Chapter 14

Aisha once again arrived at the shop before Terry and Bossy. She wouldn't complain because having a minute of quiet time was a treat. She loved living close to her best friends but lately it seemed to be one crisis after another with them. Between Terry and her sleepless nights and Bossy's hesitation to make a long overdue life change, Aisha was plain tired.

Before leaving for the shop this morning, Aisha treated herself to a bubble bath, a glass of herbal tea, aromatherapy candles and more importantly, an hour of quiet. As she soaked in the relaxing tub, her mind drifted back to her life with the only man she'd ever loved, her ex-husband, Pete Jackson.

Pete was two years ahead of her in high school and always had a crush on her. They had met six months after Aisha was raped. He hadn't known her personally but had heard about the tragedy around the jets. Aisha never knew it, but it had been one of Pete's brothers, who was locked up in the county at the time, that saw to it her rapist, David Lawford, received what he had coming to him.

During a high school football game at the Rayen High School's home field, Bossy, Aisha, and Terry were hanging out by the ticket gate when Pete walked right into Aisha. She practically jumped out of her skin. Pete apologized, introduced himself, apologized again, and turned to leave. As he was walking away, he heard one of the girls say, "Why didn't you say anything, Aisha, I think he likes you." There was no reply, just silence as Pete continued to walk away. The question required no reply because everyone, including Pete, already knew the answer; it was just too soon after her ordeal for her to trust a man she hardly knew.

Aisha was still having nightmares about that night and as a result, was sleeping in the bed with her mother. She refused to stay home alone and spent all of her time next door with Bossy or on the south side at Terry's house. Three times a week, a counselor from the rape crisis center stopped by to check in on Aisha, but their visits weren't doing much good. David Lawford had robbed her of more than just her free spirit and childhood, he took away her virginity. Her mother had always preached that the most precious thing in the world is a girl's virginity. It tore Aisha up inside that she could never get that back.

After that night, Pete and Aisha would see each other around school and on those rare occasions that Aisha would be hanging outside with Bossy. Due to Pete's patience, they slowly became friends and just before his high school graduation, she became his girlfriend. That summer the two were inseparable and the old Aisha slowly resurfaced. As September 1986 approached, their love was full blown and the reality set in that Pete would soon be off to join the air force.

"What am I going to do when you're gone? I was lucky to have you in my life; you wanted to be with me even though you knew about what happened to me. No one else is going to want me," said Aisha, apprehensively.

"Don't talk like that; any man in this world would be lucky to have you as their own. Just because I'm leaving doesn't mean I'm letting you go. I'll always love you and will be here when you need me."

"That sounds good and I know you mean it but maintaining a long-distance relationship isn't easy. I can't travel with you because I'm still in high school and my mother would never allow it. I don't think I can live without you."

It was then that they came up with a plan to stay together. Three weeks later, Aisha told her mother she would be staying the weekend at Terry's and joining the family on a weekend trip to Cincinnati, Ohio. Mama Bev gave her permission, thinking a weekend at King's Island Amusement Park would do her daughter some good. Just as Aisha suspected, her mother gave her a pocketful of money and told her to have a good time.

Late that Friday afternoon, Pete and Aisha were on their way to Illinois to get married. That night Pete made love to his young bride and made her feel like a queen. Aisha's first experience at lovemaking was everything she feared it never would be. Rape was brutal, forceful, and about power. Making love was about sensitivity, tenderness and love. She felt so much love that she cried.

"What's wrong, baby, did I hurt you?" Pete asked concerned.

"No, you've done everything right. I never thought a man could make me feel the way you have or that a man could love me after I'd been damaged."

"Please stop talking like that, Mrs. Aisha Jackson. I love you, forever."

That was almost twenty years ago and Aisha still longed to feel that way again. The marriage lasted about two weeks before Bev found out and made her get an annulment. Pete went away to fulfill his commitment to enter the air force. He continued to keep in touch with Aisha and claimed he still loved her although he was now married with four-year-old twin daughters of his own. He sent Aisha pictures of Alexis Monique and Alyssa Monae every Christmas; it seemed they were his pride and joy.

Recently, Aisha had begun dating a man the color of chocolate and as sexy as L.L Cool J with a voice like Lyfe Jennings himself. Leroy Harland was no pretty boy but he was eye candy. She met him one day when he was substituting for the shop's regular mailman. They'd gone out on a few dates before he was invited into her apartment. Uncertain if she could trust him, Aisha let Terry and Bossy know that she'd be entertaining and to listen out for any commotion.

Aisha cooked steaks, served drinks and decided it was time to see how the booty worked. The sex was a little above average but Aisha felt that after a couple of sessions, he'd be working it the way she liked. Unfortunately, she never got to find out. After their first time together, Aisha invited Leroy to join her in the shower. A half hour later, he went into her bedroom while Aisha dried and lotioned herself in the bathroom. Upon returning to her room, she couldn't believe her eyes. There he was, as if he were at home alone, sitting in the middle of her bed, butt naked clipping his toenails. Eeee! Completely turned off, Aisha couldn't get that fool out of her apartment fast enough. She was still having problems getting the vision out of her head.

Aisha's workday started stressfully and almost immediately she longed for another hot bath. *Damn that, soon as I can, I'm taking my ass to the spa,* Aisha promised herself. Before the doors even opened, the electricity went out because some fool hit a pole one block down from the shop. Aisha was just glad it happened on a Sunday when business would be scarce. It being the third Sunday of the month, all of the workers, including Talissa and Caron, were to come in for a staff meeting. Everyone was on time except for Caron. That child was truly trying everyone's patience and Aisha was ready to cut her lose. When she did show up, she had the nerve to have her boyfriend with her.

"Hey y'all, what's going on? I know I'm late but y'all know how it is, right?" Caron tried to show off the boyfriend.

"Little girl, you are tripping; haven't you been told how important it is to have respect for other people's time? Being late for our staff meetings is not respectful," said Sirenna while rolling her eyes up in her head.

"I'm not a little girl and I'm only a half hour late, dang," Caron shot back with much attitude.

"That is it!" Aisha was fed up with the young girl's nonchalant attitude. "Caron, may I see you in the office, alone."

Once in the office, Aisha let the child have it. "I'm going to get straight to the point, Miss Caron. You aren't working out and tomorrow I will contact the agency and have Ms. Houston find a better-suited place for you. Please gather your things and leave." Caron opened her mouth to protest but before she got one word out, Aisha gave her a look that could kill and Caron thought better of arguing. She packed up her things, including her boy, and left.

When Aisha pulled in front of their apartment building, she was happy to see that no one was home. *Good, I can rest before meeting with Mama for dinner. Why did I promise to meet Mama anyway? We were just there yesterday. Damn, we have got to find her a man.* Aisha laughed at the thought of finding her mother something she didn't even have for herself. The idea of having a minute to herself was short-lived when Aisha spotted Ant's deuce and a quarter pulling up behind hers. *Now what does this fool want? I am not in the mood for his ass today.*

"Bossy's not here, Ant, but I'll let her know you're looking for her." Aisha tried to keep him from getting too far out of his car. After the day she'd just had, making small talk would take entirely too much damn energy.

"I ain't looking for Bossy, I want to talk to you and Terry," Ant said smugly. He stood looking down on Aisha, trying desperately not to show the fear inside of his heart. Ant knew that he was taking the biggest gamble of his life but felt he had no other choice. The panic state fueled Ant to make the only move he believed would get him out of debt with the new drug connection.

"Why, you don't have anything to speak with us about," replied Aisha. She shifted all her weight to her left leg, positioned her purse onto her right shoulder and placed her hand on the butt of her little friend. Just in case Ant's ass wanted to show off.

"Yes I do. Our drug house on Warren Avenue got busted today and over two hundred thousand dollars worth of straight profit for my ass is gone. If y'all stuck-up asses had of let my boy stash that shipment at ya spot," Ant paused and took one too many steps closer to Aisha, "none of this would have happened and somebody gon' pay."

"Ant, I don't have time for your immature bullshit. If you and Twan can't handle the weight you're digging into, ease up off it. Before that shipment was even picked up, storage for it should have been planned and confirmed." Taking her cue from her opponent, Aisha took two steps closer as she continued. "The two of you have been doing shit ass backward so you getting that cherry busted was bound to happen."

"Look, bitch . . ."

"No, the hell you didn't come at me sideways

and call me out my name! You don't want to get yourself into a name-calling match with me. I understand you being upset but I am not the one," warned Aisha. The gun was now in her hand securely and Aisha's only dilemma was whether to fire one into Ant's ass or give him a break, and just shoot one through his ride. Aisha wasn't worried about her neighbors calling the police on her; shit, she was on the bottom of the south side, on a Sunday—what?

"Fuck that, we ain't got the money to re-up now and no way to recoup that type of paper. You two bitches better find a way to get us out of this shit or we all gon' be in trouble. If I go down, I ain't sinkin' alone," bluffed Ant.

The two stood frozen in the moment for a brief second, with Ant worried he may have crossed the line and Aisha knowing damn well that he had. Ant must have forgotten that Aisha was born and raised in the jets.

"You picked the wrong day to fuck with me. I can't figure out if you crazy or just stupid?" Aisha screamed back, "when it comes down to it, ain't no partnerships in the streets and ya ugly ass know that. See I ain't nobody's bitch, especially not some ugly-ass runner from smurf village [a small neighborhood situated at the bottom of the south side of the city]!" Aisha had had enough when she pulled out the .32 she'd been gripping and pointed it at Ant. "If you think I won't cap one in ya knees, try me. I dare you, motherfucker. I dare you to make a move, monkey." Ant stood frozen, mouth open.

"That's what I thought. Now retreat ya ugly ass

back into ya car and ride the fuck on." Ant did as he was told but not before Aisha put one bullet in each taillight of his prized deuce and a quarter. Aisha stood watching as his car disappeared up Falls Avenue and over the hill.

All I wanted was a minute to my damn self, now this ugly-ass fool got me into something I have no place being. Ain't this a bitch!

A Heart that's Pure Won't Be Denied

Chapter 15

Never in her wildest dreams did LaJetia imagine she'd experience the things Twan had exposed her to—a beautiful home, and nice cars, regular trips to the hair salon and even a cruise to Mexico. For a girl who became a teenage mother at fourteen, LaJetia's life was a fairy tale. Unfortunately for LaJetia, the one thing Twan hadn't given her was security.

Their vacation together helped LaJetia open her eyes and recognize how good a provider Twan was to his family. She thought about how Twan had taken on the responsibility of raising children not his own, never treating Kiara and Tyler differently than he did the son they shared together. LaJetia reflected on how comfortable she'd become, never worrying about the lights, gas or phone being cut off or where her next meal was coming from. She had refused to reapply for assistance after moving in with Twan because she couldn't stand the way those state workers talked down to her.

"Name of the fathers, please? Are you working?

Are you still living in a section eight home? Are you attending school? How long do you think taxpayers are going to take care of you?" Just because she needed assistance didn't mean she was triflin'. It meant she needed help at the time and anyway, she felt a man was supposed to take care of his family. Just because she grew up in poverty with a selfish mother didn't mean she was ignorant to the roles of men and women. LaJetia knew how hard her father, Barry Rose, worked to care for his family when he was alive. LaJetia could remember their lights being disconnected only one time and it was due to her mother being irresponsible and spending the bill money on a bus trip to Atlantic City. After that, Barry Rose paid all of the household bills himself.

Spending time together was all LaJetia yearned for from Twan and on the cruise, she got what she wanted. From sunup to sundown, it was just the two of them. Most importantly, they talked to one another.

"Why don't you smile like this when we're at home?" inquired Twan.

"I never smile because I never see you. We don't spend time together and that's mainly what I wanted from you," explained LaJetia in a sincere tone.

"Don't I give you everything? I mean, don't I take care of home?"

"Yes, you do Twan and I'm not trying to take that away from you. If I were honest with myself, I'd have to admit that I'm lonely. It's nothing new because all of my life, I've felt this way. Now let me ask you something."

"Ask me whatever it is you need to know."

"Why don't you let me ride with you on your out of town trips?"

Twan stood dumbfounded; surely LaJetia wasn't that fuckin' insecure to risk losing her children and her freedom just to keep tabs on him. Was this bitch for real?

"I know I don't even have to answer that stupid-ass question. Next one!"

The look on Twan's face made LaJetia hesitate to even ask her next question. If she didn't know any better, LaJetia would swear that Twan was about to pounce on her and whip her ass for suggesting she ride along on a drug run. *Damn, I was only asking.*

"Are you going to leave me?" LaJetia held her breath as she waited for the answer.

"How could you ask me that? Everything I've given you and you're still insecure? What do I have to do to make you believe I'm not going anywhere?"

"Come home at night, take time to help me with the kids and make time for me, for us." Tears formed in LaJetia's eyes as she spoke.

Twan promised to do better and honor LaJetia's request. He even brought up the subject of adopting Kiara and Tyler and wanting to give them his last name. LaJetia was elated. For a few weeks after they returned home, he'd done just that. When he slipped back into his old ways, it wasn't a gradual transition; it was at the snap of the fingers. He still helped with the kids in the mornings but that was about it. No more dinners with the family and Twan came and went whenever he pleased.

LaJetia felt betrayed and stupid. This broken

promise could mean only one of two things: either Twan had deliberately lied to her, never intending to giving his family his precious time or he was out fuckin' around on her . . . again. All in all, he'd done well just long enough to keep LaJetia quiet. She'd listened to every one of his speeches about *livin' da life* and LaJetia was beginning to understand it better, but, living the life was one thing and just being plain disrespectful was another.

The alarm clock went off at eight in the morning blarin' LaJetia's favorite song by Youngstown's own No-Joke. LaJetia joined in with the rapper as he sang:

I don't know if you notice it girl . . .

Reappearing in the bedroom from the adjoining bath, LaJetia stood over Twan as he snored loud enough to wake the neighbors. She spent the previous evening contemplating a way to test him. She wouldn't rest until she found out for sure if he were cheating on her and if so, just who the bitch was.

"Mommy, Mommy I need some help!" whined three-year-old Tyler.

"What it is, baby, are you hurt?" LaJetia couldn't run fast enough to her sons' room. When she arrived, it took all she had inside of her not to laugh at her precious child. Recently, he'd been attempting to act like a big boy and dress himself. Some days he did great and other days not so great. Today he had managed to get both legs in the same side of his jeans and his T-shirt was on inside out and backward.

Tyler looked exactly like his grandfather Barry.

LaJetia would do anything in the world to have her father back in her life. She still couldn't come to terms with him taking his own life. It was a subject she refused to discuss and fell into a deep depression whenever her thoughts returned to the night his body was found.

No one knew where the handgun had come from and there was no note left behind to explain what seemed to be his selfish and cowardly actions. LaJetia's mother Kate Rose had always maintained *her* life, making the mistake of thinking that once her only child became a teenager she didn't need her mother anymore. Kate liked to make it appear that her financial standing was higher than it really was and making appearances was more important to her than both her husband and daughter.

When Barry killed himself, his wife put on airs and played the grieving wife to a T. Kate came off as shocked, bewildered and confused when in truth, she knew exactly why her husband had chosen to commit suicide. He'd always suffered from severe depression and medications never seemed to help. Just days before the tragedy, Barry discovered his wife of eight years was sleeping with two of his best friends and had a gambling addiction. In just three months, she had managed to gamble away what little savings Barry had saved. He was disgusted when he discovered that Kate had even emptied out LaJetia's college fund. On top of all that, Dr. Roberts informed Barry he was in the advanced stages of prostate cancer, a result of him putting off his annual physical for five years. Had the disease been caught early, his odds of beating it would have been much greater.

The weight on his shoulders was just too much for him to bear. As he thought about the pain, medication and medical bills resulting from the cancer, the decision was made. Purchasing the .357 on eBay was just as easy as buying a hammer from Sears. After praying and asking the Lord for forgiveness, Barry sat down in his favorite lounge chair, relaxed, closed his eyes, and pulled the trigger.

Waking up to the sounds of laughter and toys clashing to the floor was normal for Twan and LaJetia's household. Twan joined the boys in the long hallway and played with their Tonka trucks as if he were a toddler himself. His head was pounding from the bottle of Grey Goose he'd consumed the night before but this time with Tyler and Trayvon was priceless. After the boys were tired out, Twan decided to return to bed and grab a couple more hours of sleep. LaJetia had other plans for him. The boys were down for their afternoon naps and LaJetia was determined to have her man to herself, if only for an hour.

The silk nightgown that hung tightly on LaJetia's nineteen-year-old frame was sexy and she knew it. To help entice Twan into staying home with her, she let her shoulder-length hair hang down the way he liked it. Twan enjoyed playing in her hair when they were intimate. No words were spoken between the two lovers; the second Twan looked at LaJetia and smelled his favorite scent on her almond-colored skin his nature began to rise.

As the nightgown fell to the ground, Twan

caressed her left breast and palmed her ass simultaneously. His lips found their way to her right breast and his tongue circled her erect nipple causing LaJetia to become moist. She removed Twan's shorts and grabbed him just the way he liked, his shaft in one hand and his balls in the other. Their kisses became sloppy and hard as Twan lay back on the bed waiting anxiously for his woman to use her mouth to please him. His shoulders relaxed and his legs tensed when LaJetia swallowed, knowing it only made Twan want her more. It was now her turn to be pleased as the man she loved and wanted desperately to hold on to went down on her. The scream she let out as she climaxed was a familiar sound to her lover. He lifted his body over his lover and entered her with force. The lovemaking turned to raw fucking as LaJetia slipped on top and rode Twan's manhood with her back facing him. Releasing the stress from their bodies was exactly what each of them needed. They lay entwined and sweating afterward and slept like babies until Tyler knocked on the door. "Mommy, we hungry."

The ringing cell phone caught LaJetia's attention as she made lunch for the three men in her life. Twan picked up the cell, walked off into another room, and whispered into the phone. Returning to the kitchen to eat, he gave LaJetia news she didn't want to hear.

"After I shower, I gotta go take care of some important business."

"What? I need you to spend the day with me."

"Girl, I'm telling' you now, do not start that shit. This can't wait and I'll be back as soon as I can."

"Whatever, Twan, you never have to worry about my asking you for any of your damn time again." LaJetia stormed off to her private room.

While Twan took a long shower, LaJetia put her plan to uncover the identity of his lover into action. She strolled through his cell phone jotting down all the numbers belonging to females.

Thirty minutes later, Twan was dressed in a crisp white tee, baggy Phat Farm jeans, and matching kicks on his feet. He took one final look in the mirror before grabbing his wallet and car keys off the dresser. He said bye to the kids before heading out of the house via the garage to avoid a confrontation with LaJetia.

Just seconds later, the front door slammed behind him as he reentered the house.

"Fuck man, this is some bullshit, fo' real," barked Twan. He grabbed the yellow pages from the top of the refrigerator and slammed it down on the oak wood table.

"What the hell is wrong with you?" LaJetia asked although she already knew the answer.

"Some motherfuckas flattened the tires on my ride. Shit, I don't need this mess today. Who would do some childish shit like that?"

"I keep telling you to park in the garage. The way you baby that car I don't understand why you wouldn't keep it safe at night."

"Shit, I moved us out here in Boardman so I wouldn't have to worry about stuff like this. A man can't even be safe at home and the thing that gets me is that no one knows where we live."

LaJetia smiled to herself at what she'd done. Trying to force Twan to spend the day with her, she snuck out while he was in the shower and let the air out of his tires. The only flaw in her plan was AAA coming to fix the flats and Twan taking *her* car because he couldn't wait for them to finish.

Minutes after Twan left, LaJetia made herself comfortable in her favorite chair and began calling the numbers she got from his cell phone call list.

"Hello!" The ghetto voice said while cracking gum.

"Yeah, who this?" inquired LaJetia.

"What the fuck you mean, *who this*; bitch, you called my house."

"I found ya number in my man's cell phone and I just want you to know he got a family and he stayin' with me," LaJetia said with conviction.

"Oh, so that's the game you're playin'. Okay, I'll play along. This is Shadaisy and who is ya man you tryin' to hold on to?" gum cracking into the receiver.

"My man is Twan, just remember he got a woman and stay the fuck out his face!" warned LaJetia.

"How old are you? About twelve, sixteen? Don't nobody but young girls make juvenile calls like this. Don't step to me or any other woman ya man might be keeping company with. I don't know you and ain't never told ya stupid ass I loved you or wanted to be with you." Shadaisy paused to take a swig of her White Mountain berry wine cooler. "That nigga Twan—yeah he fine and all but he ain't my type. Those fine niggas take up too much energy; I like my men ugly as a monkey. So you got me bent." Not having time for much more antics, Shadaisy cracked her gum one more time and hung up the phone.

LaJetia began to dial the next number on her list when she heard a knock at the door and assumed it was the AAA guy letting her know he was done working on Twan's tires. Forgetting to peek out before opening the door, LaJetia stood frozen at the sight of her visitor.

"Where's Twan at? And don't give me any bullshit answer because I'm not in the fuckin' mood," warned Bossy as she stared through LaJetia like she wasn't shit.

"He ain't here and how do you know where we live?"

"Tell Twan to call me as soon as possible. It's a matter of life and death. Ant's life to be exact and Twan's too if I find out he had anything to do with that bitch-ass stunt."

Bossy turned and left just as quickly as she'd come. Her blood pressure was high, she was craving a blunt, a shot of liquor, and a quickie as she sped off down the street.

LaJetia closed and locked the door as Bossy walked away. She had no idea what was going on but for Bossy to come to their front door meant Twan was in deep trouble. At that moment, LaJetia tried to think of a way to protect her man from whatever was threatening him. Besides, her love for him consumed her. Unfortunately for her, LaJetia had no idea what world she was attempting to step into.

Can You Live With Your Mistakes?

Chapter 16

Ant was pissed as he drove around the city contemplating his next move. His initial plan of intimidating Aisha was a bust. He'd fully expected her to fold like a blanket but instead she ended up turning into someone totally opposite to the Aisha he knew. The woman pointing the gun at him was strong, confident, and straight-up ghetto. In all of the years Ant had been around Bossy, Aisha, and Terry, Aisha had always come off as timid, soft, and ladylike. Terry was moody and at times, just plain unapproachable and Bossy, was well, just not to be fucked with. As the saying goes, "never judge a book by its cover." Ant had done just that and it could have cost him either his life or his ability to walk.

According to Shadaisy, officers Powell and Meeks stormed the house and left with the stash of drugs but didn't arrest her. Ant couldn't believe that those two crooked cops had remained on the force as long as they had. Every hustler in the city had had a run-in with those two so-called "officers" at one time or another and the outcome was always the same. No arrest, just robbery and a shake-down. As Ant pulled up in front of the drug house, he racked his brain to come up with a way to stop the criminal rule of officers Powell and Meeks and recover his loss.

Minutes after Ant stepped into the Warren Avenue house, Twan pulled up in LaJetia's Lexus. Ant's heart stopped for fear that word had gotten back to Twan about his encounter with Aisha last night. He stepped out onto the porch to greet his boy.

"What it do, pimpin'? You all right?" Ant asked nervously.

"I'm pissed, man. Someone let the air out of the tires on my ride." Twan paused to regain his composure. "What a bitch move."

As Shadaisy stood inside the screen door, she overheard the conversation and thought to herself how right Twan was. Bitch moves were only made by bitches and LaJetia was most likely the bitch in question. Armed with that information and the phone call she received not long ago, Shadaisy couldn't wait to school Twan on his girl.

As soon as Twan stepped through the door, Shadaisy went to work.

"Hey Twan, did I hear you right? Someone came out to the 'burbs and fucked with ya ride?"

"Yeah, ain't that some shit for ya ass? Whoever did it better hope I never catch up with 'em." Twan's anger grew as he recalled the number-one sin to a man: fuckin' with his ride. You might get away with disrespecting his mama before you'd get away with disrespecting his ride.

"Are you sure you don't know who did it? I mean, after that phone call ya girl made to me a little while ago, I'd be looking at home first before trying to look in the streets for who disrespected you like that."

Shadaisy tried to drag out the information as long as possible. She was jealous of the way Twan took care of home, especially since Ant didn't think enough of her to put her in a home of her own. Instead he had her living in a drug house where at any time her life and freedom could end.

"What the hell are you talking about?" Twan was getting frustrated with Shadaisy.

"Ya girl called me to let me know you have a woman and family and that you ain't going nowhere. She told me to stop fuckin' with you. Apparently she thinks you messin' around on her." Shadaisy's heart smiled as she delivered the news.

"Are you serious? Naw, LaJetia didn't do no shit like that. How did she get the number?"

"I don't know but I'm guessing from your cell. Did you leave it unattended?" Shadaisy knew that was how LaJetia had gotten the number because that's how she would have, if needed.

Twan thought back to everything that had taken place at home and realized LaJetia did have access to his phone while he was asleep or in the shower. She had tried hard to get him to stay home that day. He felt bad about breaking his promise to her but he had to take care of business. Recouping lost money from the drugs that were stolen from them was priority. Although Twan had been spending money like it grew on trees, he had managed to put a little to the side. It wouldn't be too hard for him to make up the five hundred grand they owed C-Lok but that meant rolling down the highway to pick up another shipment from his Colombian contact. Besides, explaining that much weight to Bossy would mean telling her about his new local connection. Twan did not want that conversation to take place, especially since Bossy had told him to slow down. Twan had gotten a little sloppy and he knew it.

"Man, who the fuck is that?" Shadaisy yelled after hearing the sound of screeching tires outside. Ant knew the shit was about to hit the fan. He'd fucked up big-time and it was time to face the music.

When he was a little boy hanging out with the street corner hustlers, he heard story after story about the boldest bitch in the city. Only those with a death wish crossed Bossy. Ant recalled hearing one tale of a drive-by done out on the Sharon line. The way he overheard it, Teddy Bear was caught slippin' at a phone booth one night after the club closed. He was parked down the street from Jitso's and some young punk rode up on him and robbed him for five hundred dollars. Teddy Bear got a good look at the dope fiend and put the word out about a reward if he was found that night. The description was a young boy with a high-top box cut, light-skinned with bad skin, wearing a blue Members Only jacket, jeans and Adidas kicks.

Bossy, Big Black and Poppy had left the club just before closing in order to get down the street to Corky's Bar before it closed for the night. Teddy Bear was comfortable being alone, at the time, because he was cool with everyone and assumed his safety around the city was on lockdown. After that night, Teddy Bear never traveled alone.

Finding the robber was easy because he bragged about the holdup while chilling in the Davis's after-hours spot just hours later. Big Black, Poppy, and Bossy were chilling in the parking lot when someone ratted on him. The fiend's name was Ali Carlson. Bossy went inside and acted like she wanted to spend some time with him. Thinking with the wrong head, Ali fell for it and he followed Bossy to her car. They took a short ride to the nearby Bailey Park and as promised, Bossy fired up a joint. Bossy led Ali away from the car so Big Black and Poppy could sneak up behind him. They had been hiding in the backseat of the SUV the whole time. Ali never knew what hit him. They beat him so bad, he was unrecognizable for months. He lay in a coma for eight weeks and awoke unable to remember his own name.

It was said that Bossy shot him in his hands and kneecaps to teach him a lesson. She reasoned that he shouldn't have been so stupid and hit a man with as many resources as Teddy Bear; as rules on the street go, business is business.

Ant never knew if the story was completely true but he damn sure did not want to find out firsthand what Bossy was capable of doing.

Twan walked away from Shadaisy and out onto the porch to meet Bossy.. He knew something was wrong because Bossy never showed her face at any spot that could be hot.

Twan had never seen Bossy in the state she was in now. Flames were coming out of her eyes and the air changed as she walked closer to her target.

Bossy did not bother with greeting Twan and Ant, she walked onto the porch barking demands.

"Let's handle this inside so the neighbors don't overhear my fuckin' business."

"Hey, you, why don't you go upstairs or to the store while I talk to these two?" Bossy dismissed Shadaisy from the room. Shadaisy turned and walked as fast as she could up the stairs. She had no problem leaving the room but there was no way Shadaisy was going to leave the house. Shadaisy was much too nosy for that.

"What's going down, Bossy," asked Twan.

"Oh, you don't know what ya partner Ant pulled out his ass yesterday?" Bossy stared into Ant's eyes as she spoke. "Why don't you tell Twan what went down?"

Ant remained silent, his tongue tied. He found it hard to breathe and feared meeting his maker within the next few seconds.

"Since his bitch ass won't own up to what he did, I'll let you know." Bossy felt her heart race and anger growing as she stared deeper into Ant's eyes. "He rode up on my spot last night and made demands on Aisha. He tried to strong-arm her into repaying him for the loss y'all took on that bullshit-ass raid." Everything inside of Bossy was telling her to put Ant out of his fuckin' misery but she promised herself years before to never take another life. Anyway, death for a dumb ass like Ant was too damn easy.

"Ant, what the fuck was you thinking?" Twan demanded to know.

"You know as well as I do that if we could have

stashed that shit in the shop, Powell and Meeks would have come up empty on their illegal raid."

Shadaisy stood at the top of the stairs straining to eavesdrop on the conversation. She could not make out everything that was being said, but she got the gist of it. Ant's punk ass had fucked up and put his and Twan's livelihood in jeopardy.

"Are you crazy? What kind of logic is that?" Twan asked.

"What I want to know is how in the hell did they get that much weight when y'all always bring it to me first for packaging?" Bossy knew she'd just busted Twan and he'd have to come clean. The look on Twan's face said he was searching for the right response and Bossy decided she would deal with his ass another time and returned her attention to Ant.

"Do you think that just because I ain't out here the way I used to be that I'm to be fucked with?" Bossy spoke calmly to Ant. She stepped close enough to Ant to stick her tongue down his throat.

"Naw, it ain't even like that. I just lost my mind for a minute and panicked because ain't no way for us to repay that bill and soon the local connect is going to come looking for his money," stuttered Ant. "Shit, Sharon, PA is only a hop, skip, and a jump from da Yo'. That nigga ain't gon' have no problem finding out what don' went down. He probably already knows we were robbed."

Busted! Bossy knew Twan had gotten in bed with someone other than the Colombians down in Florida, she just didn't know who. Now she did thanks to Ant. There was only one local hustler big enough to handle weight of any magnitude.

Ant's knees finally buckled from fear, thankfully, the couch behind him caught his fall. Bossy bent over, never taking her eyes off her opponent in hopes of scaring Ant shitless.

"I'm going to say this one time. We are no longer affiliated with one another. I don't fuck with bitch-ass men, which to me, you have shown yourself to be. If you ever cross paths with me again, it will be the second biggest mistake of your life. No one has ever fucked with me and gotten away with it and that includes you." Bossy stood straight and turned to face Twan.

"Don't mistake this statement as a choice, Twan. You cut this bitch loose or our relationship, business and personal, is over." The room was silent except for the screen door slamming behind Bossy. She knew that one day she'd have to see Ant before he tried to see her. Bossy had no problem being the last one standing. Experience had taught her when to handle things personally and reach out for assistance. She knew just who to call to take care of this problem.

The babysitter arrived thirty minutes after LaJetia made the call requesting her services. Auntell lived three doors down and had placed flyers around the neighborhood advertising her babysitting services. LaJetia was one of the first to use her services and the kids loved Auntell Patterson. She kept them busy with movies, books, games, and storytelling. As a perk, she even gave them their baths and never let them stay up past the bedtime their parents set for them.

"Thank you for coming over on such short notice. I won't be gone longer than a couple of hours and please call my cell if you have any problems," instructed LaJetia.

"Yes, ma'am, we'll be fine," said Auntell.

"Just one more thing and this is very important. Should anyone come by the house, do not open the door for anyone. Do you understand?"

"Sure, don't open the door for anyone. Don't worry, I promise the kids will be fine. They are in good hands," Auntell said with a smile.

Driving toward her destination, LaJetia was determined to get to the bottom of what was going on with Twan. Her instinct told her that whatever it was had to be serious for Bossy to show up on their doorstep. No cars were parked on the corners of Hillman Street and St. Louis Avenue so that meant all of the employees of KAT69 had left for the day. The clock in the Toyota Sienna read 4:21 PM and it being Monday, LaJetia wasn't surprised she'd missed them. She parked in the lot and thought about what to do and where to go next. *It would be a suicide mission for me to show up at the apartment down on Falls Avenue but maybe I can find Ant at the house on Warren.*

Waiting for traffic to clear and allow her to make a lefthand turn onto Hillman Street, LaJetia saw Ant's deuce and a quarter speed by. *That's it, I can follow Ant and he'll lead me to Twan.* LaJetia sped right past a police car parked in front of New Bethel Baptist Church. The sound of the sirens drew her out of her daze, frightening her. *Now what the hell do they want? Shit, I don't have time for this.* LaJetia pulled her van into Mr. Charlie's Car

Repair lot and waited for the officer to approach her driver-side window. To her surprise, they rode past her and stopped Ant.

A block away, Ant made a right onto Myrtle Avenue and two officers exited the patrol car and approached him. LaJetia parked her van and walked the block to join the small crowd watching the traffic stop.

"License, registration, and proof of insurance please," requested Officer Meeks.

"What's the problem, Officer?" replied Ant.

"The problem is we clocked you doing fifty in a thirty-five. Now please provide your documents." Ant was actually only going five miles over the speed limit and the crooked officers had no intention of writing him a ticket. That would only provide written proof of their confrontation with the right-hand man of the drug dealer they had been trying to get next to for months now.

"Please turn off the engine and wait here." Officer Meeks turned on his heels and headed back to his patrol car.

After Teddy Bear was killed, the officers lost a good part of their income because Twan refused to pay them the way his mentor had. Being from New York City and growing up fast and hard, Officer Powell knew how to set a trap and lure in his prey. After months of planning, it was time to get things started.

While off duty one evening, Officer Powell spotted Twan leaving a house on the east side of town. John Powell couldn't let the grand opportunity pass him by so he carefully followed the unsuspecting drug dealer for miles. At best, Twan would lead him to his home; at worst, he'd lead him to one of his hangouts. Either way, Powell felt he would gain some information on Twan. Twenty minutes after first seeing his prey, Powell saw Twan pull up in front of a ranch-style home in Boardman. Thanks to the Internet, Powell later discovered it was the home Twan shared with his girlfriend and three children.

Officer Robert Meeks returned to the driver side of Ant's antique car after fifteen minutes and demanded he exit the vehicle.

"I'm sure that everything is up to date and the insurance is active so what's the problem, Officer?" demanded Ant.

"Please get out of the vehicle and keep your hands where I can see them."

Following department procedures, Officer Powell frisked his suspect down. Ant prayed that they would write him a ticket and let him go home; at that moment, he needed a stiff drink.

Once they were comfortable that Ant was unarmed, they asked for permission to search the vehicle. After searching his mind to confirm the officers wouldn't find anything and wanting the entire scene over with, Ant granted their request. Officer Powell carried out the search while his partner stood in front of the squad car with their nervous suspect.

"We aren't going to find any drugs or weapons inside the vehicle, are we?" questioned Meeks.

"No, I ride around with my children in that car," lied Ant. "Don't you see the car seat in the back?"

Returning with a ziplock bag containing a white

powdery substance, Officer Powell asked Ant if he'd like to rethink his answer. Ant stood dumbfounded and nervous, wondering where the drugs could have come from. Ant was certain he didn't have anything on him. The only answer was that the officers were setting him up for this bullshit.

"Well, looks like we need to do a more extensive search of your vehicle," announced Officer Meeks, "We're going to have you sit in our patrol car while we finish the search. For your sake, you'd better hope we don't find any."

Minutes later, Ant listened from the backseat as Officer Powell recited a list of a variety of charges he'd soon face, including possession, evading arrest, and lying to an officer. Ant shook in his skin at the thought of going to county jail, especially after what had happened to him during his last stay in the county.

"Officers, I swear those drugs aren't mine. Someone must have put 'em there. I love my children too much to put them in jeopardy like that. You have to believe me," pleaded Ant. His eyes began to water at the thought of spending a night in the county.

"We believe you but we doubt that any judge will even listen to a defense like that," mocked Officer Powell. "Especially with a record and known association with drug dealers."

"Please, there has to be a way to clear this entire thing up without taking me to jail."

The partners looked at each other both knowing they had the young punk exactly where they wanted him. Meeks, being the senior officer and knowing how money-hungry drug dealers thought about saving themselves first, got a hard-on at the thought of getting a nice share of Ant's dirty money. The one thing in life he'd always wanted and could never seem to hold on to was money. His life and dreams revolved around having money.

The youngest of eight children, he'd known poverty his entire life. His father worked hard at the local steel mill to keep food on the table and a roof over his family's heads. His mother broke her back cleaning floors for both white and black families. Officer Meeks, his five brothers, and two sisters would rub their mother's feet and massage her back every night for hours. He promised his parents that when he was able, he'd take care of them. Both of his parents were so proud the day their youngest boy graduated from the police academy. Robert was proud himself and vowed to provide a better life for the two people who'd sacrificed their lives for him.

At first, living on a police officer's salary of $35,000 a year in the Youngstown area worked out pretty well. The cost of living was low and he could afford to pay his rent and that of his parents with no problem until he got married. After he married and began having children of his own and his mother was moved into a nursing home, his salary could only be stretched so far. He needed fast money and quick. With the help of his partner, thus began his life of hustling the hustlers.

"There is a way to get out of this situation but I'm not sure you can handle it," teased Meeks.

"Tell me what it is. I'll do anything, what is it," whined Ant's bitch ass.

"We know that if the drugs aren't yours, they belong to a friend of yours, Antwan Glover."

"How do you know anything about my boy Twan?" Ant didn't even see where the crooked officers were leading him but he went willingly.

"We know everything about him and you. We know where you both live, what both of you drive, that Antwan has three children and that you visit your dear mother every morning. Today Antwan had a visitor that didn't look too happy."

"What are you talking about? Have you been watching us?"

"Let's just say we have our sources. Now what we need from you is further information to help fill in the gaps." Officer Meeks paused to search Ant's face for some type of reaction. "We know who Bossy Tucker is and where she lives but what we can't figure out is how she falls into the drug ring you and your boy run."

Officer Meeks turned his body to look at Ant and get a feel for which way to take the conversation. The officer noticed Ant had stopped shaking and seemed to be thinking about what they were saying.

"We want information on Antwan Glover, Bossy Tucker, and Clifton Boyd. We want to know what their roles are and how deep this thing goes. Don't start out by lying to us. We know Mr. Boyd is your supplier. We suggest you find a way to get us close to Antwan, Bossy, and Clifton because if you don't, you will be doing federal time and taking the rap for everyone. That means your dear mother will have to travel a long way to see her only son," warned Meeks.

"Y'all are putting me in a tight spot," Ant whined. "I can't even get close to Bossy like that. She won't even invite me in her apartment to take a piss let alone open the door for me to scope out how she runs shit. Besides, having her as an enemy is not something I want to do. Those badges don't mean shit to her and if y'all fuck with her you better bring the entire police force with you. She's as connected as Teddy Bear used to be," warned Ant.

"The prosecutor has enough evidence right now to arrest Antwan and send him away for at least twenty years," Meeks exaggerated. "So what's it going to be? Are we taking you downtown? Before you answer, think about what will happen to your dear sweet mother if her only living child is behind bars," Officer Powell threatened.

Ant sat contemplating the deal the officers had placed before him. He knew that Bossy would be looking to punish him for approaching Aisha the way he did; she'd made that clear less than an hour ago. Ant knew that one way or another, his days were numbered and Bossy was certain to make sure of that. By the way Twan reacted when he found out what he'd done, it was a good chance that he was about to cut him loose. Bossy had told him to do so and Ant knew that Twan had no other choice. That would mean Ant's money would dry up along with his clout around the Yo'. No one, including the new local connection, Clifton "C-Lok" Boyd would dare fuck with him. He never thought he'd do it, but Ant reasoned it was better for him to get Twan and Bossy before they got him.

"All right, man, I'll do it. How y'all want this shit to go down."

Officer Powell smiled like a kid at Christmas and damn near came on himself at the thought of getting next to so many high-level players. The higher up on the chain a hustler is, the higher up the figure to remain free.

"Right choice, Ant. We will all benefit from this, you've made the right decision."

"In order for us all to see tomorrow, you better hope so," said Ant, in a whisper. The thought of what he was getting into scared him more than the earlier confrontation with Bossy. But Ant reasoned that Bossy had made a threat she would surely follow up on. *Fuck that bitch, I can live with this but I damn sure can't live with being an enemy to Bossy.*

Summertime in the Yo

Chapter 17

August had finally arrived and the streets of the Yo' were booming. It was as if all of the players had added amps, speakers, and TV's to their rides. The strong sounds of bass played everywhere.

The brains behind the annual block party, Danny Levy, added something every year to keep people coming back. Even those that grew up on Kenmore Street and had moved away always returned home for the event. Last year, Danny added a car show and parade. This year, he added little amusement park rides for the kids.

Bossy, Aisha, and Terry were in their own apartments working on different projects in preparation of the block party. It was less than three hours away and being the biggest sponsor this year gave them the perfect opportunity to get word out about the changes KAT69 Hair and Nail Salon were in the midst of implementing. By spring the salon would become a full-service day spa offering child care for its clients. Terry and Aisha had marketing items—flyers, ink pens, Frisbees and beer mugs—made up to be handed out at the block party.

The women arrived on Kenmore Street and helped their staff hand out the marketing items. They held a raffle for spa and salon services; there would be five lucky winners. Other participating merchants also held raffles to raise money for Danny's nonprofit organization. The money benefited residents of Kenmore Street who hit hard times, the local little league football and basketball teams, and helped beautify the street. A scholarship program was also in the works that Danny Levy and his mother, Sass, were very proud of. Participating artists made donations and he graciously accepted them.

After novelist Tysha, raised on Kenmore Street, read from her current and future projects, it was time for the free concert to begin and the crowd was hyped. First up was No-Joke, who blew the stage up. Rufus Black and Dollar kept the crowd hyped and Lyfe Jennings sang his soul out and laid it down.

Twan and LaJetia had brought the kids out to enjoy the clowns, petting zoo, and food vendors. Twan couldn't wait to get his hand on a homemade candy apple and get the kids on the rides. The residents of Youngstown had not seen so much fun since Idora Park Amusement Park closed down.

"I'm going to let the kids ride and have some fun," LaJetia informed Twan.

"Cool, I'm going to buy the CD's from those acts that performed. Do you want that book by

Tysha?" asked Twan. "She'll probably give it to me for free. Me and her little brother Jay-Jae are real tight."

"Yeah, I do and see if she'll autograph it for me but you need to pay that girl for her book because I'm sure she had to pay for it. And Twan, try not to be gone too long."

"No problem, just hold it down with the kids and I'll be right back."

Knowing Bossy was somewhere, LaJetia watched as Twan disappeared into the crowd. As the kids went around in circles on the train ride, LaJetia stood watching back and forth between the kids and trying to locate Twan. With the type of personality Twan had, LaJetia expected him to get lost in the crowd for a while. Everyone who knew Twan expected him to make them laugh and by the looks of things, Twan knew just about everybody out at the block party.

After riding all of the rides, Kiara informed her mother that she and her brothers were hungry. LaJetia put Trayvon back into his stroller and led Kiara and Tyler to the line for hot dogs, fries, and drinks. She and the kids found a table to eat at and again LaJetia looked for her man. He stood laughing and talking to her hairdresser, Sirenna, her husband, No-Joke, and Bossy. Jealousy was instantly aroused in LaJetia and it took all she had not to go the hell off.

Twan congratulated No-Joke on his performance and asked if he needed sponsorship to help promote himself and his CD. The two men got to know one another and made plans to meet in a couple of days while Bossy and Sirenna stood by listening.

"Hey, Bossy, is everything goin' okay?" Danny stood next to her scanning the crowd. His cocoa complexion glistened under the sun and Bossy couldn't help but notice how good he smelled and looked. That was Danny's trademark—to look good—and he wasn't afraid to try new styles.

"Yeah, I'm good and you can't complain about the turn-out so I'm guessing you're doing well yourself. Looks like another success," responded Bossy.

"As long as things hold up this well for a couple more hours, I'll be on cloud nine. Are you and ya girls coming to the party tonight in Warren?"

"Only if the age limit is thirty-five and over."

"Damn, girl, then I couldn't even get in."

Bossy and Danny conversed a few more minutes about the after party, business, and made small talk until it was time to get the party jumping again. Danny returned to the stage and asked the crowd to invite the entertainers back.

As everyone made their way around the stage, Bossy kept her eyes on those standing around her. Out the corner of her eye, Bossy noticed Ant standing off to the side. It was as if he was hiding. *What the hell is he doing here? I know I told his ass to stay the hell away from me.* Sensing trouble, Bossy scanned the crowd for Aisha and Terry. By the time she looked back in Ant's direction, Bossy could not believe what she was seeing. Ant had his hand in the donation tin. *This nigga must think I'm bullshitin' with him! It's time to lay him the fuck down!*

Bossy caught the attention of Danny and Twan who rushed over and cornered Ant until the three off-duty police officers, including Powell and Meeks, could get to the scene.

"Man, what the fuck is wrong with ya punk ass?" fumed Twan. "Are you that hard up that you got to do a petty-ass theft for some chump change?"

Ant stared blankly at Twan, never attempting to search his brain for a response. Before a crowd formed around the commotion, Powell and Meeks led Ant away and pretended to arrest him. Instead, they set up a meeting time and place and told him to run off and not show his face in the streets until they told him to. Ant's robbing the block party was money-hungry Officer Powell's idea. He lived, breathed, dreamt, and shitted for money.

Three hours, four trips to the Porta Potti, and two rest breaks had passed when Twan returned to his family. The kids were now worn-out and cranky. Twan and LaJetia made their way to the van and loaded the three kids inside. On the short ride home (less than fifteen minutes), the kids fell asleep watching a video and Twan told LaJetia what happened with Ant.

"I'm not surprised; you know he ain't ever been right. Following you around like a sick puppy," voiced LaJetia. "That reminds me, the other day I saw the police stop Ant, search his ride, and put him in a patrol car, but he wasn't handcuffed. It looked like they found some drugs in his trunk too."

"Straight up?" quizzed Twan.

"He sat in the back of the police car for at least

thirty minutes before they let him go," explained LaJetia.

"How you know how long he was in the cruiser?" inquired Twan.

"'Cause a crowd stood around watching and I saw someone I knew standing on her porch. I recognized his car, so I parked the car at the corner and walked down the street right along with the nosy-ass neighbors," LaJetia halfway lied.

"Do you remember the numbers that were on the squad car?" Twan prayed it wasn't the officers he was thinking of.

"No, but I recognized their faces. It was them cops that be robbing everybody, the ones that was just walking around the block party. Powell and Meeks is they names. My friend told me a couple of stories about them."

Twan remained quiet for the rest of the ride home; he racked his brain about what Powell and Meeks's crooked asses could have possibly wanted with Ant. As Twan pulled into his garage, it hit him. The only thing that made any sense was that they were setting Ant up to be a snitch. *Fuck dat nigga, I ain't goin' down wit his punk ass. Bossy was right about him and I've got to cut him loose. The price of life and freedom is just too high,* thought Twan.

Back at the block party it had gotten late and the crowd was thinning out. The after party would begin in two hours at a hotel in downtown Warren, Ohio and it was time to drop off the kids, shower, and play dress up for all the partygoers.

Bossy grew angrier and angrier thinking about that bitch-ass Ant. Her senses told her Ant was up to something much bigger than stealing a few dollars from the block party. Bossy wanted to pop his ass the moment she saw him with his hand in the cookie jar.

She had put off making a crucial phone call long enough but it was now time to return to her roots—some straight-up survival-of-the-fittest type shit. The street in Bossy was on high alert and the situation was a code ten. Unsure of who she could trust, the set she and her two best friends threw every year would be canceled. Bossy knew that once she placed the call and put a plan into action, there was no turning back. *Shit, as soon as I decide to leave this shit alone, they got to pull me back in. Damn! Summertime in the Yo' is about to blow the fuck up.*

You Have Two New Messages

Chapter 18

It was hard to tell who was more excited about the changes that were in the works at KAT69 Hair and Nail Shop, the owners or the staff. Terry, with Aisha's help, had critiqued and refined her idea for implementing her spa and day care idea. The plan called for an extension to be built onto the back of the building. The spa would be accessible from the front by walking past the beauticians or through a door in the back where a receptionist would greet customers.

Terry would have to hire another receptionist for the new spa area along with three masseuses. The new floor plan called for the nail techs to be moved from the beautician area to the spa. The hard part would be hiring the right number of people to keep watch over the children in the day care area. The state of Ohio requires a certain number of sitters to a certain number of children based on the ages of the children. Terry would be overstaffing the day care area in order to stay one step ahead of the state. Aisha and Bossy suggested that Terry hire a firm to run complete background checks on each applicant for the day care area. In order to keep all supplies stocked before and during construction, Terry and Aisha were taking inventory. Talissa volunteered to help take inventory and organize the storage closets.

Over the past few weeks, Aisha and Terry had watched fifteen-year-old Talissa grow into her own. Talissa was like a caterpillar transformed into a butterfly, no longer shy, passive and uncomfortable in her own skin, thanks to Terry's mentoring and friendship. Working with Terry and Aisha along with such a variety of personalities, like Nolicka's crazy ass and Donnie's outspoken ass, Talissa was learning work ethics, business skills and how to get along with others. She also discovered that it was okay for her to have thoughts and dreams of her own. Even if those thoughts and dreams differed from that of her parents and friends.

Today Talissa was wearing her hair down with soft curls thanks to the shops beautician Nolicka Williams-Robinson. She was wearing a cute pair of form-fitting jeans and a light pink crop top.

"Wow, look at you, don't you look cute today," Aisha complimented.

"Thank you, I bought this outfit last week when Terry took me shopping."

"Yeah, I think Talissa likes to shop just as much as I do," said Terry.

"With your hair down like that and the way that outfit hugs your curves, you look just like Terry did when we were your age," said Aisha.

Aisha had noticed other similarities between Terry and Talissa but thought it best not to mention them to Terry. To Aisha, the two of them looked very much alike and Talissa had the same interests Terry did at that age. They even shared some of the same mannerisms but with the nightmares and depression Terry had been experiencing remembering her baby daughter she was forced to give away, Aisha didn't dare bring up what she had suspected for months now. *Terry is much too fragile to even fathom the thought. Anyway, what are the odds that Talissa is . . . ? Aw, I'm tripping.* Aisha shook her head to remove the thoughts she was having and went back to work.

The three talked and laughed as Aisha and Terry told stories of their high school days. They talked about dances at the Elks and Union Hall, the sounds of Rob Bass, Slick Rick and Doug E. Fresh.

"Shit, it wasn't a dance at the Union Hall that me and Bossy wasn't at. We'd walk our asses over to the spot. Back then we were too wild and crazy to consider missing a dance like that. On our side of town too? Shit, what?" Aisha danced around as she spoke and Terry shook her head at the thought of all the things she'd missed out on because of her overly protective parents.

"Yeah, y'all asses closed down a lot of those parties with ya girl whippin' up on somebody's ass," Nolicka said. She was passing by the storage closet and overheard Aisha reminiscing. They'd known each other for years but had heard of each other back in junior high and high school before ever actually meeting. Nolicka was from the east side and was known to fight a bitch in a second herself.

After sharing another story or two, Nolicka

returned to her client and Aisha, Terry and Talissa returned their attention to the task at hand.

Aisha put on another old school mixed CD that DJ Chocolate Thunder had recorded for her years earlier and they danced around the stockroom. Talissa swayed back and forth as she raised her hands above her head, causing her crop top to rise revealing her midsection.

Aisha and Terry both stopped in their tracks when they caught sight of the heart-shaped birthmark on Talissa's flat stomach. Terry thought she was dreaming and was afraid to move for fear of waking herself up. Aisha didn't know what to do or say either. Her best friend wasn't in the best emotional state to deal with the possibilities right now, but the proof was staring them dead in the face. Talissa caught sight of Aisha and Terry and asked, "What's going on? Is everything okay? Why y'all staring at me, did I put the perms in the wrong spot?"

Terry was in shock and couldn't make her mouth work. Aisha was fast with a reply telling Talissa that everything was okay but they'd just remembered something that had to be taken care of in the office.

"Come with me, Terry, so we can make that call, we only have ten minutes." Aisha reached for Terry's hand and had to pull her out of the room. "Talissa, we need for you to stay here and keep working. We'll be right back."

Terry's heart was racing and her breath became short. She thought she would hyperventilate. Once in the office, Aisha and Terry simultaneously whispered, "It can't be." They'd both saw the proof for themselves. Youngstown is a small city but Terry gave birth in Toledo.

"What are the odds that it's her? I mean, is it possible that she's been in Youngstown all this time?" Terry began crying as she weighed the possibilities.

"You saw the birthmark at the exact same time I did. And I noticed long ago how much she looks like you. Her eyes, nose and facial structure are exactly like yours. Come on Terry, you both have the same interests and she even has the same mannerisms as you. Haven't you considered it in the last few months?"

"I thought I was just seeing what I wanted to see because I've been dreaming about my daughter for months. What do we do, how can we find out for sure if it's her? Oh my God, Aisha, my heart is racing."

Terry started hyperventilating, sweat formed on her forehead and her palms got sweaty. Aisha sat her down and rubbed her back, attempting to calm her down. After Terry regained her composure, Aisha decided the best way to find out if Talissa was the baby girl Terry gave up for adoption, was to simply ask.

"We ask her some questions and I know the perfect ones. The answers will tell us just what we need to know."

Aisha and Terry sat in silence for a few minutes, allowing Terry to regain her composure. They rejoined Talissa in the storage room and found that she had completed taking inventory and had started her next task. Aisha thanked her for her work and started up with small talk again.

"Wow, Talissa, you ain't playing around. The stockroom looks great," complimented Aisha.

"No problem. That's what you pay me the big dollars for," laughed Talissa.

While they were gone, Talissa figured that her plan to expose her birthmark had worked. Since the first day she met Terry, she knew down in her soul who she was. Talissa just couldn't figure out a way to bring up such a personal conversation. If Terry rejected her, Talissa didn't think she would be able to handle it.

"So, Talissa, will you be able to get your driver's permit anytime soon?" inquired Aisha.

Terry stood next to Aisha, staring at Talissa as if she were seeing her for the first time.

"I already have my permit and by the end of the month I'll have my license. I just finished driver's training. All I need now is a little more driving time with an adult."

"Oh, why didn't you say something, we would have been happy to take you out driving," Terry found her voice. She felt like she was going to faint and grabbed hold of a shelf for support. The walls were closing in on her and making it hard for her to breathe.

"We can go driving tonight or tomorrow morning if you'd like," interjected Aisha.

"Yeah, that would be good, but aren't you worried about your Avalon? What if I wreck it?" asked Talissa.

"That's what insurance is for, baby girl," said Aisha, "but what I want to know is when is your birthday? We may want to do something for you and we'd hate it if we didn't acknowledge the birthday of our newest best friend."

That made Talissa feel good; she knew that asking about her birthday was just their way of confirming her identity.

"I actually have two birthdays," explained Talissa.

"What do you mean you have two birthdays, how is that possible?" Aisha and Terry both stood looking perplexed.

"I was born on August thirteenth, 1989 and I don't think I've ever mentioned it but I was adopted when I was just a few hours old. My other birthday is the day the adoption was finalized, September twenty-second, 1989."

"Oh my God, August thirteenth, oh my God. It's you!" exclaimed Terry in joy. Aisha stood next to her trying to fight back her tears. Aisha grabbed Terry's arm, attempting to get her to calm down. It was still possible that they were wrong and this was all just a huge coincidence.

"Talissa, do you know who Terry is?" asked Aisha.

"Of course I do, look at us. We look so much alike that it was obvious the first time we met. My adoptive parents have been very good to me and I've known I was adopted my entire life. They wanted me to know how special adopted children are, because they are chosen. I'd always planned on looking for my mother once I turned eighteen. There are so many things about yourself that can only be answered by your birth parents."

"What changed your mind about searching now?" asked Aisha as Terry was frozen in place with tears rolling down her cheeks.

"I wasn't searching. The first day I met Terry and looked into her eyes, I saw it. I saw the resemblance and I felt something inside of me that told me who she was. My parents told me the story surrounding my adoption and I know how hard it must have been to give me away. So I figured my birth mother had probably studied me and memorized everything about my little body. I knew that if Terry saw my birthmark, she would instantly know who I was. I've been praying I was right and that she wouldn't reject me."

Talissa held her breath and walked closer to Terry. She had to know if finding out who she was made Terry happy or simply didn't matter. Talissa wanted so badly to be accepted by her birth mother and now that the moment of truth had arrived, she was anxious. Talissa and Terry stood silent for what felt like an eternity. They studied each other's eyes, nose, hairline and lips. For the first time, Terry realized they were mirror images of each other.

"You haven't said anything, how do you feel about finding out who I am?"

Still unable to speak, Terry reached out and pulled her daughter close to her for the first time in sixteen years. Mother and daughter cried in each other's arms, as Aisha watched on. Her heart filled with joy for Terry and Talissa.

"Oh my, baby girl, Anissa Renee, this is better than getting two messages that I've won the lottery."

WHERE YOU AT TWAN, WHERE YOU AT?

CHAPTER 19

Bossy finally made the phone call she'd been putting off for too long. Because of Ant's immature ways of thinking, she had given him the benefit of the doubt after he disrespected Aisha the way he had. Even after she'd warned him not to fuck with her again, Ant did not take heed to her warnings. For that, Bossy would make him pay.

It took about an hour to drive to the Pittsburgh Airport. Bossy couldn't help but reflect on old times. The night she had taken a life was the one thing she didn't want to reminisce about, but it was the one thing that kept coming to mind. After leaving baggage claim and finding Bossy's 2006 Chrysler 300, Jalil "Big Black" Perry got right down to business.

It had been about twelve years since they'd seen one another but Bossy and Big Black kept in touch with monthly phone calls. He'd always promised her to be there if she needed him and true to his word, here he was. The only change in twelve years was his weight. Bossy didn't think it possible, but

Big Black had actually gotten bigger. He'd always been a big man at six feet, six inches and 270 pounds. He had smooth skin the color of fudge brownies and eyelashes that most women would kill for.

Unbeknownst to Bossy, about two months ago, Big Black received a call from his lifelong friend C-Lok. In the years that Big Black lived in Raleigh, North Carolina, the lines of communication stayed open between them. They never discussed business over the phone so when C-Lok brought up the subject of Bossy and explained the problems she was having with Ant, Big Black knew shit was serious. He knew how Bossy was getting hers and it sounded as if this "Youngblood" Ant was putting her livelihood in danger.

Big Black knew if Ant crossed the line, Bossy would need his help but he'd come only if she reached out to him. So he packed a bag and waited for the call.

"You told me about this punk but you never said how you, of all people, got mixed up with him," questioned Big Black. It was evident in his tone that he was annoyed with the entire situation.

Bossy filled Big Black in on Twan's relationship with Teddy Bear and his current status in the streets. She was totally blind to the fact that Big Black knew all about Twan and his role in her life.

"How does his punk-ass boy play into this?" asked Big Black.

"They've been best friends for years and Ant was in the game too. So naturally, Twan made Ant his right-hand man." Bossy was disgusted by and suspicious of Ant's behavior. She'd made sure Ant was kept at a safe distance away from her but he was still close enough to mix things up for her business.

"Let me guess. Ant either got greedy, jealous or both, right?"

"You know you right," laughed Bossy. "They got big-headed and started slinging money around like they were millionaires. I couldn't believe how often Twan was bringing me kilo after kilo to store, chop, mix and bag. At one point, he even got into messing with prescription drugs and that white-boy drug, meth."

"So what changed?"

"Ah, you know me, Black. I let him know he had to slow the fuck down or I wasn't gon' fuck wit' him no more." Bossy shook her head at Twan's sloppiness.

"I bet his boy didn't like that," laughed Big Black.

"No he didn't and he had the nerve to attempt to threaten Aisha. You know the project girl surfaced in her."

Big Black and Bossy laughed and joked about how Aisha could go from a prissy woman to a ghetto girl quicker than a crackhead could make a fifty-dollar rock disappear on a hot pipe.

"Girl, you still crazy," laughed Big Black, "but back to the matter at hand. I'd like to meet this Twan and get a feel for him. Tell me this, where do you think his head is at?" inquired Big Black.

"I think Twan is a good guy but still in his twenties he's impressionable. His loyalty to his best friend made him blind to Ant's greed and jealousy. In everything that's gone down, Twan has never disrespected me and has never lied to me, even when the truth put him in an unfavorable light."

"We should have a meeting with him once we hit the Yo', right after I get settled in. Besides Aisha and Terry, the fewer people that know I'm in town the better it will be for all of us. Especially if I end up doing what I think I'll have to do."

Twan was in line at the liquor store when Yvonne walked up behind him.

"Hey, Twan, I haven't seen you at the bar lately," greeted Yvonne.

"What up wit' you, girl?" Twan turned and greeted the attractive woman with a hug and kiss on the cheek. "I just been laying low for a minute and spending a little time with the family."

"From what I'm told, it's not enough time," teased Yvonne.

Twan paid the store clerk for the fifth of Absolut and returned his attention to Yvonne. "What is that supposed to mean?"

Yvonne paid for her purchase and walked outside with Twan. "About two weeks ago I got a phone call from some chick advising me to stay away from you."

Twan wasn't surprised because he'd heard this same thing from other female friends of his.

"Damn, Twan, I've known you forever and never knew you could put it down like that. Got that girl acting all ghettofied to keep you?"

"Man, I'm sorry she did that shit and put you all up in my business like that."

"Don't sweat it. We been cool since we met and

you know I got much respect for you. But on the real, you need to check ya girl. She's also called a few other girls we both know and you're now the topic of gossip because of it."

"Damn, it's like that?" Twan was getting angrier by the minute.

"Yeah, you know how small this city is. Those with nothing to do feed on shit like this. It'll die out soon, though, and another baller will take your place." Yvonne tried to make light of the situation.

Twan and Yvonne made small talk for a few minutes before he left to sit in his Envoy for a few minutes gathering himself before driving off. When he left the liquor store parking lot, he made a right onto Southern Boulevard headed for the lower east side to check on his drug house. Careful to maintain the posted speed limit, Twan coasted down the hill. When he switched lanes, he noticed a familiar ride two cars behind him. Brushing it off as a coincidence, Twan shook his head and put on some classic DJ Quik. Relaxing in his leather seat, he checked the traffic surrounding him and again spotted the familiar car that appeared to be following him. *This has to be some kind of fluke*, thought Twan. He slowed down as he approached a traffic light. As the light changed from green to yellow, he sped through the light in an attempt to get away from the Lexus. *If this car runs the light, it's following me.*

Glancing in his rearview mirror, he saw that the Lexus was right behind him. Twan immediately picked up his Nextel and paged LaJetia. She responded immediately.

"Hey, Twan what's up?" LaJetia innocently asked.

"Nothing, I'm just checking on you and the kids. Where are you?" He hoped she wouldn't lie to him.

"Just chilling in the park with the kids."

"Liar! I'm looking at you in my mirror. What the fuck you doin' following me?"

"You trippin, Twan . . ."

"Take ya conniving ass home and quit following me. You ain't got shit else to do but run up behind my ass!" For weeks now he felt someone was following him and he thought it was the police. He never considered that it might be his own woman. Twan hung up his cell, exited the highway, and made a sharp right onto Himrod Avenue while LaJetia turned left to circle back onto the highway.

Her eyes blurred with tears knowing she'd been caught and Twan would demand answers the second he got home. If he came home at all. She may have just lost everything she had.

Deciding to put his rounds on hold, Twan headed home to confront LaJetia. She'd crossed the line by making those junior high school–type phone calls and now she was following him. He didn't know how much more he could take. Ignoring the fact that the babysitter, Auntell, was still there, Twan let LaJetia have it before he got both feet in the door.

"So what is it? Have you lost your mind or are you that damn bored?"

"Twan, calm down, please. Auntell is still here and you're embarrassing me," LaJetia responded calmly.

"I don't give a fuck if ex-President Clinton was

sitting up in this bitch with you. You should have thought about that shit before you copied those numbers out of my phone. And you really should have considered the consequences of you following my ass like you the fucking police or some shit."

LaJetia had no idea he knew about her making those phone calls. The only way for him to find out was for one of those bitches to run her mouth. "Please calm down; you know the kids don't like to hear us arguing." She was sure that mentioning the kids would make him at least lower his tone.

"Quit talking about everything besides your fucked-up actions. Why, LaJetia? Are you that insecure that you got to put my personal business on the street like that? Do you think that if I was fuckin' one of them bitches she'd tell you the truth? You need to grow the fuck up! I ain't down for this at all."

"When a man don't come home until the wee hours of the morn—"

"How many times do I have to explain to you ? As a matter of fact, I am done explaining the same shit to you. I am done justifying anything to your stupid ass." Twan cut her off. "Don't answer that because you obviously will never get it. You've fucked with me for the last time, LaJetia. I'm out of here!" Twan marched off to the bedroom to pack a few things with LaJetia on his heels.

"No, Twan, please don't leave me. I'm sorry; just tell me what I can do to make it up to you? I can make this right."

"How can you make this right when you haven't done shit right since I got with ya ass?"

Those words cut her to the bone but LaJetia was determined not to let Twan leave her. "You can't leave us now Twan, I'm pregnant!" LaJetia froze as Twan faced her with a look of hatred in his eyes.

"What did you say?"

"I'm pregnant, Twan. I'm going to give you another child and then we can get married and you'll be able to adopt Kiara and Tyler like you said. We'll be a real family. So now you know why I did what I did. When I found out I was pregnant, I had to hold on to you."

"You are stupid if you think that lying to me will hold on to me. Did you getting pregnant hold on to any of them other niggas?" Twan reached into the closet and grabbed his duffel bag to throw a couple of outfits into it.

LaJetia sat on the corner of the bed crying and trying to convince Twan of her love and that she'd never lie about being pregnant. Twan walked into the private bathroom and returned with his toothbrush and deodorant. As he walked out of the room, he turned to look at LaJetia and told her, "You should have realized a long time ago that the one and only thing you had to do to hold onto me was just trust me."

The oversized duffel bag landed in the trunk with a thud. His cell phone rang and the caller ID read KAT69-1. It was Bossy calling.

"Hey, girl, you all right?"

"Yeah, I need for you to get over here to my apartment as soon as you can. We have some things to talk about."

"I'll be there in fifteen," replied Twan.

As he drove away from his lavish house, he wondered if he'd ever call it home again. His Escalade took him away and he never looked back to see the three kids looking out the bay window just as their mother had told them to do.

"Well, Bossy brought me up to speed on ya boy," Big Black said to Twan.

"I can't believe he flipped on me the way he did. Money has really changed him," said Twan.

"Correction, Youngblood, money didn't change him; it just brought out who he really is."

"Twan, let me ask you a question," interjected Bossy. "Do you trust him?"

"That's an easy question—hell no! LaJetia told me something that will never allow me to trust Ant's bitch ass ever again."

Twan went on to explain the details of the traffic stop involving Ant and the two corrupt officers.

"Did you say Officers Powell and Meeks?" Big Black sounded confused.

"Yeah, man, they've been robbing hustlers all around the city for years. I can't believe they've been getting away with it for this long," complained Twan.

"Neither can I, but the fact that Ant might be fuckin' with them two bitches makes me worry even more about my girls," Big Black said between gulps of his third forty ounce. Big Black's physique was intimidating but his heart was filled with love for Bossy, Aisha, and Terry.

"I wouldn't put it past him to flip on me. He

knows my operation from top to bottom." Twan picked up his watered-down Belvedere and orange juice.

"Haven't I always told you there ain't no friends in this business? Seriously, you know I got love for you like a little brother but you don't know my shit all like that. My girls don't even know everything there is to know and that's for both their protection and mine," Bossy informed Twan.

"I've heard enough. This fool done stepped to Aisha, stole money, and layin' down with five-oh. That's three strikes and that lets me know it's time to send Ant on a permanent vacation." Big Black ended the topic of conversation.

Twan rose to leave but Bossy had one more question for him. If he answered it honestly, she knew she would be able to trust him.

"Twan, before you leave I want to ask you something."

"Come with it."

"Who's your new contact?"

"Clifton 'C-Lok' Boyd," answered Twan.

He passed the test.

GIRRRL . . . LET ME TELL YOU WHAT HAPPENED

CHAPTER 20

Terry was dressed and off to work an hour early so that she and Aisha could start interviewing prospective contractors for the expansion to their shop. Aisha arrived shortly thereafter with two hot cups of coffee and breakfast sandwiches.

"Thanks, girl, what did y'all end up doing last night with Big Black's silly ass?" inquired Terry.

"Nothing to brag about. After you left Bossy's apartment, we played a couple of rounds of three-handed spades and tonk with Big Black and laughed about our days in the projects. We raced over to Bellaria Pizzeria right before they closed." Aisha paused to take a sip of her coffee before continuing with her story. "You know that everybody that comes home for a visit has to get a pizza from Bella as soon as they feet hit the Yo. When we got back to the crib, me and Bossy watched Big Black scarf down a twelve-inch double cheese, extra pepperoni and mushroom pizza in five minutes flat. Then, his big ass washed it down with another forty ounce of beer. Anyway, after that, I called it a night and climbed the stairs and turned in."

"I wanted to visit longer but I had to double-check the plans to make certain we weren't leaving anything out," explained Terry while nibbling her breakfast sandwich. Her stomach had been doing cartwheels all night due to her excitement about the shop and she didn't think any food would stay down but she was hungry.

"You've gone over everything at least one hundred times. I'm sure all is well and nothing has been left out," Aisha said reassuringly.

The first contractor to be interviewed arrived on time. Terry opened the door to welcome the applicant in and was shocked at the sight before her. The overweight, gray- haired man had to be at least eighty years old and said he was still very hands-on with any work his company did. The two women were dumbfounded by the information because of the pop-bottle glasses the poor man wore. It was obvious he could barely see one foot in front of him. Aisha and Terry took his written bid and contact information before thanking him for coming.

"I hope this first meeting doesn't set the tone for the rest of the day," sighed Terry.

By lunchtime, six construction company representatives had come and gone and Aisha and Terry were both getting worn down.

"I am going to run down to Mickey D's on Market Street and grab us some lunch. We should be able to eat before the next appointment. It's not for another forty-five minutes," explained Aisha as she headed for the door.

While Terry had a little free time, she logged on to her computer and made sure the bills setup with auto bill pay had gotten paid. She then checked on the beauticians and nail techs' scheduled appointments for the next two weeks. As she scrolled down the month of September, someone knocked on her office door.

"Come in, please." Terry's eyes never left the computer screen.

"Hello, I'm Pete Jackson representing Jackson and Company Construction. I'm a little early but I was hoping—"

"Oh my God, Pete Jackson! What the hell are you doing here?"

"Looking for a job and a hug from an old friend. When I saw the letters K.A.T., I should have known it was the three of y'all. Some things just never change." Pete walked toward the desk and Terry jumped up out of her seat and into the arms of the man who'd once been married to Aisha.

"I can't believe you're in town. How have you been? Aisha and Bossy are going to be ecstatic to see you." Terry thought back to a conversation she and Aisha had just a week before. Aisha had been feeling lonely and wondering if she'd ever be blessed to have the type of love she desired in her life. Terry reassured her that when it was supposed to happen, it would happen.

Aisha struggled to carry the lunch orders from her car as the old school sounds of MC Breed blared from a classic 1977 Nova strolling up Hillman Street. Aisha's thoughts were led back to days free of care. Days when all of her thoughts revolved around high school basketball games, fifty-cent basement parties (with a flyer) and Sunday night skating. Breed sang that when he got his Jeep he was putting Breed on the chrome and Aisha wanted to drop the bags of lunch and break out doing the smurf.

"Hey, Aisha, you need some help with that?" asked nail tech Jessica Hopkins.

Aisha snapped back to the present to find help standing in front of her. Jessica was considered the comedian at KAT69 Hair and Nail Salon. She was always good for a sidesplitting laugh, a smack-ya-mama-good pot of spaghetti and a forty-ounce bottle of Colt 45 in her water cooler, all habits learned from her daddy, Jesse "Bubbles" Hopkins.

"Girl, I saw you bobbin' ya head to the Breed joint. I was ready to break it down myself," joked Jessica as she reached out her hand to assist her boss with the lunch orders.

"You ain't said nothing but a word, girl. That song made me wish that the Breakout Lounge was still open. Now that was the club back in the day. I remember counting down the days to my twenty-first birthday so I could get up in there."

"Girl, you too? You know that Jeff Smith ran a tight spot and he checked ages very carefully. He'd tell you exactly when you could come back if he had to turn you away. Remember?"

Aisha and Jessica laughed but it was true. The owner would look at an ID and say, *You ain't old enough, come back in three months and two day. Next.*

After handing out lunch to her staff, Aisha made her way down the hall towards Terry's office. Aisha was already tired from staying up late with Bossy and Big Black the night before and she wasn't looking forward to interviewing another incompetent or overpriced contractor. Her head was beginning to hurt and Aisha was looking forward to lunch because she knew it was a hunger headache.

Glancing at her watch, Aisha knew time was ticking away and she'd probably have to rush and eat before the next appointment showed up. "I bet as soon as these contractors realized they were dealing with women, dollar signs flashed in front of them. Little do they know we did our research and will recognize game at any angle," Aisha mumbled to herself.

The closer Aisha got to Terry's office door, the more she could have sworn she heard voices. She first assumed that the one o'clock appointment had shown up over a half an hour early but standing outside the door she could hear that the conversation was more personal than professional. Aisha took a deep breath, tapped on the door, and turned the knob.

In the office, Terry was grinning from ear to ear waiting for Aisha to lay eyes on her first and only true love. Terry could barely contain her level of excitement. While getting caught up with Pete, Terry had called Bossy and told her their old friend was in town and bidding on the construction of the building addition.

"Terry, I hope I didn't give your salt-free fries away to one of the girls but Jessica helped me hand out the food and you know she doesn't care who gets what as long as her order is right," said Aisha, out of breath. She kept her eyes on the bags in her hands, never noticing that Terry had company sitting across from her.

"Aisha . . ."

"What girl, dang I'm hungry too, wait a minute," ordered Aisha.

"Aisha, we have company," said Terry as she looked in the direction of her guest. "Our one o'clock is a little early but I'm very happy that he was." Terry smiled at Aisha, trying to get her to turn around and greet her guest.

"Oh, I'm so sorry and didn't mean to be rude," said Aisha as she turned around to face their guest. "Oh my God! Pete, what are you doing here? Give me a hug."

"Girl, look at you. You look even better than you did back in the day. Time has treated you very, very well," said Pete as he looked his former teen bride over from head to hips to lips and back down to her thighs.

"You have aged pretty good yourself and I can't believe you're here. I didn't know you were a contractor, let alone with your own business," said Aisha with tears of joy in her eyes.

"Girl, he's been in business for years and it sounds like he's been doing very well for himself," interjected Terry.

"Not to brag, but I've turned a profit every year we've been in operation. Business has been great and life is starting to look up," explained Pete.

Aisha was beside herself at the sight of Pete Jackson, her first love, former husband, and good friend. He still looked the same, tall with a caramel complexion, toned, firm frame and a bald head that glistened in the sun. *He must still condition his scalp twice a day. Whenever we would go out, Pete spent more time in the bathroom primping and priming his sexy ass than I did.* Aisha's thoughts were making her panties moist and she just couldn't have that. Seeing Pete again was wonderful but this was a place of business and he was there for business and business only. *At least for now.* Aisha smiled to herself.

Two hours later, the business meeting drew to a close and Terry and Aisha told Pete that they'd work together on the numbers but not to worry, the job was his. In less than a week, Pete and his crew would begin transforming the hair and nail salon into a fully functioning day spa with child care services.

Terry could barely contain herself as she soaked in her Jacuzzi tub thinking about how well things were turning out. With Pete doing the work to make her plans for the shop a reality and finding the baby daughter she thought she would never see again, Terry was feeling blessed.

After relaxing and washing away another workday, Terry dressed in a pair of boxer shorts, a small T-shirt, and slipped her pedicured feet into her new Air Jordan flip-flops. She and Talissa had been shopping almost every other day and they'd bought matching shoes, pajamas, outfits and jewelry. They were like long-lost best friends reconnecting their relationship. Terry almost skipped down the stairs and into Bossy's apartment. She couldn't wait to review the evening's events with Bossy and Aisha. Terry was finally up to talking about her parents with her best friends. *No, maybe I'll just go to Mama Bev about this. I'm positive that sooner or later, my baby girl is going to ask questions about her grandparents and her father. I have to be able to provide answers for her; she deserves that much from me. Mama Bev will know how I should deal with them.*

* * *

Talissa could not have imagined that revealing her identity to her birth mother would have gone as well as it had. She couldn't have been happier. Talissa had always known she was adopted, her parents made sure of that. Joseph and Sylvia Croomes were supportive of Talissa's desire to find her birth mother.

"Babies are blessings from God but not all couples are blessed to conceive one of their own. You were a blessing to your birth mother and she was responsible enough to share her blessing with us." Sylvia Croomes would recite those words to Talissa every night as she tucked her into bed.

As Talissa grew older she began asking questions about her birth mother and her parents would always answer her to the best of their ability. Although her life was full of love, Talissa always planned on one day tracking down the woman who gave birth to her. She couldn't help but wonder if she looked like her birth parents and if so, what features they shared. Talissa wanted to know if she had any brothers and sisters or any other family members. Now that Talissa had found her birth mother, she could ask her questions directly to Terry.

A dinner was planned for Terry and the Croomeses to meet for the first time and it went off without a hitch. The evening was perfect and Terry could not stop thanking Mr. and Mrs. Croomes for loving and raising her baby girl. While the evening went well, Terry still left feeling a mixture of emotions that she had learned to ignore years ago. She felt homesick in a way.

Terry could not help but to think about her own parents, to whom she had not uttered one word since the day her baby girl was taken away from her. The pain, selfishness, and betrayal Terry felt because of her parents was just overwhelming. In a few short days, her baby girl would turn sixteen and Terry became full of rage at missing out on all of those years. Every day Terry drove past the street she had been raised on but was never tempted to stop by and reconnect with her parents. After meeting Mr. and Mrs. Croomes, Terry couldn't fight the urge to make that left turn onto Cohassett Street.

It was dark so Terry couldn't see much but what she had noticed was the silhouette of her father passing by the front room window. Her heart skipped a beat as memories of her childhood washed over her. Terry gripped the steering wheel tight and picked up speed to get away from that house.

When Terry had discovered she was pregnant, the first person she called was her college boyfriend, Raymond Elkins. He was in his junior year and being scouted by NBA agents. Raymond was a tall, muscular, dark chocolate brotha from Flint, Michigan. He and Terry met while she was pledging Delta Sigma Delta. He was a Alpha Phi Alpha and caught Terry's eye during a party. Raymond was a smooth operator and Terry fell in love with him just days after their initial meeting. He showered Terry with attention and endless compliments until the day she broke the news to him.

"Raymond, we have a huge problem to deal with," said Terry.

"Oh, really? The only problem I have is deciding whether or not to enter the draft this year," bragged Raymond.

"Well, I'm pregnant," announced Terry.

"That's too bad but I know you not trying to say it's my baby," responded Raymond. "Naw, ain't no bitch trappin' me like that."

Terry couldn't believe her ears. She wasn't even sure that Raymond was the same person she'd fallen in love with. He was acting like she was beneath him and he was offended by her presence.

"What the hell is wrong with you? You trying to play me like I ain't shit?"

"Honestly, you ain't shit. At least not to me," snapped Raymond.

Bam!

Terry picked up a vase and knocked the shit out of Raymond, causing him to need stitches.

"Fuck you, nigga! You ain't even worth my energy. I ain't got to trap you and I damn sure don't need a thing from you. With a head as big as yours," said Terry as she walked toward the door to leave, "you won't get far in life. Anyway, karma is a motherfucker. Believe that."

Terry left Raymond laying on the floor bleeding and went back to her dorm room and called Bossy and Aisha. They rushed to be by her side and have yet to leave her. Unfortunately, she couldn't say the same about her parents.

As the years passed, Terry's hurt had turned into anger while her love for her parents became obscured by her rage. Thinking about all of the things she missed by not being a part of Talissa's life made her furious. The anger inside of her was almost blinding. Never seeing her baby girl crawl, take her first steps, speak her first words; not being able to take her to her first day of school. Thinking of all the milestones she'd been robbed of was devastating. Terry was mad at herself for even considering trying to reconnect with her parents. Terry thought of going over there just to make them share in her pain, but the sounds of her ringing cell phone drew her out of trance and saved her parents from her current state.

Terry reached over and answered her cell phone. It was Aisha checking up on her, saving the day as usual.

After dinner, Talissa ran straight to her room to document the evening in her journal. Just as Talissa completed writing down her thoughts, a knock on her bedroom door drew her from her thoughts.

"Yes, come in." Talissa closed her journal and looked up to find her father standing in the doorway.

"I hope I'm not interrupting."

"No, Dad, come on in."

"Thank you," replied Joseph as he walked over to Talissa's mahogany computer desk that held the Dell desktop computer he'd given her last Christmas. After pulling out the mid-back leather manager's chair, Joseph sat and looked at his baby girl for a minute before speaking.

"Is everything all right, Dad?"

"Yes, I just wanted to tell you that I thought Terry was nice. Your mother and I are very pleased that you wanted us to meet her. It means the world to us that we can share in this miracle with you."

"Of course I wanted you and Mom to meet Terry. I'm very proud of you both. I really like Terry and I knew you'd like her too," said Talissa with a huge smile and love in her eyes.

"So, will we be seeing more of Terry? You know she's welcome here at any time." Joseph hoped his daughter felt the sincerity in his words.

"I'll let her know you said that. Terry was worried that you and Mom might think negatively about her because she was a young, unwed mother when she gave birth to me."

"How could we think negatively about the person who gave you life? Please let Terry know that your mom and I have nothing but good thoughts and feelings about her."

"I'm so happy you feel this way because it's very important to me that I build a relationship with her."

"I know, baby, I know," Joseph said lovingly, before he rose to leave the room.

Although the shop's basement was being renovated and the rear entrance was lined with various construction materials, KAT69 was open for business as usual. Talissa was in Terry's office learning how to keep the accounting books for the business. Terry and Aisha kept true to their word and were teaching Talissa all the ins and outs of running the business. Talissa had mastered ordering supplies and taking inventory in no time at all. She worked as shampoo girl and on slow days, Diane

Jackson would teach her how to do manicures and pedicures. Aisha, who loved to be pampered, was always willing to be Talissa's test dummy. Terry played test dummy a few times while Bianca Hill showed Talissa how to create different up do's. The women were very careful to play "beauty shop" after hours because someone from the state board could walk up in there at any given time.

Talissa's concentration on the computer screen was interrupted by someone yelling her name.

"What?" Talissa hollered out to whoever was calling her.

"Come up here and help a sister out, please."

Talissa identified the voice as Nolicka's and knew instantly she needed help shampooing her clients.

"Thanks girl, I'm trying to raise up out of here on time today. I got tickets to that Erykah Badu, Queen Latifah, Jill Scott, and Floetry concert in Cleveland tonight," said Nolicka to Talissa and anyone else within earshot.

Nolicka, or Nikki to her friends, was real cool and always ready to put a rude customer in their place. She even told a couple of them not to come back until they learned to appreciate her talent to make an ugly woman look good.

"It's no problem, that's what I'm here for," replied Talissa.

Talissa began shampooing clients for Nolicka and the other three beauticians. She was willing to do anything to keep herself busy because it made the day go by faster. She and Terry had plans to spend the night together and Talissa couldn't wait for the fun to begin.

The shampoo bowls were close to the waiting area and Talissa could overhear various conversations in between washes. She didn't like the one she was currently hearing.

"You can't trust Bossy or her girls. That bitch is the reason me and my man ain't together. That's all right though, cause they all gon' get theirs one day," voiced the disgruntled customer. The voice sounded familiar to Talissa but she couldn't place it.

"Whatever, girl, ain't nobody trying to hear that bullshit. They cool with me and anyway, the best beauticians in the city work up in here so I don't care nothing about your beef with the owners. Can't nobody, especially a young, uneducated ghetto girl stop me from coming here," countered voice number two. The woman checking the disgruntled client sounded like one of the regular clients, Theresa Smith, at first, but when no cusswords were included in the sentence, Talissa knew she was wrong. She happened to be Christine Bell, an old friend of Terry's from childhood.

"Whatever, just watch them three bitches is all I'm sayin'," said the disgruntled customer.

Talissa recognized the voice—it was that girl, LaJetia. She was always whining about her man whenever she got her hair done. Nobody paid her much attention because every woman in the city knew Twan and the things LaJetia would say about him just didn't add up. Twan was known as a generous hustler and cool as hell. Talissa decided she would teach LaJetia not to talk about her mother and her two aunts.

When it was LaJetia's turn at the shampoo bowl, she strolled over to Talissa like she owned the place.

"I hope you know what conditioner to use on me? My hair is accustomed to Paul Mitchell products and nothing else." LaJetia tried to speak with some sort of superiority.

"Don't worry, I know exactly what you need," said Talissa, smirking. "Just have a seat and I'll get started."

LaJetia sat down and allowed Talissa to drape her with a cape as she prepared to wash her hair. Talissa got the water at a comfortable temperature and instructed LaJetia to sit back, allowing the chair to recline and position its occupant comfortably to have her hair washed. Talissa took proper care to wet and lather LaJetia's hair. As she massaged and cleansed, cleansed and massaged, LaJetia closed her eyes and began to relax. Talissa massaged her scalp longer than usual to ensure LaJetia was enjoying the extra care she was receiving. Just when LaJetia allowed her body to loosen and enjoy the pampering the shampoo girl was giving her—it happened.

"Ahhhh, that burns!" screamed LaJetia.

Talissa turned the cold water off and aimed the hose directly in the middle of LaJetia's head, forcing the scalding hot water to burn her scalp. Talissa's hand was pushing down on LaJetia's forehead preventing her from moving as quickly as she wanted.

"What the fuck is wrong with you!" yelled LaJetia. She jumped up and ran around in circles.

The scream that LaJetia let out startled everyone in the shop and was even heard by the construction crew working in the basement. Everyone within earshot ran over to the shampoo bowls to find out what was going on.

"Talissa, what's going on? What happened?" Sirenna asked with concern.

"This wench was over there talking about my mother and my aunts. She was calling them bitches and she needed to be put in her place." Talissa's anger was so out of character for her and everyone was surprised by what she'd done to LaJetia. The customers were confused as to who Talissa was referring to when she said, "my mother and two aunts."

Aisha and Terry had run out of their offices in time to overhear Talissa explaining what she'd done. LaJetia had since jumped up screaming and crying hysterically. Sirenna and Nolicka tried to calm her down so they could see what type of damage had been done to her scalp.

"Why are y'all asking her simple ass what happened?" fumed LaJetia. "Everybody running over to her to see if she all right and I'm the one in pain. Her petty ass burned the shit out of my head. Fuck that little bitch, she needs to be fired!" LaJetia cried out.

The shop was in an uproar with not only the staff but the clients all trying to get a piece of LaJetia. Two of the staff members, Donnie Barnett and Virginia Faircloth, went to work calming everyone down and Terry pulled Talissa off in a corner to find out exactly what was going on. The two customers, Christine and Smitty, walked over to defend Talissa.

"Terry, this girl ain't done anything wrong. The stupid-ass young girl was telling me and everyone else sitting over here to watch you, Aisha, and Bossy because y'all took her man from her or some shit like that. Talissa was defending y'all, she didn't do nothing that one of us wouldn't have done if we overheard someone talking about one of our loved ones," explained Smitty.

Terry hugged her daughter and told her that she shouldn't have done what she did though she understood her reaction to hearing someone talk about her, Bossy, and Aisha. She explained that LaJetia could easily file a lawsuit against them and that there were other ways to better handle the situation. After a few minutes, everyone had calmed down and returned to where they were before all the action started. LaJetia was still raising hell and Aisha decided it was past time to shut her ass up.

"LaJetia, why in the hell you thought to come up in here and run ya mouth is beyond me so whatever type of pain and hair loss you encounter," Aisha paused for effect, "is on you. Now get out of my establishment and never return."

"Who is going to fix this? Y'all need to make this shit right."

"Tell that shit to someone who gives a damn!" Aisha turned, smacked herself on the ass, and walked back into her office.

Terry composed herself enough to tell Sirenna to do what she wanted to with LaJetia's hair and then send her on her way.

"Oh, I will be back until my head is fixed," LaJetia said pointing to her head.

"You just don't know when to quit running that mouth of yours, do you? That's why Twan left ya simple ass, not because of us." Terry was pissed and changed her mind. "I was trying to be civil with you but you just fucked that up. Get up out of my shit!"

"But look at me. What am I supposed to do?" whined LaJetia.

"I don't care what the fuck you do! Get OUT!"

LaJetia left with a wet hot head of hair and an attitude. She didn't know if she was embarrassed or just pissed off. By the time LaJetia drove the fifteen minutes home, she knew that she was embarrassed and would be the talk of the town.

Back inside the shop, a recounting of the event was still in progress.

"The shit was funny as hell," Nolicka chuckled as she returned her attention to her client. After molding and setting her last client under the preheated hair dryer, Nolicka flipped open her cell phone, dialed someone and said, "Girrrl, let me tell you what had just happened up in this bitch!" The shop erupted into laughter once again.

Home, BitterSweet Home

Chapter 21

LaJetia walked through her front door on smoke, both physically and mentally. Her scalp was throbbing with pain and it still felt like it was on fire. She could not remember ever experiencing such an intense level of pain, except during childbirth. LaJetia felt humiliated.

"Oh my God! Miss LaJetia, what happened to you? Are you okay?" Auntell was sitting with the kids while LaJetia got her hair done. She had been watching the new Disney movie with the kids for the sixth time when she heard LaJetia come in. Wanting to give LaJetia her phone messages out of earshot of the kids, Auntell excused herself from the family room to follow LaJetia into the front of the house. Auntell never expected to see LaJetia with her hair looking like that of a crackhead's after she'd just left the hair salon.

Not wanting to explain what she had just gone through, LaJetia lied and told Auntell she was fine, hoping to avoid a long conversation. All LaJetia wanted to do was go to her room and let some cold water cool down her scalp and afterward have a shot of E&J.

"I can see you're not okay but I won't pry," said Auntell with concern in her voice. "If you'd like, I can stay with the kids a while longer."

"Thank you, Auntell. Sometimes I don't know what I'd do without you," LaJetia said, fighting back tears.

LaJetia turned to walk away when Auntell stopped her to give her the news she had been waiting a week to hear.

"Miss LaJetia, Mr. Twan called and said he would be by tonight."

LaJetia stood frozen, unable to move, speak, or believe what she'd just heard. Could Twan be ready to come home? Maybe he did still love her and finally realized he couldn't live without her.

"He hasn't been home since the night he left," said LaJetia more to herself than to Auntell. "Auntell, are you sure he said he will be by tonight?" LaJetia hadn't meant to make her statement out loud but it wasn't something Auntell didn't already know.

After Auntell confirmed the message, LaJetia ran to her bedroom to search for the perfect outfit to wear for Twan. She walked into her closet and grabbed jeans, dresses, nightgowns, and blouses. Nothing seemed right for the occasion until LaJetia realized she had no idea what Twan's visit meant. *Maybe he's coming home for good. No, he's probably just coming to see the kids. He probably doesn't want to talk to me anyway, so what I wear won't matter,* thought LaJetia. All of the enthusiasm she felt about seeing Twan made LaJetia forget about her injured scalp. After looking at herself in the full-length mirror, LaJetia stepped into the shower and allowed the cold water to ease the throbbing pain she felt.

Twenty minutes later, LaJetia swallowed a Percocet with the help of a glass of E&J. She lay down to wait for the medication to take effect. After the medicine took effect, she was able to comb and brush her shoulder-length hair into a loose ponytail. LaJetia then got dressed and waited for Twan to arrive. She took a look at herself in the full-length mirror and decided her outfit was all wrong. The tight fit of her favorite pair of jeans would confirm Twan's suspicions that she was not pregnant, so LaJetia wore a mid-thigh length lime-colored sundress in anticipation of Twan's visit. Maybe the looseness of the dress would give the illusion that she was in fact carrying his child.

It was past eleven o'clock and the kids were tucked nicely into bed by the time Twan knocked on the front door. LaJetia's excitement about his visit had dwindled around nine and she was just tired and frustrated. After unlocking the door LaJetia turned on her heels without speaking to Twan. He knew instantly her mood was not a good one.

"Hey, where are the kids at? I don't hear anything."

"They're 'sleep, Twan; do you know what time it is?" LaJetia pointed at the kitchen clock.

"I didn't realize it had gotten so late. Time flew by but I swear I meant to be by here earlier than this." Twan felt there was no need to get into the reason for his late-night visit because he was sure it wouldn't make any difference to LaJetia anyway.

"So are you here to stay?"

"I just thought we should talk about some things. YOU have to work out your insecurity issues and the lack of trust that you have for me."

"You made me this way, Twan," LaJetia said through clenched teeth.

"We have to sit down and talk and try to talk with cool heads. Do you think that's possible?"

Even after the Percocet and brandy cocktail, LaJetia's head still hurt but nothing was going to stop her from doing what Twan was asking of her. *I'll be so sweet and submissive to his request that guilt will bring him home to me.*

"Yes, Twan, we can do that."

The dysfunctional couple sat opposite of each other and looked into each other's eyes before Twan broke the silence.

"Look, LaJetia, no matter what our situation is, I miss seeing the kids every day and I'd like to set up a reasonable schedule for me to visit with them."

LaJetia wasn't expecting the conversation to begin so abruptly and to start off with the kids. *Visit the kids? What about me? What about us?*

"How can we make up a schedule when the streets never shut down? Ain't that what you always told me when I wanted your time?" snapped LaJetia.

"Come on now, girl. I'm trying to do what's right."

"Why all of a sudden you want to do what's right? Twan, you left seven days ago and haven't had the time to see the kids not once."

LaJetia knew that the old saying out of sight out of mind didn't hold true with children or for a woman who loves her man. When Twan first left, the kids asked for Daddy every day and night. After a couple of days, their questions eased up but it hurt LaJetia not to be able to comfort them by telling them when Daddy was coming home.

Twan was happy to hear LaJetia say the kids asked about him. It meant that they were keeping their secret guarded. Thanks to LaJetia paying Auntell a fortune to babysit whenever she needed her, Twan was able to sneak by the house to visit with the children without bumping into LaJetia. Luckily, LaJetia had needed Auntell every day for the last week for one reason or another and Twan took full advantage of his time with Kiara, Tyler, and Trayvon.

While LaJetia was out of the house, the kids would call Twan on the special cell phone he'd given them. Five-year-old Kiara, who was going on fifteen, was in charge of the phone. Kiara especially liked the pink cover and the way her name lit up on the face. If Auntell confirmed that LaJetia would be gone for over an hour, Twan came to visit the kids and always brought gifts. Kiara and Tyler were young but old enough to know better than to tell their mother about their father's visits. Since he'd been gone, they have been witness to her unwarranted tantrums over anything under the sun. Twan thanked God and Kiara for keeping their secret.

"I know I've done wrong by the kids and I want to make things right. If it's okay, I'd like to come by to see them at least three times a week."

"Twan, come whenever you want. I won't give you a hard time about the kids," lied LaJetia.

She and Twan both knew that the kids were her only tool to get Twan to do what she wanted. LaJetia had every intention on doing what she had to do in order to wake up with Twan each and every morning.

"I didn't expect for you to be so cool. What's up?"

The door was finally open and LaJetia was about to charge right through it.

"Ain't nothin' up, it's just that with the morning sickness and me feeling tired all of the time, it would help if you spent some time with the kids. At times I just need a break." LaJetia pouted like a toddler.

Twan expected for LaJetia to bring up her imaginary pregnancy again. He couldn't believe how transparent she could be.

"Not that I believe you're pregnant, but how far along are you?"

Instead of answering his question, LaJetia walked over to the stack of papers on the kitchen counter. She thumbed through the pile until she found what she was looking for. As she sat back down, a huge smile of victory filled her heart. She believed this would bring Twan home and they would be a family again.

Twan couldn't believe what he was looking at. He sat staring at the black-and-white image and finally accepted the fact he didn't know the mother of his children at all. He wondered how LaJetia was able to disguise the true her for so long.

LaJetia scanned Twan's face, searching for a

hint of emotion she expected from him. Knowing the love he had for Trayvon and the unconditional commitment to Kiara and Tyler, LaJetia was certain that the thought of having another baby would bring Twan back to her. Unable to read him, LaJetia broke the silence.

"I know you didn't believe me about being pregnant so now you have proof. We're going to have another baby. Aren't you happy?"

"I'm happy for the person this sonogram belongs to but this is not yours. I knew you'd do some scandalous shit to get me back, but damn! How much did you pay for this picture?"

"You ain't gon' sit in my face and call me a liar. I am pregnant and we have to deal with it." LaJetia desperately tried to worm her way out of the corner she had backed into. Her plan was to make Twan believe she was pregnant, he'd move back home and she would have him all to herself again. It was looking as if her plan was unraveling and she failed to have a plan B.

"There is no way you are pregnant, at least not by me," vented Twan.

"I have not been unfaithful to you. Not ever, and I am pregnant."

"Not by me."

"How can you say that?" cried LaJetia.

"It wouldn't be the first time you didn't know who you were pregnant by. Shit, you'd probably break the record if you were a guest on Maury. I can see it now. *LaJetia has been here twelve times searching for her daughter's father. Fifty men have been tested and still, no father.*"

The truth of Twan's words hurt LaJetia to her

soul and without thinking she slapped Twan with as much force as she could muster. She never thought in a million years that Twan would say such mean and ugly things to her. Livid, LaJetia stood and threw the cordless phone at Twan's head. He ducked just in time.

"How in the fuck you gone say some foul shit like that to me? This is your baby."

"I had a vasectomy after Trayvon was born," announced Twan with venom.

Caught!

Caught!

LaJetia had to think fast. *What do I say now? How can I get out of this and still have Twan want to be with me?* Her brain could not plot quickly enough for her to regain control over the mess she had made. *Maybe the truth can set me free. I'll just tell Twan it was a scheme to get him to come back home; that's just how much I love him. He will understand, forgive me and love me.*

"What could you possibly do with another child? Make another generation of welfare recipients? Try telling the truth for once, if you can. You're not pregnant, are you?"

"No, Twan but please understand that—"

"That no matter how it affected me, you would do anything to get whatever you want." Twan was beginning to feel sorry for LaJetia.

"That's not true. Don't you know that I love you and I can't stand the thought of letting you go?" LaJetia caught herself from crying and decided the only way out of the situation was to tell the whole truth. "I did lie about being pregnant because you seem to love the kids so much. I knew it would be easy for you to leave me but you could never leave the kids."

"But why go to so much trouble to keep me here?" Before LaJetia could respond, Twan said, "You know what? It doesn't even matter. I'm out of here."

Furious, Twan headed for the door. He knew that he had to get away from LaJetia before he put his hands on her and choked the shit out of her crazy ass. Just as he reached for the doorknob, a vase went flying past his right ear.

"Fuck you, Twan! You ain't the end all to be all. You act like ya shit don't stink. Where you goin', to that bitch Bossy? Well, fuck her too." This time LaJetia threw a castiron skillet and it connected with its mark. Twan ignored the searing pain echoing through his back long enough to charge at LaJetia like a professional linebacker. Twan wrapped his fingers around her neck and slammed her against the side-by-side refrigerator, Twan threatened, "Bitch, if you ever fuckin' hit me with some shit like that again, I'll kill ya' simple ass right after I fuck you up." Twan's grip around LaJetia's neck tightened with each word.

Twan released his grip, allowing LaJetia to catch her breath and her senses as she fell to the floor. Hatred filled Twan's heart at the speed of lightning. Watching the mother of his children gasp for air while tears ran down her face, Twan felt nothing but contempt. It was taking everything inside of him not to beat LaJetia down like he would a nigga on the streets. Twan knew that if he didn't put some distance between them, he just might do something to land himself in prison for a very long time.

"I will continue to take care of my financial responsibilities and I'll visit the kids when you are not home. You are to stay as far away from me as possible. I will not be held accountable for what I might do to you if I ever see ya stupid, simple ass again." Twan took a step backward, called LaJetia a scandalous bitch, turned on his Nike-covered heels, and slammed the door as he left.

LaJetia lay on the tiled kitchen floor whimpering like a hurt puppy.

"He'll be back. He still loves me."

What's Done in the Dark Will Come to Light

Chapter 22

With Ant loose on the streets acting like a bitch in heat, lives were in danger, including Bossy's. She knew with Big Black involved, once the shit hit the fan, nothing would ever be the same again. Bossy just prayed that the right people were left standing.

She drove more than forty-five minutes to her destination. She hadn't been out that way in years and took a couple of wrong turns making the trip longer than it should have been.

Bossy slowed her car down as she searched for the house number that read 6789. She exited her car as fast as possible so the three young men manning the corner wouldn't mistake her for a customer.

The guarded front door opened wide as Bossy climbed the stairs. C-Lok's frame blocked Bossy from entering his house without first greeting him with a hug.

"Girl, you look good. It's been a long time," said C-Lok.

"I have missed you too," replied Bossy, smiling.

They walked into C-Lok's office where a couple of his runners waited. There was no need to introduce Bossy because they had known about her for years. Bossy never knew that C-Lok looked out for her almost as much as Teddy Bear had. The two runners greeted her and exited the room.

"Tell me what brings you this far away from your comfort zone?" C-Lok stared into Bossy's eyes.

"I need to talk with you about Ant and Twan," responded Bossy.

"I heard about the rift between those two," C-Lok shared.

"Some things never change. It's never a good idea to mix business and personal. Twan mixed it and shit has gotten hot."

"That's what I hear. But I take it you think I should know about something more."

"Yeah, I believe ya boy Ant is in bed with them two bitch-ass police Meeks and Powell. Watch ya back closely and keep Ant closer." Bossy went on to explain about Ant fucking up and the info about him chilling with the cops.

C-Lok listened intently to Bossy.

"Good looking out and coming to me like this."

"You know what's up," stated Bossy. She had never stopped loving C-Lok but had long ago accepted that they were not to be.

"How is Devin? That nigga keeping his head up behind those concrete walls?"

"You know he's straight. If he can keep his nose clean, he can see daylight the next time he comes up for parole. Lord knows between the two of us, we've paid that damn prosecutor enough. By the way, thanks again for helping me."

Bossy and C-Lok began having a sexual relationship four years after the arrest of her brother. She was alone and lonely until C-Lok came to see about her one night. The two friends sat drinking and puffin' on joints all night. They talked about Devin, Teddy Bear, the streets, and Bossy's lack of security her whole life. As the saying goes, one thing led to another.

Not long after, what was supposed to be a sex thing turned into a real relationship only with untraditional roles. Bossy was never the type of woman to be taken care of or to depend on a man. C-Lok was a typical man who wanted to take care of home by providing for his woman. That was hard to do when it was his woman supplying the keys he was putting out on the streets. Her prices beat his supplier hands down and the product was better. They stuck it out for a couple of years but Bossy and C-Lok both knew their type of ghetto love would never allow them to make it work.

"Look girl, no matter what I'm always going to look out for you. You never have to doubt that I'll have your back," said C-Lok tenderly.

"I know you will and I love you for it but you know me, I'll be just fine."

That was the last conversation the two lovers ever had but C-Lok was always true to his word and looked out for Bossy. Bossy just never knew it. Sitting across from him now, she still didn't know all of the things her first love had done for her since their breakup. She felt her heart flutter at the thought of feeling C-Lok's strong arms around her. As quickly as the thought entered her mind, Bossy forced it away and refocused on the reason for her visit.

C-Lok and Bossy visited another hour and Bossy headed back to the Yo' with more thoughts of intimacy swimming in her head. Big Black was waiting for Bossy when she walked in.

"What took you so long; I know C-Lok's ass ain't trip on you."

"Naw, it wasn't nothing like that. He was straight and we got caught up on a few things. I was telling him about me wanting out." Bossy hadn't told Big Black of her plan to go legit and waited anxiously for his response.

"It's about time, girl. You just made my fuckin' day. Do you know how much sleep I've lost over the years worried about you? Since that night we lost our boy Poppy, I've wanted you out the game. You just ain't the type of woman to take to somebody telling her what to do," confessed Big Black.

"The time has come and after this shit is finished, I'm out before some of the things I've done in the dark come to light." Bossy released a sigh of relief.

SOMETHING DOESN'T SMELL RIGHT

CHAPTER 23

"Good morning, Ma. You need anything done besides the grass cut?"

"No, son, I'm fine. What I don't have the good Lord will provide," Olivia Quarles solemnly answered her son Ant.

"Aren't you feeling well today, Ma?"

"Mama hasn't been sleeping too well these last few days. I've been having an unsettling dream that something bad is going to happen to you."

"Ma, ain't nothin' gon' happen to me. You just worry too much."

"I had the same dream right before we lost ya brother. Baby, the Lord speaks to me in my dreams. He's never steered me wrong and you need to promise me you'll be careful out there."

"I have something in the works and if everything goes as planned, I'll be able to take care of you the way I want to."

"Anthonie Quarles, you know I'm a simple woman with common sense. I know how you make your money. It's the devil's dirty money and I'll have no parts of it."

Ant wondered how he could have been so dumb to think his mother didn't know how he was living.

"It's just temporary until I save enough to do what I need to do and I'm almost there."

"I've raised you and your brother to know right from wrong, to understand what hard work is all about. I've lost one child and Lord knows I can't live through the pain of losing another. But you're a grown man and you decide your lot in life. All I can do is pray for you son, just pray."

Ant left his mother's house feeling lower than a snake's belly but he had to do what he had to do. He'd chosen to jump into bed with Meeks and Powell and he was in too deep to turn back now.

The meeting was set for three in the morning at Volney Rogers Park. It was a dark area that no one frequented after the sun went down. Ant arrived ten minutes early, giving him too much time to wrestle with himself about stabbing his only friend in the back. *Twan was gonna keep me in his shadow picking up his crumbs. I'm bigger than that. Teddy Bear slept on me and so did Twan, thanks to Bossy.*

Thinking of Bossy made Ant refocus on his plan. *Getting Bossy out the way will leave Aisha and Terry to fend for themselves. Aisha won't be a Billy-Badass no more. I'll show that bitch to pull a gun on me and not use it. Bossy won't be in Twan's ear when both they asses is sitting behind bars.*

A car turned into the parking lot, making Ant nervous. He wasn't sure he could trust Meeks and Powell. This could be a setup for all he knew. Ant doubted the two crooked cops even trusted each other.

"I hope you have something for us. You've had plenty of time to get it," spoke Meeks sternly.

"Slow down, man. Twan's due to make a run to our connection in Florida early next week. You can catch him with a few keys of cocaine on him."

"Prices must be pretty good to travel that far." Hearing about a connection in Florida gave Powell ideas of making trips to the state himself.

"Yeah they are, and Twan makes the runs like clockwork," explained Ant.

"That'll give us Twan, now what about Bossy and C-Lok?" questioned Meeks.

"Twan takes his stuff to Bossy for packaging and warehousing the same day he gets back in town. We still owe C-Lok money so Twan will have to give him something to hold on to before C-Lok comes looking for us." Ant went on to explain Twan's routine and the complexity of gaining entrance into Bossy's apartment building. Powell and Meeks were already familiar with the difficulty in obtaining access to Bossy's home; they had to come up with a plan to get past the security alarms and cameras.

"If y'all time things right, Bossy and Twan will be in possession of some major weight. The rest is up to y'all." Ant allowed himself to believe his assignment was complete.

"Look, Ant, we're going to go with the information you've supplied but we want you to keep one thing in mind," said Officer Meeks.

"What's that? I've given y'all what you asked for," Ant nervously responded.

"Not quite yet. You've given us a means to get what we want but if this doesn't pan out the way you said it will, let's just say there will be repercussions. And you'll be the one doing the paying," warned Meeks.

Just as Bossy and Big Black had expected, for the last two weeks, Officers Powell and Meeks had been parked up and down Falls Avenue in unmarked vehicles trying to figure out Bossy's daily routine. The task was more difficult than expected because nothing about Bossy was routine. Some days she never left her apartment and some days she went to work at the hair and nail salon as if it were her full-time job.

While surveying the residence, Powell and Meeks argued about the best way to gain entrance into Bossy's domain.

"Man, you saw the steel doors and security alarm just like I did, how else do you suggest we get in?" Powell was losing patience with his partner. It didn't seem as if his heart was in the plan to take down Bossy and Twan. For years, they had been blackmailing, stealing, and strong-arming people but neither man had any intention of fuckin' with C-Lok. Powell and Meeks may have been bold but they were nowhere near stupid. Stepping sideways to the biggest drug dealer in the northwestern part of the Pennsylvania area would mean instant death. C-Lok maintained bodyguards armed with assault riffles twenty-four hours a day and seven days a week.

"Are you crazy? From what we hear about this

woman, she ain't no ordinary mark. You think she's not smart enough to read a warrant served on her? And say we do find a judge willing to issue a legal warrant, then what? How do we get what we really came for without being found out by the department?" Meeks was right and Powell knew it but from where he sat, what other choice did they have?

"Look, you're probably right about Bossy and the warrant but our first objective is gaining entrance into the queen's kingdom, anything after that we play by ear. Besides, what can she do to us once we are on the inside?" Powell argued.

"Okay, but we have to time this right. Her best friends cannot be home and we have to strike while Twan is there. That way we know Bossy and Twan are conducting business and the drugs will be in plain sight." Meeks remained opposed to the plan because something didn't feel right. In his opinion, the entire scheme was sloppy.

The next morning Aisha and Terry left for work at the same time and the apartment building remained quiet for a few hours. Just as Ant had said, Twan showed up at Bossy's apartment during the early afternoon hours. Twan did not disappoint the officers when he pulled his rental car around the back of the brick apartment building and exited the vehicle carrying a couple of packages.

"This is it, partner. It's time for us to do what we came to do," said Powell.

The sound of the doorbell rang, letting Bossy know she had company. She got up from her comfortable position on her couch and pressed the button to the intercom system she'd recently had upgraded. It was equipped with a hidden spy camera.

"Yes, who is it," asked Bossy with the sweetest voice she could muster.

"Police, open up, we have a warrant," replied Officer Powell.

Bossy took her time unlocking her front door and then that of the security door. She stood and looked her two visitors up and down before stepping aside, signaling for them to come inside.

"Come on in, officers, I've been expecting you."

THE PAST WON'T LET ME GO

CHAPTER 24

Aisha sprung up out of bed in a cold sweat at four in the morning. She covered her mouth with both hands to muffle the sounds of her crying. Unable to fall back to sleep, she decided to give her apartment a good cleaning, starting in the front room that she used to house a fifty-gallon tropical fish tank and a variety of house plants. Aisha watered, dusted, and sang to her plants after feeding the fish.

Next, she broke down her living room by running the vacuum, rearranging the cream Italian furniture, and cleaning the smoke glass end tables. Still feeling wide awake, Aisha moved into her dining room and sprayed Windex on the dining room table that matched the coffee and end tables in the living room. The glass chandelier proved to be more complex than she initially thought but Aisha gave the two-hour project her all. By the time she finished, it was going on 7:00 AM and she finally felt like she could drift back to sleep. The only problem was that Terry would expect her at the shop no later than ten.

Aisha decided to slip a note under Terry's door letting her know not to expect her at work that day. It was rare for her to take off but there was no way she'd be able to be productive. Knowing Thursdays are busy at KAT69, Aisha decided to ask Bossy to cover for her.

The phone rang four times before Bossy answered with a groggy voice.

"What's wrong, Ish?"

"Bossy, please forgive me for waking you up but you know I wouldn't if it wasn't important. I had a bad night and haven't gotten any sleep. I need you to fill in for me today at the shop."

"No problem . . . but you have to promise me that you'll talk to Mama Bev about those nightmares."

"I'm going over to the house today and talk to Mama. I just need to get some sleep for a few hours. My ringer will be turned off until I get up."

"That's what's up. Do what you need to do and don't worry about the shop today," reassured Bossy."

"Let me get off this phone and back to bed. Thanks again for helping me."

"You know I got your back," said Bossy before hanging up the receiver.

Aisha slept for three hours before she woke again in a cold sweat. Instead of forcing sleep to return, she decided to dress and go visit her mother.

The bay window in Bev's kitchen supplied an ample amount of natural light and temporarily blinded Aisha as she walked in the side door of the house. Bev sat at her smoked glass kitchen table reading the *Vindicator* and sipping on coffee when

Aisha came in. The cordless phone lay to Bev's right and a pack of Newport 100s and an ashtray holding a lit cigarette was to her left.

"Hey, Mom, how are you today?" Aisha drew her mother's attention from her newspaper.

"Girl, you like to scare the shit out of me!" Bev jumped at the sound of Aisha's voice. "Why aren't you at work?"

"I decided to take a day off but you didn't answer me. How are you feeling?"

"I'm fine, girl, don't be worried about me," Bev's voice trailed off as she returned her attention to the newspaper article. "Have you read today's paper? There was a home invasion last night just a couple of blocks away from here."

Aisha had been concerned about her mother since her two-day hospital stay a month ago. Bev had gone to the emergency room with pain in her right side and was diagnosed with kidney stones. She was okay now but had decided to use up some sick days she'd accumulated over the years.

"No, Ma, I haven't seen the paper but I'll read it later," Aisha said as she poured herself a cup of coffee and joined her mother at the table.

"I'm glad you came by. It'll save me a trip to the south side. I want you to give Terry a book for me."

Bev loved to read almost as much as Terry. Bev's best friend, Daria, worked as an editor for a big publishing house in New York. Daria always sent Bev copies of novels that weren't yet available to the public. By the time new African-American titles were released, Bev had already retired them to her bookshelf.

Finally offering her full attention to Aisha, she

could see something was wrong with her daughter. "Aisha Shawntay, you look so tired and something must be wrong for you to take a day off work." Bev knew Aisha better than she knew herself.

Aisha dropped her head and burst out in tears. Bev rose from her seat as quickly as she could and embraced her daughter. It was exactly what Aisha needed; her mother's loving embrace always made her feel safe and secure. Although she didn't yet know the cause of Aisha's pain, Bev did know that she'd be there for her daughter unconditionally.

"Let it out, baby, let it out. You cry if you need to cry," Bev whispered into Aisha's ear as she rubbed her back.

"I can't sleep, Mommy. The nightmares about the rape are haunting me," Aisha whimpered.

"Oh, baby, if I could bear this pain for you I would," Bev cried with her daughter. Unbeknownst to Aisha, her mother had experienced nights of unrest due to bad dreams and regrets. Bev blamed herself for what happened to Aisha so many years ago.

Being a single parent is a challenge for every woman, especially when she's trying to improve life for herself and her children. Sacrifices must be made. The greatest sacrifice a single mother makes is time with her children.

Bev worked her fingers to the bone at minimum-wage jobs in order to provide for her only child. She was often forced to leave Aisha alone at night, as she was working midnight shifts. Other times Aisha was left to prepare herself for school in the mornings and make her own snacks every day after school. By the time Aisha entered junior high school, Bev's luck had changed and she was offered a job at Tile Supply from 7:00 AM till 3:00 PM with weekends off. Finally mother and daughter would have more time together and Bev could not have been happier. She wanted nothing more than to make up for lost time.

Her goal was to get to know the young woman that Aisha had grown into. Despite living in the projects, Bev always came home to a clean house and oftentimes to a cooked meal. Aisha had mastered doing the laundry, washing dishes, and mopping the floors all on her own. On Sunday evenings, Aisha would iron clothes for the week both for herself and her mother. Aisha kept good grades and always showed her mother the utmost respect. With the new job, Bev would have time to take care of Aisha instead of Aisha taking care of her.

It was during one of the days Bev was working mandatory overtime that Aisha was violated in that terrible way. That day would be forever etched into Bev and Aisha's memories. Bev was working hard putting items through the machine that ironed and folded garments. Her supervisor, Patte Smith-Eiland, ran to Bev informing her of an important call on hold for her. Instinctively Bev knew that something was wrong with Aisha. Nothing could have prepared Bev for the information she received from the caller.

"This is Beverly Woods speaking."

"Miss Bev, this is your neighbor, Bossy, and you need to get home as soon as possible. Aisha has been hurt and the police and ambulance are on their way."

Bev dropped the phone, frozen with fear and

panic in her heart. Bev somehow managed to tell Patte that she needed to get home. Although she lived not five minutes away by car Bev had to walk to work because she couldn't afford an automobile at the time. Patte could see that Bev was in no condition to be alone and volunteered to give her a ride home.

"Come on, Bev, I'll drive you home," offered Patte. The two women made it to Westlake Projects in three minutes flat. They arrived to find police cruisers, fire trucks and an ambulance. Just as Bev opened the car door, two men were wheeling Aisha out of their apartment on a gurney. "Wait, where are you taking my daughter?" Bev screamed while running to Aisha. A young police officer stepped over to Bev and broke the news no mother ever wants to hear about their daughter.

"Ma'am, are you Beverly Woods, the mother of Aisha Woods?"

"Yes I am, please tell me what is going on." Tears streamed down Bev's face. Patte knew in her heart that whatever happened, it was bad. She put her arm around Bev to offer support for the news she was about to receive.

"Ms. Woods, your daughter will be okay," the young officer stalled and searched his mind for the right words to say, "but she is being transported down the street to St. Elizabeth Hospital."

"Okay, but why? Would you tell me what has happened to my child? What is wrong?"

"I regret having to tell you that she has been beaten and raped." The officer had said the words and braced himself for Bev's reaction.

Bev knees gave out on her but she quickly regained control. She needed to be with Aisha and Aisha needed to be with her. Patte helped Bev walk over to the ambulance where Aisha lay bruised and battered. It took all of the will inside of her not to cry but Bev was determined to be strong, just as strong as she needed to be now, almost twenty-five years later.

After Aisha cried her last tear, Bev got a clean rag and washed her child's face for her. She then led Aisha into the living room and sat her down on the micro-suede opal couch. Bev sat next to Aisha and held her hand in hers.

"Aisha, you are the strongest and bravest woman I know. A lot of women, let alone girls, who go through the horrible ordeal that you did, don't survive. Not only have you survived but you've succeeded. You went on and made something of yourself when you could have wallowed in self-pity and given up on life. I've never told you this before but I blame myself for what happened that day." Bev paused to catch her breath and the tears in her eyes won the fight and began to fall from her eyes. "If only I were there, if I hadn't taken the job at Tile Supply, if, if, if. I almost let all of the what-ifs destroy me but I didn't because of you. I got my strength from you during that time."

Aisha was confused at what her mother was saying. "Mommy, how could I be your hero when I got my strength from you? You went on to become a registered nurse after that day. I haven't always done right after David Lawford stole my virginity and dignity from me."

"You're right but you were still a child with growing to do. Listen to me. No one has the power to take your dignity unless you give it to them. Also, you did nothing to be ashamed of and you have to believe that," advised Bev. "You were supposed to go through a rebellious stage. Don't get me wrong, there were some days I could have put my hands around all three of you girls' necks, but I didn't. When you, Bossy, and sometimes, Terry would get caught doing wrong and I wanted to kill the three of you, I'd have flashbacks to my teenage days. Girl, your mother did some things in her day that you still aren't old enough to know about." Bev broke out into a light laugh. "See, I tried not to be one of those parents who acted as if they never made mistakes growing up. I was a better parent because I'd personally experienced most, it not all, of the things you were going through. I mean by the time I was sixteen, I'd been smoking weed, drinking liquor, sneaking out of my bedroom window to go find trouble. I can't tell you how many times I had my hot ass out there clubbing when I wasn't even old enough to drive a damn car," confessed Bev.

"Ma, I didn't know all of that. You never went out when I was coming up. The most you did was have Miss Daria, her sister Angela, and your friend Jada over to play cards and listen to music. I can't believe you were a wild child."

"Child, I never went out because by the time you came along, I had done everything there was to be done out in the streets. I was bored with the clubs and the streets by the age of twenty-five. But Aisha, you went on and on and on with your life, never missing a beat. You got through the physical and emotional anguish that bastard put you through and you didn't allow him to win so don't you dare step out of the winner's circle now."

Aisha gave her mother a hug and kiss after allowing her words to sink in. Her mother was right, she had survived and she now knew that she could continue to forge ahead. Aisha felt so much closer to her mother and no matter what Bev said, Aisha would always get strength from her. She was her hero.

"How long have you been having these nightmares?"

"Honestly, Ma, I haven't had a nightmare or thought about the rape in over twenty years but someone from the past has resurfaced in my life and as a result, so have the nightmares."

"Oh, you mean Pete Jackson coming into the shop unexpectedly? Well, that makes sense because he played a huge part in your getting past the pain of that night. Pete may have taken you across state lines and married you behind my back, but he was a godsend when you most needed it."

Aisha was so happy she'd come to talk with her mother. She'd never before put the two together: Pete returning and the nightmares. Bev spent the rest of the afternoon babying her daughter by cooking her a lunch of potato cakes from scratch with fried green tomatoes and two slices of Canadian ham. It was just what Aisha needed to lift her spirits—her mama's love and attention.

Aisha couldn't believe that Pete still thought of Red Lobster as being an upscale restaurant. *Where has this fool been hiding? Taking me to Red Lobster after making such a big deal about where we would eat on our first date. This is going to be an early night.*

"So, Pete, how have you been since the accident?"

"I've been holding up pretty well considering everything. Taking care of twin girls is very difficult but Alyssa and Alexis are the best and they are truly a blessing. They help me go on each day."

Pete looked as if he were remembering a happier time. The day he walked into KAT69 and reunited with Terry and Aisha, Pete had told them of the mysterious illness that had taken the life of his beautiful wife, Marty. He explained that for months, Marty was unable to hold down food or any liquids. She suffered from severe stomach cramps, weakness, and hair loss. Pete had seen to it that Marty saw the best doctors but none of them could diagnose the ailment. Sadly, Marty had succumbed to the illness during her last hospital stay just a week before Mother's Day. Since her death, Pete had been raising their five-year-old twins with the help of his mother.

"Do the girls ask about their mother often? I mean, at five years old, do children truly understand death?" inquired Aisha.

"Yes, they do ask about her but we've explained to them that Mommy is an angel in heaven keeping watch over them. Let's talk about something else." Pete needed to change the subject fast. "This is supposed to be a happy occasion, remember? Pete Jackson and Aisha Woods back together again." Pete held up his glass in an attempt to make a toast. Aisha didn't follow suit. "What's wrong, Aisha, did I say something wrong?"

"I just don't know what you meant by Pete and

Aisha back together again. I think I should let you know something now."

"Please don't tell me that you are already involved with someone else," whined Pete. The tone in his voice turned Aisha off and the expression on her face probably showed it.

"It's not that, Pete. At this point, I'm not looking to be in a committed relationship with anyone and I'm sorry to say this but that includes you." Aisha hadn't meant to be so harsh but after the words were out, they couldn't be pulled back.

"Ouch! I'm sorry, Aisha, I just assumed you still had feelings for me. The moment I laid eyes on you after all those years apart, my heart began to flutter. I still care for you."

Aisha was surprised to hear Pete say that. His wife hadn't been dead long enough for him to be looking for a relationship with anyone. Although Aisha still cared for Pete, she was not so out of touch with reality to think they could just pick up where they'd left off. People change over the years and she knew that she was not the same person she was at sixteen.

"Like I said, at this point in my life, I'm not looking for love. So let's just take things slow and see where it goes. Who knows what might happen?" Aisha lied. *Shit, this nigga must be crazy telling me he wants to be with me after all these years. And bringing me to Red Lobster for an upscale meal lets me know his ass is cheap. No cheap-ass nigga can afford or keep up with my ass. This fool got me fucked up believing I'd invite him back into my life without reason. Note to self: never be alone with him again.*

I'M SORRY, HAVE WE MET?

CHAPTER 25

The day Terry had held her breath for had finally arrived. Seeing the work sketched on paper didn't do the actual results justice. Thanks to Pete and his crew, the work had been finished one month before the projected date of completion. After explaining the differences in various floor plans to Terry and Aisha, and in order to easily separate the noisy areas like the day care, reception, and pedicure areas from quieter ones, like the massage and meditation rooms, Pete went with appropriate insulation. The only disadvantages to this plan were the additional cost for heating and cooling. Pete explained how he had saved them money in other areas so the financial plan would balance out.

As soon as the construction crew cleared out of her way, interior designer Cheryl R. Hill got to work choosing quality fabrics, furniture, and color palettes to give the spa a feel of tranquility and relaxation. Bev had used Cheryl when she had her entire house made over. Cheryl had also worked on the mayor's house and a few local banks; her own office was a testament to her skills. Terry had no problem giving Cheryl free reign after explaining what her vision was for the new space.

One week later, Cheryl had completed the assignment and once again, she did not disappoint. The mixture of deep purples, lilacs, whites, and yellows fit the reception and pedicure areas perfectly. The three massage rooms and two meditation rooms were designed in a mixture of warm and neutral colors. The yellow, orange, gray, and blacks immediately gave a feel of tranquility. Each room was vibrant, contemporary, and soothing in its own way. The day care area was done in bright rainbows and letters of the alphabet hung on the walls. Terry couldn't compliment Cheryl enough on her vision and style; she was always on point whether the job was residential, commercial, or small business. Cheryl was always professional and exceeded expectations.

Everything had just fallen into place and Terry was so excited that she couldn't sleep at night. She lay awake thinking of various ways to improve the business even more. Talissa and Bossy suggested the start of a book club. Terry and Aisha agreed it was a good idea and that a lot of the clientele would think so too. Of course, Terry did not want just another book club; she wanted a book club worth joining. Aisha came up with the idea of closing down the shop one Sunday a month to host the book club meetings. She even had the idea to hold spa parties after the meetings once a quarter, collect small dues, and vote on annual group outings. Maybe visit the AABC (African American Book

Club) in Atlanta, the Harlem Book Festival, or the Sea Summit. Whatever the outing, it had to be literary based. The club would be called Shades of Everyday Women Book Club at KAT69. Bossy, Aisha, Mama Bev, and Talissa were all so proud of Terry and joined in her excitement. Terry promised them all that her business plan over the next five years would allow them all to live very comfortably.

In just two days, the new KAT-69 Hair, Nails, and Day Spa would open its doors offering clients every service imaginable from head to toe. With all of the contract work completed, hiring a cleaning company was an option that everyone knew Terry would pass on. Being a fanatic for cleanliness, she had to do the cleanup herself; or at least be a part of the cleaning team. Mama Bev slipped out on her girls just before the last of the interior decorating team left. The girls all knew better than to ask where she was headed but this time, they didn't have to chance it. Mama Bev voluntarily provided an excuse for her leaving without lending a helping hand to clean. She had a date. Bossy, Aisha and, Terry were all happy to hear that she had met someone.

"Please save your questions for later. Mama is running late but y'all come on by for lunch tomorrow and we will talk," instructed Mama Bev.

The four women giggled like preteens as they offered advice and dating rules.

"No kissing and don't go back to his place. Write down his license plate number if he drives but it is best to drive your own car. As a matter of fact, text me the make of his car and plate number." Bossy, Aisha, and Terry all agreed upon the advice. Mama Bev gave the girls the "talk to the hand" stance and started off on her way.

After a good laugh, Terry said, "Let's get to it so we can get out of here. I don't know about all of y'all but I'm getting a little tired."

"I hate this part and you always make us do this. I don't see why we have to pay for a cleaning crew if we're going behind them redoing everything," whined Aisha.

"And I don't know why you always whine. It's not like we do renovations every weekend. Girl, this is a celebration. You've heard of painting parties, right? " asked Terry. "Just think of this as a cleaning party. The faster we work, the faster we'll be out of here so quit acting like a big baby!" Terry chastised Aisha while pouring cleaning solution into an industrial-size bucket.

The three friends mopped and waxed the floors, cleaned windows, and reminisced about the old days while old school rappers YoYo, MC Lyte, and MC Breed played in the background. Terry's heart filled with pride as she realized her dream had come to life and she was able to share it with her best friends and for the first time, her baby girl.

"Looks like I showed up at just the right time," Twan's voice drew Terry from her thoughts.

"So you think," teased Terry, "go grab that vacuum cleaner in the corner with your name on it."

Stomping his feet and swinging his arms wildly as if to mimic a toddler, Twan did as he was told.

Bossy, Aisha, and Terry all laughed at Twan's antics, causing him to laugh at himself.

The friends cleaned and played around with each other, forgetting about the various issues going on in their individual lives.

All of the fun allowed Aisha to forget about the loneliness living deep inside of her soul. She had lied to Pete when she said she didn't want a committed relationship. Her strong desire for companionship, love, and commitment rested in the back of her mind. With Pete recently losing his wife, raising twin girls alone, and having a business that required him to leave home for weeks at a time, Aisha wanted no part of it. Aisha didn't realize that the distraction of cleaning and playing around with her friends was allowing her to breathe.

The smile on Terry's face contrasted with the look of stress she'd carried around for weeks while the work was being done. To see her five year plan come alive four years earlier than expected was exciting and frightening at the same time, but remembering old days as a shy young girl, tucked away in her bedroom reading books and making journal entries gave Terry insight on how far she had come to get where she currently stood.

Not once while Twan was pushing the mop and broom had his cell phone rang. Its silence was welcome and Twan felt good to have a break. Since his last encounter with LaJetia, when she threw a cast-iron frying pan at his back, things had gotten more and more chaotic. LaJetia had begun acting more neurotic than usual. Twan took in the laughter and old school music and allowed himself to relax as he thought, *It feels good to feel this way. I just don't appreciate playing maintenance man!*

Sitting inside the rented silver Honda Civic less than one block away from what used to be her favorite hair salon, LaJetia grew more and more impatient waiting for Twan to leave for his next destination. So far, Twan had been inside of KAT69 for over two hours. LaJetia couldn't figure out what could possibly be going on inside the shop for so long. *I'll sit out here all night if I have to. One way or another, I'll find out who it is keeping Twan from coming home to me and our family.*

Unbeknownst to Twan, LaJetia had resumed following him around town. Being caught in the act taught LaJetia a valuable lesson: never use your own car to play private detective. She now used rental cars that were financed by the household bill money Twan gave her. Every bill in the house had just enough money put on it to maintain the service. Twan had cut off LaJetia's pocket money. Apparently, he didn't like having a potential deadly weapon thrown at him.

LaJetia had no intention of losing the best thing she ever had in her life. Her heart believed Twan still loved her and wanted to be with her. She had convinced herself that it was another woman keeping him from her and the kids. Facing reality was not an option for LaJetia because doing so meant she'd have to admit to herself that it was her who drove Twan away. Youth and inexperience wouldn't allow LaJetia to take ownership of her role in the breakup of the relationship that she held so dear.

The ringing of her cell phone drew LaJetia's attention away from the KAT69 parking lot.

"Hello."

"Hi, Miss LaJetia, it's me, Auntell."

LaJetia felt important every time her babysitter addressed her as "Miss LaJetia." The respect helped LaJetia hold her chin up so she never saw the need to tell sixteen-year-old Auntell to relax with the formal way she addressed her. Although Auntell was only three years younger than LaJetia, their roles should have been switched. Auntell was a much better role model for LaJetia's children. She cared for Kiara, Trayvon, and Tyler with the love of a doting mother. Caring for the three of them had her planning to decide on one day becoming an elementary school teacher, a principal, or perhaps open up a chain of day care services.

"What's up, Auntell? Are the kids giving you a hard time?" LaJetia failed in her attempt not to sound annoyed.

"The kids are fine. It's just that you said you'd be back an hour ago and I have plans tonight with my boyfriend, Rayshaun. He's going to be at my house soon to pick me up and I still need to go home and get ready," explained Auntell in a panic-filled voice.

Time was the last thing on LaJetia's mind. Glancing at her watch, she realized that it had now been two and a half hours that Twan was inside of KAT69. It was time to find out just what in the hell was going on.

"I'm so sorry, Auntell. You know I wouldn't do this to you on purpose." LaJetia had to think quick or all of the time she spent following Twan around that night would wind up being a big waste of time. *Damn, now is not the time for this interruption.*

Auntell became impatient with LaJetia. Over the past few weeks, she'd been with the kids so much that they had begun slipping up and calling her Mommy. The pay was good but not worth sacrificing so much of her time as a teenager, when she should be out kickin' it. Auntell had promised her parents that she would tell LaJetia she couldn't babysit for her anymore but she had no intention of quitting until she bought herself the beige Coach bag she just had to have.

"Miss LaJetia, are you still there?"

"Yes, I'm still here. I'm sorry for being so late. I have an idea, why don't you look in my closet for something to wear out with Rayshaun. That will save you some time and by the time you get dressed, I'll be home."

The idea of rummaging through a closet that held nothing but high-end name brands made Auntell excited enough to lose her attitude with LaJetia.

"Oh my God! Are you sure? I mean, you haven't even worn most of the stuff in there."

"Don't worry about that. Wear whatever you want and don't forget to match the outfit up with the shoes. You wear a size eight, right?"

"Oh yeah, now that's what's up."

"I'll be home by the time you find an outfit, shower, and get dressed. Just call ya boyfriend and have 'im pick you up from my house. You got to look good if you want to hold on to that cutie," laughed LaJetia. When she met Rayshaun, she thought he was as ugly as he wanted to be. He had a face only a mother could love but he was a sweet kid.

After pressing the end button on her cell phone, LaJetia started up her car and slowly drove into the parking lot adjacent to KAT69. From this position, LaJetia saw there were three cars in addition to Twan's parked in the front of the shop. She immediately recognized one of the cars.

"Fuck that! This nigga must think I'm stupid. I knew he was fuckin' her."

Having long finished the cleanup, Bossy, Aisha, Terry, and Twan sat drinking glasses of champagne in celebration of the addition to the shop.

"This still feels like a dream. I just can't believe all that work was completed in such a short time," Terry slurred.

"Well, believe it, girl. Here we all are to see it," replied Aisha.

"That's what I'm talkin' about. Business brings money and money brings about more business," declared Bossy.

"I can't believe y'all even came up with the idea for all of this. Do y'all know how much money is about to be pulled in here? For real, Terry and Aisha, I need y'all to help me go legit with a business idea that's going to flourish." Twan had been thinking about leaving the game since all of that mess with Ant trying to double-cross him. The thought was haunting him more and more after Officers Powell and Meeks walked through Bossy's front door a couple of days ago. Bossy questioned the warrant and let it be known that Clifton Boyd had a lawyer rushing right over. Fortunately for Bossy, Twan and Big Black, Officers Powell and

Meeks's plan to rob them was quickly defused by the mention of C-Lok's name. The officers apologized for their mistake by explaining the address on the warrant was a clerical error. They left empty-handed with their tails between their legs, yet determined to return with a new plan.

Terry and Bossy had already started putting their next business idea on paper. With Big Black complaining about the shitty-ass lineup some barber had given him, Terry's mind started spinning. It was too early to say anything because no details had been worked out yet but a barbershop might be the next project for Terry to put her great business skills into.

"We have another idea in the very early stages that might be just right to bring you in on," explained Bossy. "Just be patient. We will look out for you."

"That's what I—"

CRASH!

A flying object hurled past Twan's left ear interrupted his thought. The red brick shattered a hanging mirror and ended the group's celebration.

"Man, what the fuck?" yelled Twan as he turned to face the direction that the potentially deadly weapon originated from. He saw LaJetia standing in the door to the salon, her face contorted with rage.

"Bitch!"

For the second time Twan lunged toward LaJetia, "What the fuck is your problem?" Twan was holding LaJetia three inches off the ground with one hand around her petite neck. Staring into

LaJetia's eyes made the hatred he felt for her begin to bubble.

"Didn't I tell you I would kill you if you ever threw anything at me again? Didn't I?" Twan's voice sent shivers up Aisha and Terry's spines.

"Twan's grip began to loosen as LaJetia began to pass out. He wanted her to suffer, to be taught a lesson.

Twan, let her go! You are going to kill her," screamed Terry.

Bossy, Aisha, and Terry finally snapped out of their shock and ran over to save Twan from catching a case.

Anger had Twan squeezing the life out of the mother of his child. He had grown so tired of her childish antics that he cursed the day they met.

With all the screaming and hollering going on around him, Twan released his long, slim fingers from LaJetia's neck. LaJetia fell to the ground, attempting to regain her breathing pattern and regretting what she'd just done. Not because Twan tried to choke her to death, but because she'd read the look in Twan's eyes—deep hatred and animosity. LaJetia finally understood that she would never get him back home. She knew she had gone too far but she reasoned that she did what she had to do in order to get his attention. LaJetia was determined not to lose Twan to Bossy.

Aisha reached out to lead Twan away from LaJetia. Before he followed behind Aisha, Twan made sure to kick LaJetia on her left side, cracking three ribs in the process.

As LaJetia lay on the concrete, still fighting for

air and gripping her side, all she could think of was how much she loved Twan.

Bossy and Terry stood looking down on Twan's intended manslaughter victim and tried to figure out what would make a person do such a thing. Bossy was too disgusted to care about LaJetia's well-being. She turned on her heels to avoid hitting LaJetia in her fuckin' head. Not only had LaJetia broken the large storefront window but she put a big-ass monkey wrench in the feelings of pride Terry had been feeling. Bossy already didn't like LaJetia, now she had a reason to despise her.

"Let me help you up. Are you okay?" Terry was always the compassionate one.

Unable to talk, LaJetia shook her head no. She needed just a few more minutes to regain her senses. *How did this go so wrong? Things weren't supposed to go like this. I just wanted to bust Twan and that bitch Bossy together. Why didn't I just throw the damn brick and run?*

"Terry, do me a favor and get that piece of shit out of here," requested Twan.

Aisha and Terry helped the young, stupid girl off the floor and outside to her car, which was still running. It seemed to take forever but LaJetia got situated behind the wheel of her car and slowly pulled off.

"I have a bad feeling about that girl. Something tells me tonight was just a preview of what she is capable of doing," said Aisha.

"Yeah, if he knows like we do, Twan better watch his back. LaJetia is not done with him yet," replied Terry.

AIN'T THIS A BITCH . . .

CHAPTER 26

Thanks to Talissa's suggestion, Bossy, Aisha, and Terry had their apartment building hooked up to allow them to use both their desk and laptop computers without all the pesky wires and cords. It was something Terry really needed in order to work from home whether she was in her own apartment or that of Bossy or Aisha.

"Instead of working all late at the shop, work from home," suggested Talissa. "All you need are computers equipped with the technology allowing you to share files and stuff. The home computers will have the same information as the shop."

As soon as the idea was put to them, Bossy, Aisha, and Terry were in agreement and took Talissa with them to find the right equipment.

The straitlaced salesman with the deep suntan had smoke shooting out his ears after the transaction was completed. He was the same salesman to turn up his nose at the four black women as if they would be wasting his time. His name tag read *Fred* and his snooty attitude cost him the biggest commission of the month. After Fred dismissed the women as a waste of time, Terry went in search of a young salesperson of color. She found a skinny young man who looked to be in his early twenties but was full of energy, flirtation, and jokes.

Deon Harris had only been working at the store for a month and was still in training.

"Hey, ladies, can I help you find anything?"

"Yes, we need some new home and business computers and we need them fast. We want both desk models and laptops set up wirelessly at our apartment building and our business establishment," replied Terry.

"I knew I was going to be blessed today but I never imagined it would be by four lovely angels. Excuse me for saying this, but the four of y'all are the prettiest women I've ever seen. And they say pretty women don't travel in packs," joked Deon.

The group laughed at the young salesman and thanked him for the compliment. After three hours of shopping and learning the various options available to them, the ladies paid the bill and were on their way. The electronics manager promised to personally oversee the installation of the computers and set the appointment for the following day.

Bossy, Aisha, Terry, and Talissa made a stop at the Sandwich Factory to pick up lunch after leaving the store and headed back to their apartment. Big Black sat just three feet away from Bossy's plasma screen television playing PlayStation 2 and listening to his trademark reggae CD.

"This singer Sizzla ain't no joke and people need to stop sleeping on him," said Big Black, bobbin' his head.

"You are in the same spot you were in when we left here. I swear men are worse than kids with them video games," vented Aisha. "Big Black, come on in here and eat with us, we picked you up a sub from the Factory."

Big Black did as he was told and joined the women at the dining room table. Fifteen minutes later, Twan knocked on the door and an impromptu set was underway. Drinks were made and gulped down, blunts were rolled and old stories were told. Twan and Talissa enjoyed learning the history of the friends and couldn't believe how wild Bossy, Aisha, and Terry were back in the day.

"Listen y'all," requested Aisha. "Who remembers the time Bossy came home from the Break-Out Lounge to find three of the four niggas she was hollering at chilling around her dining room table?"

"Oh my God, I can't believe you bringing that shit up. That night was crazy as hell," said Bossy.

"What happened? I know my girl didn't get caught slippin' like that," said Twan.

"See, I used to tell niggas not to claim me on the street because they weren't the only one. I also had a rule not to ever drop in without calling me first because . . ."

"They weren't the only one and they just might get their feelings hurt," recited Aisha, Terry and Big Black in unison. They all laughed because Bossy used to use that line so much in the early to mid-nineties.

"Anyway, I come home one night and find Aisha and Terry sitting on my couch with stupid looks on their faces. They kept looking from me to the dining room and after I caught on, I follow their eyes to see three men sitting at my table."

"Oh my God, Aunt Bossy what did you do?" inquired Talissa.

"Shit, they were in my crib and had broken my rules. I walked in here, grabbed a deck of cards, and started dealing them. I said to all three of them, 'House rules are joker, joker, duce, no French cutting, and no overbidding.' "

Twan couldn't believe what he was hearing. Bossy couldn't have had game like that. "Are you serious? They stayed and played spades with you?"

"Yeah, they did until that fourth nigga walked in the door, without knocking and broke up the game," explained Big Black.

"Who had it like that?" asked Twan.

Aisha, Terry, and Big Black looked at Bossy and waited for her to answer Twan's question. Bossy took a toke of her blunt and a sip of her drink before looking at Twan.

"C-Lok."

"What?" said Twan in disbelief.

"You heard me nigga, I said C-Lok. We used to kick it for a minute so we have a lot of history together." Bossy had hoped that her relationship with C-Lok could be kept from Twan. Him having knowledge of their past meant that he might see Bossy as being in a position to mediate between Twan and C-Lok regarding the money owed and the fallout between Twan and Ant. Bossy didn't want to use her clout with C-Lok like that and now that the cat was out of the bag, she hoped Twan wouldn't ask it of her.

The rest of the night was filled with more laughter and old stories. It was after three in the morning by the time everyone left for their own apartments. Twan had been staying in the spare apartment across the hall from Bossy since he left LaJetia. Apartment A was fully furnished and used to house some of the money Bossy made. The walls were specially constructed along with the bathroom floor to hide her stash. No one knew about it except Bossy, that way no one would ever be forced into giving up all of her trade secrets.

The next night, all of the computers had been installed and were running perfectly. Aisha and Terry were in Bossy's apartment playing around with their new toys while Bossy worked on Twan's shipment.

It was that time of the month to pay bills and time to cut Pete his check for a job well done.

"These numbers in here don't look right. Where is the paper copy of Pete's invoice?" Terry was happy to use computers to keep records but she also kept paper copies for backup. Minutes later, Terry located the invoices and began breaking down the cost of the renovations.

Bossy was in the mood to work hard and that meant playing her favorites to help set the mood. Ice Cube, DJ Quik, Busta Rhymes, Snoop and Dr. Dre helped Bossy concentrate on the task at hand. She was in the kitchen dancing and waiting for the pots of water to start boiling. She danced her way back into her dining room and found Terry still in deep thought. Bossy danced over to her bar and poured herself a drink while Big Black sat in the living room playing his video game.

"Y'all done in there?" asked Big Black.

"Naw, Terry is going over the last invoice from Pete. When she gets into a zone, like she is now, do not disturb her," explained Bossy.

"You mean like you get when you're weighing that shit up and breaking it down?" teased Big Black.

"Exactly." Bossy and Big Black laughed in unison and fired up a blunt to help set the mood.

As the background music that had been playing came to an end, Terry's growing frustration was heard by Bossy and Big Black.

"Something isn't right here. I have to be reading this wrong or transposing numbers some place and just not seeing it," vented Terry.

"What's up, T, what has you stressing out?" asked Bossy.

"Bossy, I know you about to be busy but come and double-check my figures for me. I've never been off like this before but the credits and debits don't balance with Pete's final bill."

Bossy sat at the computer to re-input the same information Terry had. On the first, second, and third tries, Bossy matched Terry's figures and not Pete's.

"See, something is wrong. Pete's final invoice is off by three times the amount." Terry hoped what she was thinking did not turn out to be true.

"How could that be? Since I'm just learning the money end of the business, you have to explain it to me."

"Either Pete's bid was gravely under budget or

Pete had packed his final bill and is trying to take us for thousands of dollars," explained Terry.

"Ah, hell no! I know damn well that soft nigga Pete ain't trying to play my girls," hollered Big Black.

"Wait a minute, everybody just calm down before this blows up and gets out of hand," reasoned Terry.

"What else could it be? Shit, Pete is a fool if he doing what I think he's trying to do." Just the thought of his girls being played was infuriating Big Black and he'd be happy to take care of the situation for them.

"Maybe the query is off someplace on the computer software. Here's what we are going to do. Call Aisha down here and have her review the formula on the software. She'll be able to locate any incorrect formulas and update all the information. At the same time, me and Bossy will do it the old-fashioned way, one invoice at a time," explained Terry.

"Let me guess, calculators, invoices, and receipts, right, Terry? We're going to review each one line by line and dollar by dollar?" asked Bossy.

"Very carefully; very carefully."

Still inside of Bossy's apartment, six hours, three pots of coffee and two blunts later, the results were in. Pete had billed them for over three times the amount actually owed. He had charged them for workers that didn't exist; midnight hours not worked and submitted invoices from fictitious businesses. Not only had Bossy, Aisha, and Terry reviewed every receipt, invoice, and payroll record, they researched the companies Pete dealt with for materials. Aisha searched the Better Business Bureau Web site and found that multiple complaints had been filed against Pete Jackson Construction. The search also revealed that Pete's business license had been revoked five years ago.

"I should have known this motherfucker was too good to be true from the start. Showing up the way he did, perfect bidding and a work crew on hand," vented Terry. "I should have known better but no . . . he was an old friend and I trusted him with no questions asked." She paced back and forth, ringing her hands and beating herself up inside.

"I should have known he was a hustler because game recognizes game. Listen to me, the only person at fault is Pete. He lied to us, we never lied to him." Bossy's voice was full of anger.

"None of us suspected anything because he was a friend of ours. We knew him and shit, I was married to his ass once," added Aisha.

"There is no use in beating ourselves up about what we should have known or done. What we need to do now is figure out what to do now," said Terry.

"You're right and I can guarantee that we aren't the first people he's done this to. The complaints filed with the BBB are proof of that. This punk-ass nigga must make a living off doing people like this." Bossy was tired of all the drama that seemed to be coming their way from every direction. As far as she was concerned, it was time to lay all the drama queens and kings the fuck down. "That's what's up and I know exactly how we can find out all we need to know. Aisha, go back on the Web and search Ohio, Indiana, and Illinois for any criminal records or outstanding warrants Pete might have out there. We about to lay this bitch down."

Big Black had been relaxing on the living room couch while the women talked and the more he heard, the angrier he became. "Research my ass, man, fuck some research! Let me have his ass alone and I'll have him paying y'all by the time I'm done with 'im."

"Calm down, Big Black, we got this. I can't believe I got caught slipping like this. See, my head ain't right and that's how niggas be getting caught." Bossy wanted to handle things the way Big Black suggested but she knew the situation had to be taken care of on a different level.

Feeling she had let her girls down by not seeing Pete for who he truly was made Bossy sick to the stomach. Preparing to leave the game and actually being out of the game was two very different ends of the spectrum. At that moment, Bossy knew one thing for certain: one way or another, Pete's bitch ass was going to pay big for his fuckup.

Pete had become restless and anxious waiting for his big windfall to finally land in his lap. He worked harder on this job than he had any other. Some nights he went back to his shady motel room and fell into a deep sleep the exact second his head touched the pillow. The renovations at KAT69 were completed over two weeks ago but some of Pete's muscles ached as if he'd just built a three-story house alone. Usually when Pete left these types of jobs, his work literally began falling apart but this job was different. He couldn't do shabby work for old friends even though he had every intention of piling his bill and making a huge payday out of the assignment.

Pete knew that Bossy, Aisha, and Terry had all changed over the years but by the look of their business, the cars they drove, and the way they dressed, their love of money was evident. Pete knew all about Bossy's hustling and that she always took care of her girls so he imagined that their bank accounts were overflowing with cash. He wanted his piece of their pie by any means necessary.

The plane Pete was scheduled to leave town on was due for departure from Cleveland Airport in two days and he still hadn't been paid for the work. Within those two days, Pete planned on collecting his paycheck, visiting the bank, and wiring the bulk of the balance to his offshore account. His plan to escape was made the same day he cemented the deal with Aisha and Terry.

"Hello," answered Pete to his ringing throwaway cell phone.

"Hey, Pete, this is Terry; how are you today?"

"I'm good, how about yourself?" Pete's heart started racing at the thought of his sizable paycheck. That had to be the reason for Terry's call.

"Oh, I'm blessed as always. Listen, I'm calling to let you know we have your check and I need your mailing address so I can overnight it to you."

"Don't worry about mailing it. Why don't I just come by the shop and pick it up?"

"Oh, I'm sorry, I just assumed you had already left town. Yeah, come on by in about an hour and I'll be in my office," instructed Terry.

Pete was so pleased with himself that his dick got hard.

"All right, he'll be here in about an hour. Let's get this set up." Terry's stomach was in knots at the thought of seeing Pete but they had to get him before he got somebody else.

"Aisha, are you one hundred percent positive that you want to handle things this way?" Bossy had to be sure that Aisha wouldn't back out on the plan at the last minute.

"Girl, what? Let's do this."

Right on time, Pete was standing outside of Terry's office waiting for a response to his knocking.

"Come on in."

"Hey girl, you're looking beautiful as always."

Whatever, nigga. I bet you won't feel that way thirty seconds from now, Terry thought to herself. Forcing a smile, Terry offered Pete to take the seat opposite of hers.

"Well, I know you're a busy man just like I'm a busy woman so I won't keep you here any longer than needed." Terry reached inside of her top desk drawer and handed Pete a manila-colored envelope.

"Thank you and I'm so happy we got a chance to visit with each other. I'm very happy we were able to work together." Pete stood as he spoke in anticipation of leaving Terry's office and running to the nearest bank. After giving Terry a hug and asking her to tell Aisha and Bossy bye for him, Pete turned toward the office door to leave. Before turning the knob, Pete took a peek inside the envelope. He couldn't believe what he was seeing and thought that some type of accounting error had been made.

"Terry, this figure on the check is incorrect."

"Oh, how did that happen?" Terry turned to her computer and pulled up the invoice history for Pete Jackson Construction to check the numbers against the check.

"No, Pete, the check is right according to the invoices, payroll records and receipts you provided to us."

"No the fuck it ain't!" barked Pete.

"Excuse me?"

"Look, Terry, don't play games with me. Me and my crew worked hard on this place and I want every penny owed to me." Pete felt as if he were about to have a stroke. His heart was racing and his forehead was forming beads of sweat. He felt weak for a minute and sat back down in his seat.

"You know what, Pete, last night while doing the books, I thought that your final bill to us was extremely packed. Three times packed, as a matter of fact, and me being me, I redid the numbers various times and I always came out right." Terry straightened her back and leaned forward to let Pete know he was busted.

"Look, I know what I'm due and you gon' pay me every damn penny. You hear me, bitch? Every damn penny." Pete had regained his composure and was standing over Terry's desk with a gun pointed in her direction.

"This is the exact reaction we expected from your thieving ass and you did not disappoint."

"What are you talking about, we expected? Just give me what I got coming to me. I don't know who you think you messing with but don't think this is the first time some shit like this has happened. Now get ya prissy ass back on that computer or whatever you got to do and write me another check," demanded Pete.

"Oh, you want what's coming to you? Not a problem. Pete Jackson, I got you."

A thud rang out, knocking the office door wide open, startling Pete. At the same time, the closet door opened revealing a tall white man in an Armani suit.

"FBI, drop the weapon!"

Dropping the gun to the floor, Pete did as he was told. He stared down at Terry as the FBI rushed over to where he stood, frisked him, and threw the handcuffs on him.

"Peter Franklin Jackson, you are under arrest for the murder of one Marty Jackson, multiple counts of forgery, theft by deception, and suspicion of wire fraud and tax evasion. Let's go!" The white men snatched Pete's ass out of Terry's office like he was a child who'd just stole something. Bossy and Aisha were waiting outside the office as Pete was being led off.

Pete was stunned by the events and couldn't believe his plan had turned so wrong.

The night before while searching the Web, Aisha came upon Pete's complete criminal history and discovered the outstanding warrants and newspaper articles outlining the death of his wife. Marty Jackson didn't die from a health ailment, her body was discovered in some woods in Illinois by some boys playing nearby. She had been beaten to death and tortured. The police investigation pointed directly to the victim's husband, Pete Jackson, and the police have been tracking him down for over a year. As the investigation progressed, the FBI got involved because of the fraudulent business practices, overseas wire transfers, and most sadly, the kidnapping and murder of his two daughters.

It turned out that Pete had been physically abusive to his wife for years but she didn't initially try to make things better, especially since Pete had brainwashed her into believing it was her fault he beat her. Marty did everything she thought would make him happy and had become very submissive to Pete until his physical abuse was aimed at their twin daughters. Her motherly instincts took over and Marty protected her babies and lost her life in the process. The five-year-old girls were witness to their father killing their mother and Pete had to be certain they never told a soul.

Pete thought he could get enough money from Bossy, Aisha, and Terry to leave the country and begin a new life somewhere without an extradition agreement with the USA. He should have realized that Bossy, Aisha, and Terry were three women like no other and after surviving the ghettos of Youngstown, Ohio, they could and would survive anything.

And My Parents Said . . .

Chapter 27

Talissa had gotten very spoiled by her birth mother, Terry, and two aunts, Bossy and Aisha. They showered her with all of the material things a girl of sixteen could want. The shopping trips were off the hook. Bossy, Aisha, and Terry had all taken turns shopping with Talissa. It wasn't enough to buy her outfits, they had to buy shoes, socks, jewelry, perfumes, everything.

The first time all four of the women shopped together, Bossy rented a Denali and they drove down I-71 to the Jacksonville Outlet Mall located halfway between Columbus and Cincinnati. Aisha explained to Talissa that the Denali was big enough to carry all of their goodies home. Talissa was in heaven on earth and not just because of all the gifts but because of the attention.

That was the one and only time they drove themselves. After shopping for hours, no one was in the mood to drive the almost four hours back to Youngstown. From then on, they rented a driver to go along with the car.

Talissa appreciated all the trips, surprise gifts, money, and work experience. However, what she wanted most was to continue getting closer to Terry and discover more of her history. Even Mama Bev had gotten in on spoiling Talissa. Bev cried and hugged the child so long and hard the first time she lay eyes on her that Talissa began feeling a little uncomfortable.

School had begun and Talissa was starting her junior year in high school. For as far back as she could remember, Talissa wanted to be a world-renowned novelist. She wrote in her journals faithfully since being introduced to it in the fourth grade. Reading was her passion and Talissa believed her purpose on earth was to be a writer. Talissa's goal was to attend Howard University and study literature and creative writing. Lately she didn't feel the same about going off to college. Working at KAT69 offered Talissa a view into small-business ownership that she never knew existed. She just couldn't figure out what business would intertwine with being a novelist, besides the obvious, a bookstore.

In addition to working at the shop, Talissa continued to give her time to children at the Urban League. Two-days a week, she read to and played with little girls and boys who craved positive attention. The children lived in areas where gunshots rang out every night and police sirens were the norm. Talissa considered her time well spent and the experience very humbling. Seeing how easy it was for a person to fall into the disadvantage trap reassured Talissa that her goal of going to college was what she needed and had to do.

Talissa's heart went out to the single mothers she saw picking up their children from the Urban League's day care program. The mothers all came in various shapes, sizes, complexions, and backgrounds but they each had one thing in common: to make a better life for their children. Some of the women worked two or more minimum wage jobs to keep a roof over their kids' heads and food on the table. It was clear they loved their children by the way they dressed them, held their hands a few seconds longer when dropping them off at the day care. Many of the women were forced to catch three different buses to get home safely every night.

Talissa thanked God every night for blessing her with devoted and loving people in her life. Her adoptive parents, Joseph and Sylvia Croomes, had raised her with love and honesty. They not only told her how special she was, they showed her by letting her get to know where she came from. Finding Terry made Talissa feel complete. Getting to know her birth mother opened the door for Talissa to get to know herself. She understood why she twirled her hair while she was reading, why her brown hair turned auburn in the summer and why she never left the house without first looking like a model: because her mama did.

Terry had explained the situation surrounding her birth and the fallout with her grandparents as a result of being forced to give her away at birth. Talissa understood how painful it must have been for Terry, or anyone for that matter to have a baby she shared a body with for nine months to be ripped out of her arms. Having been raised in the church, Terry knew that forgiveness was important and necessary. After sixteen years the hurt and disappointment she felt in her parents should have subsided by now, but it continued to linger. For months now, Terry had prayed for a miracle, for a door to open and her parents to walk through it and apologize for what they put her through, for what they put their own grandchild through. Talissa had dreams filled with a family reunion, fun-filled holidays and Sunday dinners resembling that of age-old traditions.

Thanks to the local white pages and Internet search engines, the search for her grandparents took all of two minutes. Apparently Richard and Cheryl Woods still lived in the same house Terry grew up in. Cohasset Street was only three blocks long but Talissa drove her new 2005 baby-blue Ford Escape, given to her by Bossy, Aisha, and Terry for her sixteenth birthday, as slowly as possible in search of the right address.

The big yellow house had been well maintained over the years. New windows and vinyl siding made the three-story house very attractive. An old-fashioned front porch with the banister wide enough to slide down enhanced the look. No front porch of its type would be complete without the white porch swing and green outdoor carpeting.

Talissa sat in her car staring at the house and daydreaming of being a little girl sitting next to her grandmother, whom she would call Ma'Dea (short for Mother Dear). Ma'Dea and Talissa would sit together for hours watching the cars go up and down the street while her grandmother broke the tips of fresh-picked string beans. Talissa stared at the modest lawn and visualized helping her grandpa with yard work, mainly just getting in the way.

A speeding car brought Talissa back to reality and she knew her parked car would draw attention to herself.

"Dear Lord, please help me with this meeting and assist me in finding the right words to say."

Talissa found herself unable to release her hands from the steering wheel. She couldn't figure out what was making her so nervous about seeing her grandparents.

What is wrong with me? I wasn't this nervous about revealing my identity to Terry for the first time. After our first meeting, I couldn't wait to get to know Terry, so what is my problem today? Talissa didn't realize she was actually sitting in her small SUV talking to herself. Never in her life had Talissa felt unable to face or overcome anything in her life. No matter how hard or how easy, how educated she was about a situation or how foreign the matter, Talissa overcame her fears and forged forward. She prided herself on tackling life's unforeseen obstacles with her chin up and her faith in God. Today, Talissa just couldn't see her way through the tunnel that was suffocating her.

Talissa wasn't experienced enough at sixteen to understand the power of fear. She was not afraid of meeting her grandparents and revealing who she was but she was afraid of being rejected by them. They rejected her even before she was born and Talissa didn't want to be rejected by those whose bloodline ran through her.

"The time isn't right," Talissa whispered under

her breath as she drove away from the Benson residence.

The house was quiet as Talissa walked down the long hollow hallway of the house she'd grown up in. This was usually the case when it was past nine o'clock at night. Her parents were in the habit of retiring to their modest-size bedroom at the same time every night.

The faint tapping at her bedroom door rattled Sylvia Croomes from her light sleep. Unlike her husband, Joseph, who had become accustomed to hearing noises that first night God blessed their childless lives with a beautiful baby girl, Sylvia was a light sleeper. The slightest noise would wake her. Talissa took a step backward and waited for her adoptive mother to open her bedroom door.

Out in the kitchen, Sylvia poured two glasses of warm milk while Talissa cut two slices of homemade apple pie. Just by looking at her daughter's face, Sylvia knew that something was weighing heavily on Talissa's heart.

Sylvia was a short woman with a medium frame. She was aging so gracefully that Sylvia looked to be in her thirties instead of her mid-fifties. Very little gray was peppered throughout her thick hair. It was so faint that only Sylvia and her hair stylist of thirty years knew where the gray strands were hiding.

It hurt Sylvia deeply that she was unable to protect her only child from growing pains and the evils of the world. She had tried to explain to Talissa that life could be unfair at times but with every experience comes a lesson. While Sylvia could never figure out how anyone could reject the miracle of a newborn life, she was forever thankful to her Lord in God for the gift of Talissa. It had taken Joseph and Sylvia four years of red tape before they were approved to become adoptive parents. After that it was another three years before they found a baby in need of their love. The Croomeses were introduced to Terry's parents by a fellow church member and were instantly willing to adopt the baby that their college daughter was carrying. The Bensons had made arrangements for the adoption even before discussing the issue with Terry.

"So, what's bothering you, baby? You look like you have the weight of the world on your shoulders." Sylvia spoke softly as she sat at the kitchen table next to her pride and joy.

"Mom, at the Urban League there are a lot of small kids at the day care who are being raised by single, struggling but hardworking mothers. Every time I'm there, I am amazed by the commitment those women have for their children."

"I don't understand why that's bothering you," said Sylvia.

"Well, some of these young girls are only a few years older than me. They're working two jobs just trying to provide for their babies. When they pick up the kids, each one looks exhausted from a hard day's work but they light up at the sight of their kids."

"And that makes you think about Terry and the situation surrounding your birth?"

"Yes, it does. From what I have learned about Terry, I am certain that she would have been one of those mothers. Working a job she hates, trying to go to school and living in low-income housing just to provide for her child." Talissa was about to cry but fought the tears from falling. "Don't get me wrong, Mom, because my life has been great with you and Dad. It's just that I have so many questions about my heritage, my relatives and especially my grandparents."

"If given the chance, I know Terry would have worked hard to provide for you. I don't know if Terry has told you the situation surrounding your birth, but Terry was not given a choice on whether to keep you or give you up for adoption. Terry was seventeen when you were born. Even though she was in college, her parents made all of the decisions for her. I know that God blessed our lives with yours but I do feel that Terry's parents were wrong for how they handled things."

"I went by their house today, Mom, but for the first time ever, I was scared to do what I went there to do." The tears fell down Talissa's cheeks like raindrops. Sylvia's heart sank and all she could do was hold her daughter and say a silent prayer.

"Talissa, all Mama can tell you is what I've always told you to do, simply follow your heart. Your heart will not lead you wrong."

"Yes, Mom."

Early the next morning Talissa made her way down Cohasset Street in search of the big yellow house. Her talk with Sylvia renewed her determination to meet Terry's parents and attempt to begin the healing process between parents and daughter.

Before leaving the house, Talissa took great pains in picking out the right outfit for the special occasion she'd hoped the day would turn out to be. The soft pink linen skirt outfit with mini–white pumps gave Talissa a look of innocence. She looked exactly like Terry did when she was sixteen.

I must have arrived right before breakfast, thought Talissa. The smell of grits and eggs made its way out the open screen door. After reciting a short prayer asking God for strength and the right words to say, Talissa knocked on the Bensons' front door.

Seconds later, Talissa found herself standing in front of a middle-aged woman whose skin tone and dark brown eyes mirrored her own. There was no mistaking that the pretty, medium-build woman before her was a blood relative. The two women, separated by only a foot of space between them stood frozen, neither speaking or blinking their eyes.

Instinctively, Cheryl Benson knew who the beautiful young lady at her front door was. How could she not? When Cheryl first looked at the child, she thought time had been turned back and she was looking at her daughter Terry.

Time stood still for the two as a warm breeze swept through the open screen door and windows causing the wind chimes to sing, breaking the silence.

"Good morning, Mrs. Benson. I don't mean to interrupt your breakfast, but my name is—No, I mean I'm here to—"

"I know who you are, child," said Cheryl Benson, without feeling.

Talissa was at a loss for words. She became embarrassed and her nerves were on end. The initial meeting wasn't going the way Talissa had dreamt last night. She expected her grandmother to hug her and say how great it was to finally meet her. Instead, the woman in front of her was cold and distant.

"So, I guess you have been in contact with Terry?"

"Yes, I have. We met by coincidence a few months ago," replied Talissa. She scanned the very proper-looking woman's face for any hint of emotion.

"You look exactly like her so it should have been obvious to the both of you at your initial meeting who you were. So, have you two bonded or was it just a onetime meeting?"

"We have been spending as much time together as possible. My adoptive parents told me about my being adopted at an early age and they have welcomed Terry into their home and our lives," explained Talissa. She could feel the coldness coming from the woman and it was making her uneasy.

"Well, how can I help you?"

"I just wanted to meet my grandparents and learn about my history. It is also my wish to reunite you with Terry."

Talissa wanted Cheryl Benson to open her arms and allow her to fall into them. In her dream, grandmother and grandchild embraced for what seemed like forever and once they let each other go, Cheryl began making up for time lost and not being able to spoil her only grandchild. She served Talissa homemade sausage, potatoes, scrambled eggs, and walnut waffles with orange juice on the side. This was not a dream and reality wasn't feeling too well. Talissa knew it was a mistake to come there.

"I don't know why you came here but I have no information to give you that you can't get from Terry. I am sorry you wasted your time by appearing on my doorstep unannounced, but if you'll excuse me, I have food burning on the stove."

Cheryl quickly turned away from Talissa as if she were a stranger on the streets and not her long-lost grandchild. Talissa's disappointment quickly turned to anger. Talissa followed her heart and was right behind Cheryl walking into the old-fashioned kitchen that was no bigger than a walk-in closet.

"Look, Mrs. Benson," Talissa's voice startled Cheryl as she turned to face her, "let me tell you something. I didn't come here to ask you for anything. My only intention was to meet my grandparents and try to reunite you with your daughter but as you said, I have wasted both of our time. I apologize for that and I'm also sorry that I am unfortunate enough to have inherited YOU for a blood relative." Talissa was livid and wanted to cuss the woman out from top to bottom but she was brought up better than that.

"My adoptive parents have taught me to respect my elders and they have also taught me that not everyone who claims to be a Christian is truly a child of God. I can tell by the hanging crosses, the pictures of Jesus, and your worn Bible that you consider yourself a believer. Well, while you're reading the Bible, don't skip over the parts about forgiveness and not judging others lest you be judged."

Cheryl Benson stood staring at Talissa with a blank stare. She was at a loss for words because she knew that the child was right but Cheryl's heart wouldn't allow her to reach out to Talissa.

As she walked back out the door in which she came, the sight of an old family portrait sat on the mantel. Terry and her parents looked happy and close at one time and Talissa wondered how they could love their child one day and turn their backs on her the next day. Talissa accepted the fact that she would never know the reason for Cheryl Benson's cold and empty heart and unwillingness to forgive.

Before pushing the screen door open, Talissa looked over her shoulder and saw Cheryl watching her.

"Don't worry, I ain't gon' steal nothing from you and I promise you will never be bothered by me again. My prayer for you is that God forgives you when you meet Him."

Talissa got into her car, turned on her music, and rode off up the street—she had to see Terry and give her a hug. Talissa's biggest fear was confirmed and her grandmother had rejected her for the second time in her life. At that moment Talissa promised herself to never become a cold, bitter person with no feeling.

Back in the Benson house, Cheryl stood over her kitchen sink watching Talissa drive off. Her husband, Joseph, appeared in the doorway and watched his wife of forty-two years. He had overheard the entire encounter and for the second time in their marriage, he realized that he didn't understand her at all.

It was Cheryl who insisted on Terry giving birth in Toledo instead of bringing her home to help her through the pregnancy. It was Cheryl who demanded Terry give the baby away and never speak of the child again. Cheryl would not have her stature and reputation in the church compromised because of her "loose daughter who couldn't keep her legs closed."

Cheryl had always ruled the roost and Joseph had always done as his wife had wanted. He stopped having opinions and thoughts of his own so long ago that he couldn't remember the last time he had an independent thought of his own. Many times in the past sixteen years Joseph wanted to call Terry or stop by her hair shop and see how she was doing but fear of his wife always stopped him. Today, seeing and hearing his grandchild for the first time sparked something inside of Joseph that he hadn't felt in so long he wasn't sure what it was.

"I heard how you spoke to that child just now," Joseph spoke to the back of his wife's head. "God forgive me but I never should have stood in the background and watched you ruin this family. No more, Cheryl, this time you have gone too far. That child you just turned away is a part of us, a part of me lives through her."

Cheryl turned to look at Joseph because she just *knew* he was not speaking to *her* with such a harsh tone. What she saw in his eyes stopped her from opening her mouth.

"You have kept me away from my only child for sixteen years and I take my ownership in that because you only did what I allowed you to do. No more! No more! I am going to my daughter and beg her to forgive me. I am going to know my grandchild with or without your support and if that means our marriage is over," Joseph straightened his back and held his chin high as he continued, "it won't be much of a loss."

Joseph grabbed his car keys and took off after his grandchild as fast as his worn legs would allow him. He had no idea how Terry and her daughter would receive him but Joseph knew that an attempt at reconciliation with them was way overdue.

"Dear Lord, please walk me through this and help me find the right words to say and carry me through to the end, amen."

As Joseph parked his car at the end of the driveway, he recognized the small SUV that had been parked outside of his house this morning. His stomach began doing turns as he made his way to the front door. Joseph rang the doorbell with Terry's name taped on it and waited patiently for someone to answer it. His heart raced with each passing second but Joseph was determined to see his daughter and make his peace. After what felt like an eternity, a voice came over the intercom.

"Yes, who is it?" asked Terry.

Joseph recognized his daughter's voice and searched for his own voice in order to respond.

"It's me, Terry. It is your father." The intercom became quiet and Joseph stood outside the security door praying that Terry would not turn him away before he was able to say what he'd come to say.

The steel door crept open slowly and Joseph held his breath. He focused his eyes on the ground until he saw a shadow come into view. Terry thought someone was playing games with her when the male voice said it was her father. The sight of him made her want to cry but she was strong, thanks to Talissa's hold on her hand.

Terry opened the door as far as she could and Joseph looked up and met two sets of eyes looking back at him—Terry and Talissa.

Frozen . . .

Silence . . .

Fear . . .

Forgiveness . . .

"Daddy!"

Love . . .

"Baby girls!"

New start . . .

The Big PayBack

Chapter 28

Figuring that his plan to bring down Bossy had worked out, Ant strove to relax. For the first couple of days after meeting with Powell and Meeks, he had been a nervous wreck. He'd only guessed about the information he gave them and wasn't sure if Twan was even making the runs to Florida anymore.

The longer Ant mulled over the situation he'd put himself in, his mother's dream and the money he still owed C-Lok, the more stressed he got. Hiding out at his mom's house for two days enabled him to do some chores for her. Ant even painted his mother's bedroom and living room. He hung wallpaper in the kitchen and rearranged furniture in every room of the three-bedroom house. He couldn't remember ever working so hard and knew he never wanted to work that hard again.

Atlantic City was Ant's next hideout. For three days he gambled, ate, drank, and slept. Ant had ten thousand with him when he left for Atlantic City and returned to the Yo' with thirty thousand more thanks to the blackjack tables. To help him relax, Ant didn't carry his cell phone with him. By the time he checked his messages, the mailbox was full. He knew instantly that the majority of the messages were from Shadaisy. He dialed her number first.

Shadaisy answered on the first ring. "Yeah."

"What up, girl? How you holding it down over there?" Ant had let the drug house on Warren Avenue slip his mind.

"I'm doin' what I do. Where you been that you can't call a bitch back?"

"Just takin' care of some shit. Anybody been lookin' for me?" Ant wanted to be sure that Powell, Meeks and C-Lok hadn't been tracking him down.

"Naw, ain't nobody come by here looking for you. I'm the only person tryin' to get with you as far as I know. Supplies are low, we gon' have to do something soon."

"I'll be through there in a few. You be ready for me, I'm overdue." A huge smile covered Ant's face when he ended the call. He was anticipating seeing Shadaisy laid out on the couch, half naked, ready to do whatever she had to do to please him.

When Shadaisy hung up from their conversation, she wanted to throw up. She couldn't stand for Ant to touch her, kiss on her, or be inside of her. Shadaisy was simply doing what she had to do in order to keep a roof over her head and live rent and utility free. To her, she was getting over, and all she had to do was give up some ass and give some head every few months. Even pimps had to ho sometimes, right?

Since seeing for herself how Twan took care of

his girl, Shadaisy knew it was time for her to find a baller higher up on the food chain. Ant was in no position to buy her a hooptie let alone a 2005 Lexus. The house Ant had her living in actually belonged to Twan.

She heard on the street that Ant and Twan had a riff in their friendship. Where before, Shadaisy couldn't have been paid to take from them, now that Twan had severed ties with Ant's ugly ass, she was going for hers. She had skimmed off some of the drugs and money for herself. To her, life had been hard, cruel, and cold but the free money and drugs were going to change things, and fast.

After showering and preparing for Ant, it was time to roll a blunt and make a stiff drink. The only way she could stand being intimate with Ant was to be as high as possible. Shadaisy decided to roll a primo for Ant. She also poured him a glass of whiskey laced with crushed Percocets. She was determined to get this date over with as soon as possible, maybe even stop it before it began. Shadaisy decided tonight would be her last encounter with Ant. After he passed out, she would rob him for whatever he had on him and begin her search for a "real" hustler.

Ant parked his car behind the house and walked in the back door. As expected, Shadaisy lay on the couch in a matching bra and panty set, two drinks on the table and two blunts in the ashtray.

"You ready to get with this, girl?" Ant sat next to Shadaisy and began running his ashy hand down her leg.

"Of course, but let's enjoy our drinks and smoke a little before we get started," Shadaisy stalled. "You know, to help relax you. It sounded like you've had a stressful week."

"Good idea; let's start this party."

Ant took a toke on the blunt and gulped down the laced drink Shadaisy had prepared for him. As the blunt and drink began to take effect, Ant's body relaxed and he fought the urge to lie back on the couch and drift off to sleep. Shadaisy sat watching Ant before slipping out the room to put on a pair of jeans and a shirt. She walked back into the room and found that Ant was no longer alone.

"What's going on in here? Looks like I'm interrupting a little party." Ant opened his eyes to find Twan standing before him. They hadn't spoken since the block party and Ant figured he had come by to collect his half of the money they owed C-Lok. Ant attempted to acknowledge Twan but found himself unable to speak.

"What's wrong with you? You send the police after me and you can't even open up ya mouth to speak to me? Ain't that some shit." Twan baited Ant.

"Don't pay him no mind, Twan, he's high as hell and probably don't even know where he is," explained Shadaisy before asking. "What you mean Ant sent the police after you? I know damn well he ain't do no foul shit like that."

"Ant ain't tell you that he made a deal with the devil? He sent Powell and Meeks to Bossy's looking for my shit."

"Naw, Ant is capable of a lot of shit but not that," Shadaisy said.

"He was pulled over on a traffic stop by Powell and Meeks and let go. He was caught trying to rip off the money from the block party and again Powell and Meeks let his punk ass go. After half of her life in the game, Bossy's house is searched out of the blue? It don't take a scientist to figure that shit out. They just happened to show up at her door the same time I would've been dropping a shipment off from Florida? Something told me to rearrange my schedule until I found out who my enemies were. Ant's a straight-up bitch," fumed Twan.

Shadaisy was shocked at what she was hearing but it all made sense. "That's why he was missing the last two weeks. He was hiding out." She immediately turned on her heels and began gathering up her shit. Getting out of the house was in her best interest. If what Twan said was true, Powell and Meeks would be looking for Ant because they came up empty in their search. Since Twan's arrival and revelations, Shadaisy decided to abandon her plan to grab the money and drugs left in the house. She knew that it would be like stealing from Twan. Shadaisy made a beeline for the door, leaving Twan to watch her smoke.

The proper-sounding, African-American news reporter, Tiffany Patterson, notified viewers of breaking news from the city's south side.

"The police are investigating the discovery of a dead body while answering a call to look into possible suspicious activity at a suspected drug house on Warren Avenue. No name has been released at this time. We'll have additional information as it becomes available."

At the scene . . .

Officers Powell and Meeks were responding to a call of reported gunshots when they discovered the gruesome scene. Minutes later, the crime scene unit was lifting prints, taking pictures, and bagging items for evidence.

"Whoever did this guy hated him and was out for revenge or was sending a message," said the newest member of the crime scene unit team.

Officer Powell stood in the corner of the room with a full view of the victim when his sergeant walked up beside him.

"What do you think, Powell?"

"Someone was determined to send a message here, sir."

"Do you think this was a professional hit?" inquired Sergeant Collins.

"With him being stripped naked, it does resemble a professional killing. But the single gunshot to each knee isn't the mark of a hired hit. With his tongue being cut out and his testicles placed in his hand, I'd say this was personal, very personal."

"Have we identified him yet?"

"Yes, he's well-known by the narcotics division. They have been trying to get him for months now. His name is Anthonie 'Ant' Quarles."

Bossy had already received word of the murder before it ran on the evening news. Things like that flowed through Youngstown like a cascading waterfall. Bossy tried to understand why she had no feelings one way or another about her hand in Ant's death. Years ago, she'd vowed to never be responsible for the death of another human being. As she thought about everything that had taken place, she reasoned that Ant had left her no other choice.

Bossy hadn't heard from Big Black since he left late last night. He said he was headed for the club but he should have come back by now. *With Ant dead, I can breathe again. When Big Black comes home I'll take a deep breath.*

Drugs, Money and Death in the Yo'

Chapter 29

Officer Meeks maneuvered his twelve-year-old Cutlass down the eerie streets toward his destination. Sharon, Pennsylvania was close to his family home of Hubbard, Ohio but traveling during the wee hours of the morning made the short ride feel more like a weeklong road trip. His partner, Officer Powell, had dozed off five minutes into the drive but sprang to life when he felt the car come to a stop. Both men were anxious to get this visit over with. Just the thought of all the money they had coming to them was burning a hole through their pockets.

"We're here, man; let's get that money," said Meeks.

"Our big payday has finally arrived. Remember, we can't trust this man, no matter what he's paying us for that kill. We need to quickly gain control of the meeting, get our money, and leave," directed Officer Powell.

"We're on the same page, partner. Let's get this shit over with." Officer Meeks lead the way up the cement steps. His dick was getting hard thinking of how many zeros he would finally have. "All that robbing and thieving has finally paid off."

C-Lok opened the door and welcomed his visitors.

"Have a seat, gentlemen, you're right on time. Let's get right down to business," directed C-Lok.

"Before we do, don't you want to introduce your friend?" asked Meeks.

"This is my good friend, Big Black," said C-Lok. "Big Black, meet two of Youngstown's finest, Officers Powell and Meeks. Can you believe they sought me out after Teddy Bear died?" C-Lok and Big Black laughed in unison.

"What they want from you? Protection?" joked Big Black as if the two cops weren't sitting next to him. The two laughed before C-Lok replied, "Naw, they wanted me to pay them for protection. Ain't that a bitch?"

Big Black and C-Lok stared blankly at Powell and Meeks, signaling playtime was over.

"He cool?" Powell wanted to know.

"This is the only person on earth that I trust with my life. Now, word has gotten back that the job was taken care of. It even made the news."

"It went very well. When we found Ant, he was high as the sky but came down fast at the sight of a weapon in his face. He begged, pleaded, and cried like a bitch in labor before he took his last breath." Meeks bragged a little too much for Big Black's taste.

"Another job well done. I trust the weapon has been disposed of properly," inquired C-Lok.

"Absolutely, this will go unsolved, as usual," Powell guaranteed.

"Here's your fee of one hundred thousand dollars each, plus another fifty-thousand dollars bonus to split between you. I'll be in touch if your services are required in the future." Normally, C-Lok would see his hired hands to the door but he had other plans for Powell and Meeks today.

C-Lok had heard about the problems Bossy was having with Ant from Twan before she'd told him. After Ant disrespected Bossy the second time, C-Lok's plan to punish him was underway. Ant's jealousy of Twan made him an easy mark. C-Lok knew it wouldn't take much on Powell and Meeks's part to persuade Ant to work with them. The only problem was when Bossy contacted Big Black. C-Lok knew that he would have to bring his longtime friend in on the plan he already had in the works. If they ended up stepping on each other toes, everything would fall apart.

The day Bossy went to C-Lok about Ant and the police, Big Black knew that C-Lok would watch his back by not telling Bossy of their partnership.

Now, here the two old friends sat together as partners for the first time in almost twelve years. The only difference was the company they were in. C-Lok and Big Black both knew that given the chance, the two crooked officers would take them out. That shit wasn't going down like that.

When Officer Powell approached C-Lok about providing protection for him, C-Lok turned him down flat.

"Naw, I'm straight on that but we may be able to work together," said C-Lok.

Officer Powell was instantly intrigued and sat down to discuss business with the powerful gangster.

"Your first assignment is to get this bitch-ass nigga Ant under ya spell. Back him as far into a corner as his dumb ass can fit. Next, get my product back from his ass."

Officer Powell knew better than to ask any questions, plus the amount of money C-Lok was offering was far too much to pass up on. The deal was made but Officers Powell and Meeks tried to backstab C-Lok by serving that fake warrant on Bossy.

There was a light tap at C-Lok's office door and the room turned quiet.

"Who else are you expecting?" Officer Powell started feeling uneasy.

"Chill, nigga," replied Big Black, "we got this."

The door opened to reveal Bossy and Twan standing outside the door. C-Lok had summoned them both to join the meeting. It was time to put the entire episode to an end.

"What's going on here? What are they doing here?" Meeks stuttered.

"Just like you, they are here by my invitation."

Bossy and Twan walked in the room and ignored the two officers. Big Black rose from his seat, allowing Bossy to take his place while Twan stood to the left of C-Lok.

"This room is a bit small for a group of this size, why don't we go into what I like to call 'the man's room'?"

Powell and Meeks looked at each other, both expecting the other to get out of the invitation. Finally, Powell found his voice.

"No thanks, man, we have to get back to the station."

C-Lok stepped around his desk and stood over the crooked officers and replied, "It wasn't a suggestion; it is what we are ALL going to do."

Bossy followed behind C-Lok with that sway in her hips that drove men crazy. With Twan right behind her and Big Black bringing up the rear behind Powell and Meeks, Bossy knew she was safe.

In the soundproof basement four large-framed employees of C-Lok's waited in the shadows. Hiring the officers was a means to an end for C-Lok and Big Black but they never figured that the men would double-cross two of the most infamous gangsters in Youngstown's history. Trying to strong-arm Bossy was not part of the plan and Officers Powell and Meeks had finally fucked over the wrong man.

"Bossy, come over here so Big Black and me can clear a few things up with you," requested C-Lok.

Bossy asked no questions and did as she was told. She had no idea what C-Lok had summoned her and Twan for but upon seeing Powell and Meeks, Bossy pretty much knew the day she was dreading was finally here.

"Baby, we have somethings to tell you and I want you to hear us both out before you say anything," instructed C-Lok.

Bossy remained quiet and shook her head in agreement.

Big Black went first. "Bossy, back when our boy Poppy was killed, the retaliation that happened as a result is what brings us here today." Bossy didn't understand where this was going but she continued to listen. "Me and C-Lok were in charge of taking care of you at the time and allowing you to pull that trigger meant that we failed. At least in Devin's eyes we did." Big Black took a deep breath before continuing on. "See, the two of us didn't know what to do in order to protect you so we paid your brother a visit in prison and to say he was pissed would be an understatement. Devin wanted to kill us both for allowing you to roll the way we did back then."

"He's right, Devin was pissed and if he hadn't already been behind bars, he would be now for our murders," explained C-Lok further. "When we left the prison that day, Devin demanded that we find a way to protect you. So we did."

"Bossy, twelve years ago when I left here, it wasn't to relocate down south. At least not the way you think. Based on our plan, I was shipped off to a federal prison to do a ten-year bid for the killings in the park that night."

Bossy couldn't believe what she was hearing. There was no way Big Black served a dime without her knowing. She'd sent him cards, money, and packages over the years. They had talked on the phone once a month and his calls never originated from any prison. Bossy stood bewildered.

"Don't get me wrong, I did do a dime but it wasn't hard time. With Teddy Bear's help, a federal prosecutor and a judge willing to receive monthly payments for his services, my time was served in a minimum security prison. I was allowed to work an outside job as long as I kept my nose clean. That's what I did."

"But how? Why would you do that?" questioned Bossy.

"Baby, I asked you to hear us out," C-Lok reminded Bossy. "Now it's my turn to confess. After we broke up and you refused to accept any help from me, I had to find a way to keep you safe and taken care of. It wasn't Teddy Bear who bought your apartment building and the shop. I gave him the money and had him make the business transaction. It was the only way I could think of that you would accept what was being done for you. I knew that you would feel obligated to me back then if you knew the truth."

"Why are y'all confessing all of this now? I mean, I'm grateful to you both for the sacrifices y'all made for me but after all this time, why tell me this now?"

Twan took a step forward and knew that was his cue to come clean on his part on what was going down.

"Bossy, that day I found out what Ant had done to Aisha and him getting in bed with them two bitch-made niggas over in the corner," Twan pointed at Powell and Meeks, "I felt guilty for introducing Ant into your life. We had just copped a huge shipment from C-Lok and the only way I could see putting a stop to Ant's stupidity, was to come out here and have a sit-down with him. That's when I found out about Big Black and C-Lok's plan to protect you at any cost."

"Yeah, Twan got heart, Bossy. He's a gangsta from the womb," said Big Black.

"So, Big Black, it wasn't you that took care of Ant?" questioned Bossy.

"It's not important who did it. All that matters is that the matter was handled," barked C-Lok.

"But what about them two over there?" Bossy wanted to put all of the puzzle pieces together.

"Originally, they were part of the plan to take care of Ant but then they made the fatal mistake of coming to your doorstep. For that, they will pay dearly," explained C-Lok.

The bodyguards had since bound and hog-tied Powell and Meeks. All that was left to do was put the two men out of their misery. The only dilemma now was which one of the three men who'd already sacrificed so much for Bossy would end the life of two police officers.

Bossy looked C-Lok in his eyes and could still see how much he was in love with her. Big Black had always been her protector but Bossy had no idea to what extent. Bossy was proud of Twan because he had been listening to her teachings. Her day had come and Bossy felt it deep inside. It was time for her to thank those who'd always protected and loved her.

Reaching behind her back, Bossy gripped her pearl-handled gun and announced, "I got this." As she walked toward the dark corner where her potential victims laid in wait, Bossy felt a strong hand on her right shoulder, stopping her in her tracks.

"No, you don't got this. I'll take care of it. Bossy, you go home."

Bossy put her gun back in place and turned to do as she was told. She knew better than argue or disagree with the man. Slowly, Bossy climbed the stairs and closed the thick door behind her knowing that no matter what, she would always be protected.

About an hour later . . .

"If only Bossy knew how much you've been looking out for her over the years, she would consider being ya wifey," Big Black said as he flashed a smile.

"She would never have it. Bossy was reluctant to get off these streets and learn a different way to hustle. She has to be independent and I need to be a provider. We just aren't meant to be. When we left that prison that day, I didn't know what we were going to do." C-Lok turned to look out his bay window and light a stogie to gather his thoughts. "When the apartment came up for sale it was a lifesaver. Bossy and her girls would always have a roof over their heads, and Devin's wishes came true. We protected his sister."

"We can never let it get out Teddy Bear paid me one million a year for taking that bid for Bossy," confessed Big Black.

"How can one woman have so many men putting their lives down like this? You did a bid for Bossy. Teddy Bear molded his game and lived his life for Bossy. And I . . . well . . ."

"And you love from a distance. What a man won't do for love," stated Big Black.

"Correction," C-Lok stated, "what a man won't do for Bossy."

And For My Final Act . . .

Chapter 30

Twan walked through Southern Park Mall in search of some new gear for the Mary J. Blige concert in Cleveland. Since breaking it off with LaJetia's crazy ass, Twan had been spending more and more time with Yvonne. They began talking as friends after Yvonne put Twan on to the fact that LaJetia had been calling all of his female acquaintances and making threats. Hooking up with Yvonne was like relocating from Alaska to Florida. Twan felt good about life for the first time ever. Bossy was safe, his debt with C-Lok was taken care of, and Terry was working on a business plan for a new barbershop. It would be built across the street from the new KAT69 Hair, Nails, and Day Spa and would be open seven days a week. Twan was the only investor and he too would be able to go legit with Terry's business savvy and his hustle mentality behind the project.

The only dark spot in Twan's life was not seeing the kids every day. Twan called every morning to speak with Kiara and Tyler but LaJetia made that feel like a street fight. As far as Twan was concerned, after the way LaJetia had shown her ass at Ant's funeral, keeping as much physical distance as possible between them was the best way for him to remain a free man. Twan knew if he were to see LaJetia any time soon, he would strangle the life out of her.

LaJetia had no one to blame but herself for Twan's distance from his family. It had been two weeks since Ant's body was found tortured and one week since the funeral. Unfortunately for LaJetia, it had also been that long since she and the kids had seen Twan. Her only hope of catching a glance of the man she loved was to make an appearance at Ant's funeral.

Twan disregarded the riff between him and his childhood friend because he knew Ms. Quarles was left alone. The history between Twan and Ant meant something to Twan and in the end, it was important for Twan to do the right thing. As most young men who die before their time, Ant had no life insurance to pay for his burial and neither did his mother. Twan saw to it that Ant had a proper burial and Ms. Quarles's needs were taken care of.

The service was simple, respectful, and quiet. That is, until LaJetia made her presence known. She walked into Mason's Funeral Home and immediately scanned the quiet room for Twan. Never one to sit with his back to a door or window, Twan's seat offered a full view of the mourners paying their respects. Twan saw LaJetia before she found him in the crowded room.

Twan jumped up from his seat and immediately confronted the woman he once loved.

"What are you doing here, LaJetia?" Twan had approached LaJetia so fast it startled her. Getting no response, Twan spoke again. "I asked you a question and I'm waiting for an answer."

"I just wanted to pay my respects to his mother and make sure you were okay," LaJetia half lied. As far as LaJetia was concerned, Ant could burn in hell with gas-soaked draws on.

"You and Ant never got along so I don't believe one word coming out of your mouth."

"You're right, Twan. I'm here because I just needed to see you. You won't answer my calls and you don't even come see the kids. Knowing how much you love them, I was just worried about you."

"This is not the time nor place to discuss this—"

"Twan, I just want to say I'm sorry. I miss you and the kids miss you," interrupted LaJetia.

"As I was saying," Twan was past annoyed, "stay as far away from me as possible. Your crazy ass could have killed somebody by throwing that brick through that window. But, I'm sure you don't see it that way."

LaJetia's heart began beating fast as she watched Twan turn his back on her and walk away. *I can't lose him, I can't live without him.*

Twan made it back to his seat just as the casket was being closed, signaling the start of the funeral services. Before he was seated comfortably, it happened.

"Antwan Glover! If you think you can just walk away from me, you got another thing coming. You hear me, Twan? I ain't goin' nowhere and if that bitch Bossy thinks she can have you, I got something for both y'all simple asses."

The room grew still and a pin could be heard hitting the floor if it weren't for LaJetia's yelling. Twan was pissed, embarrassed, and mortified. It took all he had inside of him to refrain from pulling his gun out and killing her crazy ass. Before any more drama and disrespect could erupt, two of Twan's runners dragged LaJetia out the building. The services began right after LaJetia was removed, kicking and screaming.

Two hours later, the burial was closed with a prayer and Twan escorted Ms. Quarles to the limousine. After the car pulled off, Twan spoke to a few stragglers and made his way to his truck. Twan hit the button on his keyless entry to unlock the doors of his Envoy. Just as the double chirps sounded, Twan noticed the scratches on his prized possession.

"No the fuck this bitch didn't!" Twan could not believe his eyes. The sun was not shining when he left the funeral home so he failed to see the evidence of vandalism to his truck. The pearl 2005 Envoy had been depreciated by thousands and so had any feelings Twan had left inside him for LaJetia. She had finally pushed him over that thin line between love and hate.

Twan was having no luck finding the right gear in the mall so he decided to hit up one of the hip-hop stores in the hood. He headed for the food court before leaving and spotted Bossy and Aisha at a table eating steak sandwiches.

"What's up, ladies? Y'all all right?"

"Hey, Twan. What got you out here in the mall?" asked Aisha.

"Trying to find something for this concert tomorrow night. I can't have my girl Mary J. in Ohio without seeing her."

"You going to the concert too? Me, Bossy, and Terry are taking Talissa to the concert. She is leaving for a visit to Howard University soon so as a treat we reserved a skybox and set up some VIP treatment. Why don't you come with us?" invited Aisha.

"Well, thanks for the invitation but I'm taking Yvonne up there with me," said Twan, blushing.

"Who?" Bossy and Aisha asked in unison. They were prepared to pounce on Twan if he answered wrong.

"Not that crazy bitch," responded Twan. It was obvious by the looks on their faces they thought LaJetia was the broad in question. "Come on now. Give a brotha a little credit. I wouldn't touch that with a fifty-foot pole."

"As long as it's not LaJetia, the invitation is still open," said Bossy.

"Yeah, chilling in a skybox will be on point. We will meet y'all there at eight if that's cool?" inquired Twan.

The three friends sat and talked for another half hour before heading out the mall. "Damn—women can do some damage in a mall," complained Twan as he struggled to help Bossy and Aisha with their bags. "What is in all of these bags?"

"Going away gifts for our goddaughter, of course," bragged Aisha.

It was just one week before Talissa was scheduled to start her college tour. With Terry's support, Talissa had decided to attend a historically black university. Howard University topped her list because it was close enough to home for comfort and still far enough for Talissa to spread her wings. Bossy, Aisha, and Mama Bev had offered to pay for an apartment close to campus but Mr. and Mrs. Croomes protested. Anyway, freshmen had to live on campus.

During an intimate dinner, held at Mama Bev's house, everyone had gathered to celebrate Talissa's going off to college. It was during dinner that Mrs. Croomes explained her reasons for putting her foot down on the idea of Talissa living in an apartment.

"I thank God every day that each of you has opened your hearts, homes, and wallets to our baby. We have watched Talissa grow and blossom since discovering her history. From day one, Bossy, Aisha, and Terry have spoiled this child with everything up under the good Lord's sun. Bev even got in on spoiling this child rotten."

Bossy, Aisha, and Terry all smiled while Joseph shook his head in protest of any further spoiling. "As Talissa's parents, we have to put our foot down and it's past time. You all are picking up any slack the academic scholarship doesn't cover and that is enough. We thank you for your generosity but Talissa, like most other college freshmen, will be fine in a dorm room."

Aisha opened her mouth to protest but Mama Bev threw her a look that let her know to shut the hell up. She simply replied, "Yes, ma'am, you're right. Between the shopping trips, vacation and the car, I guess we have gone a little overboard."

The dinner guests all laughed, agreed that

Talissa would spend her freshman year in a dorm room and enjoyed the rest of the evening surrounded by loved ones.

Now with one week to go, Bossy and Aisha were at Southern Park Mall picking up a new fall and winter wardrobe for Talissa. They reasoned that Talissa may have to live in a dorm room but she was going to be the best-dressed student on campus. Freshman or not.

The bright sun was blinding as Bossy, Aisha, and Twan exited the mall. Unable to block the rays with their hands, the three stood just outside the mall doors while Aisha and Terry searched several bags for the new Fossil sunglasses they had just purchased. Twan waited patiently for the women to find what they were looking for and tried to make small talk to pass time.

"Y'all got me out here sweating under this hot-ass sun and I'm too cool for that," complained Twan.

"Then chill ya' cool ass out. We got four more bags to go," laughed Bossy.

The glasses were hard to find because neither Bossy or Aisha could remember what store they had bought them from. Five more minutes passed before Aisha finally found their new shades. As the trio struggled with the bags and searched for their cars, they had no idea their every move was being watched. By the time they saw danger coming, it was too late.

"Twan! Watch out!" screamed Bossy.

The car seemed to come out of nowhere and was speeding toward them. The closer it got, the slower time seemed to move. It was like they were costarring in a movie with the driver of the car gunning for them.

"Twan!" Bossy and Aisha screamed. More screams were heard coming from mall shoppers witnessing the out-of- control vehicle headed toward a potential disaster.

Twan turned around in time to see the five-thousand-pound weapon gunning for him. It was too late to run, no time to move and no voice to scream. Just darkness followed by nothing.

STRANGER IN THE MIRROR

CHAPTER 31

Bossy was sitting on her couch with a drink in one hand and a joint in the other. The apartment was dark, quiet and lonely, which matched the way Bossy was feeling inside. She allowed tears to fall from her eyes for the second time in over twenty years. Bossy recalled all the pain she had felt in her life and all the loved ones she'd had taken from her. The pain and guilt she lived with had become overwhelming since the day Twan was snatched from her life.

The tears fell like rain for what seemed like hours. Bossy held knees close to her chest attempting to ease the pain that had been building since childhood. For the first time since her brother was led off to prison, Bossy felt vulnerable. The pain had been a part of her for so long she didn't know if she would be able to let it go.

Bossy wanted nothing more than to turn back the hands of time. Back to when Devin still had his freedom, to before Poppy lost his life, before she took her first life. The need to speak with Teddy

Bear was overwhelming and Bossy never realized how much he meant to her until he died. Teddy Bear had looked out for Bossy when her own mother left her for dead. He had been her father figure and her friend.

The afternoon at the mall had begun as such a fun and carefree time that Bossy had let her guard down. She was blaming herself for being off her game and not paying attention to what was going on around her. Bossy felt that if she had just been cautious about her surroundings, she would have spotted LaJetia before LaJetia spotted her. If she had just looked over her shoulder to make sure no one was watching her, Twan would still be alive. The guilt was so strong that Bossy feared sleep. Bossy was having a recurring dream about Twan.

In her dream, Bossy is a teenager again and Twan a little boy. They are at a playground playing on a swing set. Bossy is pushing Twan as high as the swing will allow until Twan's grip slips and he begins to fall off the swing. Bossy runs to catch him and break his fall but she always wakes up before the dream reveals if she gets to Twan on time.

Bossy doesn't move when she hears Aisha and Terry whisper her name. They have been practically camping out in Bossy's apartment for almost a month. It had been that long since Twan lay in Bossy's arms dying from the car's impact.

"Bossy, it's us. Are you okay?" Aisha speaks gently.

"Come on, Bossy, it's time for you to try and eat something," says Terry.

"Thank you both for being here, but I'm not hungry," answered Bossy.

Aisha and Terry have been afraid to leave Bossy alone for any significant amount of time. In the twenty-three years of their friendship, Aisha and Terry have never seen Bossy depressed. She had always been the strong one, the friend with the dominant personality, the daredevil of the group. Bossy was their rock and support system. Seeing Bossy in her current state hurt Aisha and Terry. They felt helpless and unable to reach Bossy. Neither was sure if they were doing and saying the right things.

"I'm sorry, Bossy, but you have to eat something. We just picked you up a salad and you don't have to eat the whole thing, but try to put a little in your system. Not eating is doing more harm than good," pleaded Aisha.

Bossy conceded and joined her friends at the dining room table. Terry turned on the ceiling light, revealing Bossy's red, swollen eyes and traces of recent tears. The sight caused Terry to begin crying herself.

Aisha could not take any more. She rose from her seat and walked down the long hallway to Bossy's bedroom. *I've put this off long enough. I know one person that can get through to her,* Aisha thought to herself. After a brief conversation on the phone, Aisha returned to her seat at the dining room table. Twenty minutes later the buzzer sounded, startling all three women.

"Who could that be?" asked Terry.

"I'm not in the mood for company. I don't care who it is, just get rid of 'em," said Bossy.

Aisha did not say a word as she headed toward the door. She stepped aside for Mama Bev to enter the apartment.

"Where is she, baby?"

"She just walked back to her bedroom," answered Aisha. "Mama, we have done everything we could think of to help her through this but it seems like Bossy is falling deeper and deeper into a depression. We just can't seem to find the right words to reach her."

"It's okay, baby, Mama's here and I'll get through to her," Mama Bev reassured Aisha and Terry. "You two go on upstairs to your apartment and give me and Bossy some time alone. Everything will be okay."

Aisha and Terry gave Mama Bev a hug, said thank you, and did as they were told. After seeing them out, Mama Bev made her way down the empty hallway in search of Bossy. Mama Bev reached the bedroom and found the door locked. She tapped lightly as not to startle her. She waited a few seconds, waiting for an invitation to enter. When none came, Mama Bev knocked a little harder and spoke through the door.

"Bossy, it's Mama Bev, can I come in?" A few seconds went by and still no response. With her patience wearing thin, Mama Bev decided to drop the sympathetic persona and be herself.

"Kayla Marie Tucker, open this door up before I get pissed."

Bossy did as she was told and unlocked her bedroom door. It had been so long since anybody called her by her government name that she had almost forgotten it herself. The only person who still called her Kayla was her brother Devin. Bossy had been so down about Twan that she had avoided her brother's last two phone calls.

The bedroom color scheme was earth tones with modern furniture and African-inspired art. Bossy's four-poster king-size bed was made out of a material Mama Bev was not familiar with. She made a mental note to ask about it at a more appropriate time. Right now, Bossy's mental health was the only issue at hand.

"Bossy, talk to Mama Bev and tell me how we can help you."

Bossy opened her mouth to tell her surrogate mother how to help her ease the pain inside of her but all she could do was fall into her arms and cry. Mama Bev held Bossy, stroked her back, and gave her permission to cry until the last tear was out. A half hour passed before Bossy was able to compose herself.

"Twan was my responsibility and I failed him. He was like a little brother to me and I just wanted to do right by him but I ended up letting him down just like my big brother let me down," cried Bossy.

"Now, you have not failed anyone and you do not owe anyone anything."

"But I do. Teddy Bear looked out for me when my own mother wouldn't. You have done more for me than my own blood relatives would do and I just wanted to do the same for Twan. His mother turned her back on Twan just like my mother turned her back on me. That's why Twan was so important to me. I didn't look out for him the way I should have and now his son has to grow up without a father."

"Bossy, you did look out for Twan and you took good care of him but that grown man was not your responsibility. Now, Twan in no way deserved what that nut job did to him, so don't get me wrong, but he made his own choices in life. You didn't always agree with the things Twan did just like I don't always agree with the things you girls do. But I know for a fact that when you saw Twan making bad choices, you sat him down and tried to get him to see a different way."

"Yes ma'am, I did, but Twan wouldn't always listen to me," cried Bossy.

"And you girls don't always listen to me. Twan was no different than any of us. Sometimes the best lessons in life are those we learn by going through the rough times. We learn more from our own mistakes than we'll ever learn from somebody else's mistakes."

Bossy decided to open up completely and explain to Mama Bev how much pain and resentment she held in her heart.

"I've never told anyone this but I blame myself for Devin being in prison. If it weren't for me, he never would have been in on robbing that store. Devin was just trying to put food on the table and buy me school clothes. That's why he did what he did."

"No it isn't, Bossy. Devin and them other boys robbed that store because they, not you, chose to. Robbing that store was not Devin's only option to get what he wanted. Devin robbed that store because he believed they could get away with it. He took a gamble and lost," Mama Bev explained. She tried to hide the anger rising inside her but it was difficult. Mama Bev felt that Devin had been putting Bossy through recurring guilt trips since his arrest. He'd made Bossy feel responsible for him and Mama Bev resented it.

Mama Bev watched for Bossy's reaction to her words and it was obvious that her words were getting through. Before continuing on, Mama Bev considered her words carefully as not to offend Bossy. For years she had watched Bossy play Russian roulette with her freedom and life. Mama Bev had tried multiple times to talk Bossy into changing the way she lived. Experience had long taught her that a person will not make changes until they are ready to do so and Mama Bev believed Bossy's time for change had finally come. Mama Bev felt it was time to open Bossy's eyes to the true effect Teddy Bear had on her life.

"As far as Teddy Bear is concerned, he wasn't right either. Bossy . . . think about the things he introduced you to. I mean really think about them." Mama Bev paused for effect. "Teddy Bear wasn't taking care of you back then; he was taking advantage of you. He used you to carry his drugs and run his money, to help his own cause. See, if you ran his drugs, he wouldn't be caught with them. Teddy Bear took advantage of a young girl who was raising herself and didn't know where her next meal was coming from. If Teddy Bear truly cared about you back then, he would have made sure you went to school. He would have sent you to college instead of on drug runs. If that man truly had your best interests at heart, he would have encouraged you to want more out of life than the life he knew."

"I never thought of it that way but you have a good point. Teddy Bear taught me everything I know about hustling and surviving the streets," admitted Bossy with a new level of awareness in her voice. "He kept me locked in that narrow and violent world, to serve his own purpose."

Mama Bev had given Bossy a new pair of glasses to see through, ones not shadowed by guilt or obligation. Bossy could feel her heart mending and her mind clearing of all the hurt and guilt she'd been carrying around for half of her life. For the first time since Twan lay dead in her arms, Bossy felt relieved.

"Thank you for coming to see about me, Mama Bev. Aisha and Terry must have been really worried about me for them to put an emergency call out to you," said Bossy, smiling.

"You know those two love you unconditionally. They were very concerned about you and were becoming discouraged because they couldn't seem to reach you. But I knew you just needed some time to mourn. Not just for Twan but for all the loss you've had in life."

"You're right, I did, but I guess I mourned a little too long for the wrong people," stated Bossy.

"What do you mean?"

"I was mourning, Devin, Teddy Bear, my mother and Twan when all along the person I should have been mourning was me."

"Mama Bev doesn't understand what you mean by that. Why should you have been mourning for yourself?"

"Because, my mother, my brother and Teddy Bear killed the person I could have become when they decided to make life choices for me. I was only a child and they all took advantage of me by deciding how I would live my life. Aren't parents suppose to want more for their child than they had?"

By looking into her eyes, Mama Bev could see Bossy's heart changing with her new realizations. However, she hadn't meant for their conversation to introduce more negativity into Bossy's life.

"Yes, they did, baby, but what's done is done and you have no control over the past. What you do have control over is where your future takes you."

Mama Bev reached out and held Bossy in her arms. It broke her heart that she wasn't able to protect Bossy, Aisha and Terry from the cruelties in the world. She just prayed that Bossy knew how much she meant to her and that Bossy would have the strength to walk away from the life she'd been living for too long.

Fifteen minutes later, Bossy walked Mama Bev to the door and thanked her for all the love she'd shown her over the years. Bossy promised Mama Bev she'd be okay and said good-bye.

Bossy had been given a different perspective on her life thanks to Mama Bev's wise words. As Bossy continued to reflect on the impact others had on her life, the hurt and guilt she felt was quickly turning into hate and anger. She was not yet able to forgive and let go and so, pouring herself another drink, Bossy sat down at her dining room table, becoming familiar with the growing resentment in her heart for those who had once claimed to love her, but eventually let her down.

Ghetto Laws and Inner-City Order

Chapter 32

The sun was shining brightly through the window, blinding Bossy's view of the passing cars. It had been one year since Twan was killed and Bossy had gained a new outlook on life. Many things had changed for Bossy and the biggest would be arriving soon. Bossy knew this day was quickly approaching but now that it had arrived, she couldn't believe it. Looking around her apartment was proof enough of the swift passage of time.

Aisha and Terry had taken care of every detail to make the day a memorable one. The decorations were simple yet festive. Mama Bev had prepared every variety of food she could think of and the bar was fully stocked. The guest of honor would be arriving within the hour. After twenty-six years behind bars, Devin was coming home.

C-Lok had arranged for Devin to be picked up from Mansfield Correctional Institution by a stretch limo complete with champagne and three paid escorts. Devin would be greeted by a surprise welcome-home party, an apartment, a new car and a job. Bossy had even gone shopping for her brother and bought him enough outfits to fill his closet.

It took some convincing but Bossy had talked C-Lok into throwing Devin a small celebration with close friends instead of the huge party he had in mind. Bossy reminded C-Lok that a lot of people had fallen off the radar in the past twenty-six years.

"C-Lok, do you know how many people left my brother for dead? Besides the two of us, Aisha, Terry, Mama Bev, and Big Black, ain't nobody else visited Devin, sent him a letter or accepted a collect phone call. Besides, most of the people Devin ran with are dead, in prison, or doing the same dirt they were doing before he got locked up."

"You right, girl. We'll just keep it small and intimate but spare no expense, the party's on me," replied C-Lok.

Bossy threw C-Lok a smile across the room as she recalled that conversation. *He could never say no to me,* thought Bossy. She had a new level of respect and love for C-Lok since finding out about all the sacrifices he'd made for her over the years. C-Lok had confessed his love for Bossy and wanted more than love at a distance but she turned down the offer. They were at two different places in their lives and Bossy knew that she wouldn't be able to walk away from the life if she allowed herself to reopen her heart to C-Lok.

"He's here, he's here!" screamed Aisha, "Everybody hide."

Bossy ran to the security door, swung it open and ran out to meet her brother. Devin was as handsome as ever, sporting a goatee and close shave. His six foot, three inch frame looked like he spent all of his time in the weight room.

"Damn, girl, look at you," said Devin.

"Naw, look at you. You look great," replied Bossy. She ran up to her big brother and jumped into his arms the same way she did when she was a little girl. Devin caught his sister, hugged her tight, and spun her around like a rag doll. He put her down and allowed her to lead him into the place she'd called home for years.

"Surprise, welcome home!" everyone yelled.

The small party lasted well into the night. The fellas played a few hands of tonk, swapped jokes, and everyone reminisced about the good old days. Bossy couldn't believe how much her brother had changed. When Devin was shipped off to prison he was a twenty-three-year-old boy; today they sent him home as a forty-nine-year-old man. Bossy just hoped his mind-set matched his age.

The next afternoon Devin woke in his own bed inside the extra apartment across the hall from Bossy. She thought having his own place to call home would be a good start for Devin. The best part was there was no rent to pay because Bossy owned the building. C-Lok hooked Devin up with an old school 1980 Monte Carlo SS. The burgundy car was as clean as the day it rode off the assembly line.

Devin was so grateful to have a fresh start in life and vowed to repay everyone for looking out for him. The only worry Devin had was making money but Bossy had that taken care of as well.

"You really looked out for ya brother, girl. Those

clothes you got me are cleaner than a mutha-fucker, for real," said Devin.

"Anything for you," replied Bossy, "if I forgot to pick up anything, you just let me know."

"You've done enough for me as it is. I'm not here looking for a handout and I damn sure ain't trying to live off you," said Devin, smiling.

"What are you talkin' about? I know that it was because of you that C-Lok bought me this building. I also know about Big Black doing that bid behind something I did," confessed Bossy.

Devin was pissed and shocked. He thought he'd made it clear that Bossy was never to find out about any of that stuff. He had no idea that C-Lok and Big Black had come clean to Bossy about everything. Bossy knew Devin would be upset with his two friends so she told Devin the story about Ant and Officers Powell and Meeks. The last thing she wanted was for Devin to lose the two best friends he'd ever had. After Devin heard the entire story, he decided to let it go because it sounded like they didn't have a choice in the matter.

"Well, all I have to do now is make that money to fill these empty pockets of mine," stated Devin. Wheels were already turning in his head as he tried to map out his first hustle as a free man.

"That's what I wanted to talk to you about. We have a job for you at KAT Sixty-nine so don't worry about that. You can work for us until you get ready to open your own business, and of course, I will invest in it."

"I ain't pushing no broom, Bossy. I took those barber classes in the joint so I already have a trade.

So unless it's a lot of women looking to get buzz cuts, I think I'll pass," said Devin defensively.

"You won't be pushing a broom, Devin. Terry and Twan had a plan under works last year before he was killed. He'd already invested a lot of money into the project; unfortunately, he didn't live to fulfill his dream of walking away from the game once the business took off."

Devin could see the hurt in his sister's eyes as she talked about Twan. He wondered if their relationship had been more than just business.

"So what's going on? I mean, is the business up and running today?"

"No, but the grand opening is next week. It's opening right across the street from the shop and the best part is that it's a barbershop. You will run it, hire your staff, and be your own boss. After working there for awhile, you can become the owner or part owner if you want," explained Bossy. She paused and held her breath before finally asking, "So what do you think?"

"That sounds good to me and I'll be happy to work there. It will probably be a great cover for my real hustle," said Devin, grinning. He couldn't believe how everything was lining up for him. Being a free man was going to be easier than he thought.

Bossy couldn't believe her ears. She knew Devin wasn't talking about getting his hands dirty after having his freedom for only one day. She tried to contain her anger as she questioned him further.

"What do you mean 'cover for your real hustle'?"

"C-Lok hooked me up with a package last night when we slipped away from the party," confessed

Devin. "Don't get me wrong, I'm all for owning my own business but that takes sweat and time so for right now, I need quick money."

"Are you serious? You been locked the fuck up for over half your life. You think you can put foot to pavement and begin your old hustle just like that?" hollered Bossy.

"Yeah, what you getting so upset about? You know I'm going to look out for you," said Devin.

"It ain't even about that because I ain't hurting for shit. See Devin, these streets have changed since you been gone. You think it's the same players out on the grind? Shit, the majority of them niggas you knew is dead or locked up. The two or three still walking the streets are strung out on the same shit they made their money off of." Bossy's anger was reaching a new high with each word she spat out to her brother. "These young boys out here ain't like they used to be. Today they don't have no respect for themselves let alone the next man. They don't understand the finality of death and they throwing bricks at the walls you just crawled out of. These kids out here are killing each other over somebody stepping on their new shoes. You think hitting the streets will gain you instant respect? Shit, you got life fucked up." Bossy was furious that she even had to have the conversation with Devin. She wondered if his release was a blessing or a setup for him to fall back into the arms of Satan.

"I can hold my own and ain't nobody gon' fuck with me because of C-Lok. Shit, I'm one of Teddy Bear's original hustlers," bragged Devin.

"Devin, do you hear yourself? Teddy Bear is laying six feet under and his name don't carry no fuckin' weight out here. Don't you know that hustling has a timetable? That life will get you an early grave or have you back on that modern-day plantation you just crawled out of. Very few of us get to walk away," Bossy vented.

She couldn't believe Devin was willing to roll the dice again. Doing all that time hadn't changed his way of thinking. Bossy was beginning to see that sitting behind them bars had just made Devin hungrier for the grind.

"What the fuck, Bossy—you think I don't know how you been keepin' ya head above water? You one of the biggest hustlers in the Yo' so who are you to preach to me?"

"Fuck you, Devin! You think I wanted this life? This fuckin' life chose me, I ain't chose it. Shit, you went and left me with a fuckin' crackhead. Then you hooked it up for Teddy Bear to take care of me. Yeah, he did a great fuckin' job too. He taught me how to run up and down the highway with enough weight to put me away for life. He taught me how to cook, weigh, package, and store the same shit I ran to get for his ass. Teddy Bear taught me how to fire everything from a handgun to a fuckin' missile. He even taught my ass how to beat a nigga's brain in so bad he wouldn't remember how to wipe his own ass."

Bossy was so angry her head was pounding in her ears. How could Devin put her on the road she walked for twenty-three years and then have the nerve to throw it in her face? It finally hit Bossy that she never really knew her brother at all. How could she when Devin didn't even know himself?

"You survived these streets though, didn't you?

How you gon' blame me for all that shit when I wasn't even here. Ain't nobody force you to do any of that shit, you chose to do it," spat Devin.

"Muthafuckin' what? How can you say I wasn't forced into this life when it was the only thing I was ever shown? What other choice does a thirteen year old have when she doesn't know where her next meal is coming from, or if she'll even have a roof over her fuckin' head from night to night. I ain't have nobody but my damn self," screamed Bossy with tears streaming down her face.

"I tried the best I could to take care of you. Why you think I robbed that store? I did it so you could eat and have clothes on ya back. Now you want to repay me like this? That's fucked up with you, Bossy," Devin replied defiantly.

"No, that's fucked up with you! All these years I've had to live with the guilt of you being behind them walls. That guilt caused me to rob people for what was theirs. It caused me to take another man's life, Devin. Shit, you talk about me, well, what about you, Devin? You sat behind big walls and inflicted fear in the hearts of men."

"What are you talking about?"

"I'm talking about Big Black giving up ten years of his life for some shit I did because you made it happen. I'm talking about C-Lok putting two policemen down, buying this apartment building, and paying ya debts for you. Shit, nigga, you the one with the power so you must not need my little apartment and business offer. You were so fuckin' big while you were locked up, so now that you're free, you must be the fuckin' man."

Devin and Bossy stared each other down, neither

willing to be the first to look away. Devin couldn't believe how Bossy reacted to his wanting to get back in the game. Bossy felt she was looking into the eyes of a stranger. The apartment remained quiet as brother and sister stood off, both determined to be the victor.

"Bossy, all I need is for you to do what you do and package them thangs for me. I know your rates, I got you."

"No more, Devin, no more," cried Bossy.

She took a deep breath and turned on her heels to leave. As she reached for the doorknob a strange feeling swept over Bossy. Something inside of her said, *Let it all go.* Something was offering Bossy a peace she had never experienced before. She felt a wave of calm move through her and she knew exactly what to do. Bossy turned back around to face her brother.

"That day you walked into that store had nothing to do with me. You made that decision without me. That was your choice in your life and I have no reason to carry that guilt anymore. I can't blame you for the things you did while you were behind bars because I'm sure everything you did for me was done out of love." Bossy paused to consider her next words carefully. "I have hustled drugs, laundered money, and sold my soul to the devil. I take full responsibility for all the choices I've made in my life. There is only one thing I regret."

"What's that, Bossy?"

"That I was a bad big sister to Twan just like you were a bad big brother to me," spat Bossy, "but at least I get to walk away."

One Year Later . . .

LOVE, LIFE AND SURVIVAL IN THE YO

The new KAT69 Hair, Nails, and Day Spa was flourishing and the owners were having no trouble keeping up with business. Terry and Aisha had increased their staff by adding three new beauticians, Tootsie, Ondrea, and JoAnn. The nail technicians included one new girl, LaTrice. There were three full-time masseuses, three child-care workers, and two new receptionists.

Terry had decided long ago not to expand the shop to include barbers but to open a new location for the men. She reasoned that men have barbershops to get away from their women and women have their beauty shops to go talk about their men. Combining the two just would not work.

When Terry presented the business plan to Bossy and Aisha, they all agreed that Twan was the perfect person to back the idea. Twan had poured money into the barbershop before Terry could envision what it would look like. The day to cut the ribbon and open the doors to Youngstown's newest barbershop had finally arrived.

Bossy, Aisha, and Terry were sitting in Terry's office making a toast before joining the large crowd outside.

"Terry, you went all out for the grand opening," solemnly said Bossy. "Did I see Tiffany Patterson and her camera crew outside?"

"Yes, I want the opening and dedication to be as big as possible and having WKBN Twenty-seven news here is free publicity," answered Terry.

Looking over at her friend and seeing the pain in her eyes, Aisha felt her heart break. It had been two years since that horrible day at the mall when Bossy had been forever changed.

Twan was killed instantly from the car's impact. Bossy had run over to Twan and placed his head on her lap until the ambulance arrived. His body was limp; life had already left it by the time Bossy reached him. Growing up poor in the projects, Bossy had seen a lot, done a lot more, and caused more problems than even her two best friends knew of, but seeing Twan's life end so tragically had given her a different view of life.

At the scene, Bossy asked the police to allow her to notify Twan's mother of his death. It was the hardest thing she would ever do, but she felt obligated to do it. Bossy promised Tracey Glover that she would oversee all the arrangements for the funeral services. After seeing that Twan was laid to rest properly, Bossy walked away from the only life she had ever known.

Bossy had written Devin about that day and her decision to leave all that hustling behind her. Devin made it obvious last month that he didn't believe his sister could just walk away from the game. After their argument, Devin became a believer and didn't press Bossy on the issue any more. Devin told Bossy he was proud of her strength and he would always love her but felt it best if they kept distance between them. Bossy agreed and Devin moved to North Carolina with Big Black.

Sitting in the office she now shared with Terry, Bossy wished that Twan had lived long enough to walk away from the streets and see his business flourish. Bossy wiped a tear from her eye and shook the thought from her head.

"Drink up, ladies, it is time to do the damn thing. Let's go out here and make ourselves and Twan proud," said Terry. "We have to be strong out there. This will put an end to this tragic episode."

"Wrong, Terry, this will mark a new beginning. The jury put an ending to the senseless tragedy last week by finding LaJetia guilty of second-degree murder and putting her away for life," replied Bossy.

"You are right about that. I still can not believe that bitch tried to get off by pleading not guilty by reason of temporary insanity. I know for sure that Twan's mother and brother are thankful for that too," commented Aisha.

"I am just glad that his mother took custody of his son Trayvon. It will be hard for yet another young black male to grow up without a father but at least he'll be cared for by family," added Terry.

"Wasn't it great that Auntell's parents adopted the older two kids so they could stay together? Those people have some big hearts," said Bossy.

"Yeah, especially since Auntell is seventeen. They should be starting the next part of their lives but instead they are starting a new family. They will be truly blessed," concluded Aisha. "Now let's get out here because me and Mama are volunteering tonight at the rape crisis hotline so my time is limited."

"We are so proud of you, Aisha. Not many women are able to live through something so terrible. You not only lived through it but you are helping others do the same," said Terry.

"Cheers, let's drink to that too," said Bossy, smiling.

Bossy, Aisha, and Terry downed the last of their champagne and walked out into the crowd holding hands for strength. In addition to the news crew and their staff, Mama Bev, Talissa, Mr. and Mrs. Croomes, and Terry's father were all in attendance. Terry briefly addressed the crowd, reading from a prepared statement before turning the microphone over to Bossy for the dedication.

"Two years, two weeks, and three days ago today, my friend had his life cut short because another human being decided it was his time to go. We came here today to honor not only the memory of our friend, Antwan Marcus Glover, but to celebrate the life he dreamed of having. We, the owners of KAT Sixty-nine Hair, Nails, and Day Spa dedicate this new establishment to the memory of our friend. It is our hope that one day, we as a people, will come together for support, uplifting, and celebration instead of negativity, violence, and death." The crowd began its applause just in time for Bossy to pause and regain her composure. "Ladies and gentlemen, in honor of our friend, we present to you 'Twan's Urban Kutz'. A place where a black man can simply be a man."